"I wanted to talk to you about this list of yours. You know, the list of sexual scenarios.

"I couldn't believe it," Dante continued. "You hit on all but one of my top fantasies!"

What? He couldn't believe it? Isabel pulled back so fast, Dante's arm slipped from her waist. "You have my..." *Oh, God.* How did he get the list? She couldn't have left it out. She turned quickly and started rustling through the loose papers on the table. But it wasn't there.

"Hey," he said, turning her back toward him. "You have nothing to be ashamed of. Sexual fantasies are normal, you know? It's the people who deny their fantasy life who have problems."

"I'm not ashamed," Isabel said honestly. "Embarrassed, yes. I can't believe I didn't notice that list was missing." Nor could she believe that Dante Luciano, the inspiration for all those naughty fantasies, was the one who'd happened to pick it up.

"Relax. I'll be happy to return it." Then, with a wicked grin, he added, "Of course, I'd be happier to *fulfill* it with you...."

Blaze™

Dear Reader,

Do you remember your first serious crush? The intense, stomach-melting rush of feelings? Those hot, sexy daydreams in which you dared to be his one and only?

That's how Isabel Santos feels about Dante Luciano. He's the baddest bad boy she's ever known. And ever since a high school kiss, he's been the one guy she's always fantasized about. Not to mention the inspiration behind her ultimate fantasy list—her Man Plan.

So when the hottie of her dreams shows up on her doorstep...well, what's a girl to do but grab on with both hands? Luckily for her, Dante not only loves her list, he has his own fantasies to add to it....

So what would *your* fantasy list look like? Drop by my Web site at www.TawnyWeber.com to send me an e-mail and let me know. While you're there, check out my blog, my latest contest or vote for the hunk of the month. I'd love to hear from you.

Happy reading,

Tawny Weber

DOES SHE DARE?

Tawny Weber

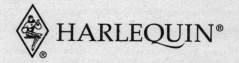

HARLEQUIN®

TORONTO • NEW YORK • LONDON
AMSTERDAM • PARIS • SYDNEY • HAMBURG
STOCKHOLM • ATHENS • TOKYO • MILAN • MADRID
PRAGUE • WARSAW • BUDAPEST • AUCKLAND

ISBN-13: 978-0-373-79376-1
ISBN-10:   0-373-79376-6

DOES SHE DARE?

ABOUT THE AUTHOR

Tawny Weber is usually found dreaming up stories in her California home, surrounded by dogs, cats and kids. When she's not writing hot, spicy novels for Harlequin Blaze, she's testing her latest margarita recipe, shopping for the perfect pair of boots or drooling over Johnny Depp pictures (when her husband isn't looking, of course). And when she's not doing any of that, she spends her time scrapbooking and playing in the garden. She'd love to hear from readers, so drop by her home on the Web, www.TawnyWeber.com.

Books by Tawny Weber
HARLEQUIN BLAZE
324-DOUBLE DARE

To my incredible critique partners Beth and Sheila—thanks for holding my hand.

To Karin and Poppy for the challenge, to Trish for "ishing," and Kimmi for advising the best use of a pool table—I couldn't have done it without any of you!

In loving memory of two beautiful souls who believed so much in my ability to do anything I set my mind to:
My Grampa, who really *could* do anything.
And Carol, an inspiration of strength and love.
I miss you both so much.

Prologue

Ten Years Before

"WE DARE YOU TO KISS the baddest boy at Western High," Suzi said, wicked glee coating her words.

Isabel Santos dug her heels into the grass to keep herself from running away. Kiss some strange boy, and a bad one at that? Were they crazy? What the hell had she been thinking?

"You want to play with the big girls," Suzi continued, "you've got to prove you've got what it takes."

"That's the rule," Isabel's best friend, Audra, explained in a soft, slightly apologetic tone. "If you hang with the Wicked Chicks, you have to prove you can handle it by taking a dare."

Isabel shot her a look that said *duh*. But inside she was shaking. It wasn't so much that she wanted to be a Wicked Chick. It was more that Audra was in the club. And Isabel felt left out. Thanks to uptight, overprotective parents, Isabel now attended an all-girls private school and hardly ever saw her friend anymore. Lately, all Audra talked about was the Chicks and what they'd done, or *who* they'd done. Wild times, apparently. Not that Isabel was the wild type; she really was more content daydreaming than partying and chasing boys. But she wanted to belong. So she'd lied to her parents—told them she was spending the night at a friend's since they didn't approve of Audra anymore—and snuck out.

"I can handle a dare," she vowed with a lift of her chin. She tried to push out her chest, too, but that was just depressing. The Chicks were all busty, definitely way ahead of her in the development department, as proven by the boobs overflowing their low-cut tops. When she made it into the club, she'd have to get a new bra.

She looked around the party. The moonlit backyard was filled with bodies gyrating to the bubblegum beat of pop music blasting from someone's boom box.

Her eyes stuck on the guy in chains and leather with greasy hair and a mean look. He looked bad, all right, as in smelly bad. Could she do this? She swallowed and pulled back her shoulders. Yes, she could. She was sixteen, not six. She'd planned it all out. If she wanted to hang out with her best friend more often, she'd have to be a part of the club. She pressed a hand against her churning stomach. Even if it meant kissing smelly guys.

"Who's the baddest boy?" she asked.

"Dante Luciano," Audra, Suzi and the third Chick, Bea, declared in chorus.

Her churning stomach almost jumped out of her throat. *Oh no.* She shook her head. Not Dante Luciano. They even talked about him at *her* school. Usually in whispers, of course.

She'd heard he was hell on wheels. He'd done more girls and drank more booze than a rock star. Everything from vandalism to public brawls. If he was even half as bad as his reputation, she was better off with the stinky guy.

"He's the dare," Bea insisted. Her red pigtails waved

in concert with her adamant nod. The pigtails went with the naughty-schoolgirl outfit, Isabel supposed. "Being wicked isn't just being wild, it's being brave. Attitude is everything, you know."

"I don't even know what he looks like," she answered in a faint voice. Like it mattered. She'd made a plan, she was sticking with it. She could hold her breath for the thirty seconds it would take to kiss and run.

Audra pointed across the lawn to a group of guys doing keg stands. "The one in jeans and black T-shirt."

Her heart did jumping jacks. She'd never seen anything—anyone—so beautiful.

"Wow," she gasped.

Suzi and Bea laughed.

Tall and leanly muscled, he had a body like one of the Greek gods she'd studied. His black hair curled over his forehead, falling in loose waves to his shoulders. She'd only known boys. Dante was very obviously a man. Her eyes traced the wide set of his tanned biceps—rumor had it from working construction after school for his father. What would it feel like to touch him? To feel that smooth skin under her fingers? Her breath caught at the image.

She'd never understood the fuss over sex. Sure, guys were cute, some really cute. But to want to rub her hands all over one? To want to press her lips to his shoulder just to taste his skin? Until this moment, she'd had no clue. But now? She wanted to do some fussing herself.

She had no clue what she'd say to him. How did they think she could kiss him? What was she supposed to do? Isabel's vision wavered as fear nipped at the edges of her awareness. Did she introduce herself and ask for a kiss? Just walk up and plant one on him? Did he have to kiss her back? Questions raced at a frantic pace through her head.

She shot Audra a panicked look, but her friend just shrugged. A look of worry, combined with doubt, lurked in the other girl's heavily lined eyes.

"You don't have to take the dare," Audra murmured.

If she wanted to be in their club, she did. She eyed Dante again, odd sensations zinging around in a wild, tempting dance in her belly. She really did want to kiss him. Suddenly, the dare was simply an excuse.

With a quick squeeze of Audra's hand, she made her way across the lawn. Moonlight flicked in and out of the trees, adding to the surreal feeling inside her.

She had no idea what to do. Her brain was on autopilot. Even the questions and panic were gone now; all she knew was she had to kiss Dante Luciano. She started to move forward, but another guy stepped between them.

"Dude, you're out of booze."

Dante slipped his hand into the front pocket of his jeans. Moonlight sparked off the small metal key. "Here, hit my dad's liquor cabinet. He's got plenty."

With a start, Isabel realized this was Dante's house. Her breath hitched. He really *was* bad.

"Real nice of your dad to share." His buddy grinned.

"Right. Like he shared his truck," Dante said with a smirk. "You gotta help me get it out of that ditch tomorrow."

Even his voice was sexy. Low, husky and filled with what she imagined sin sounded like. Dante Luciano had the worst reputation in the county. Even Audra, who was a known hell-raiser herself, was in awe of how much trouble he stirred up.

"Looks like someone's waiting for you," the guy said, his laugh a little mean this time. It took Isabel a few seconds to realize he meant her. At their stares, her cheeks flamed and she would have turned away except the look on Dante's face had her rooted in place. She barely noticed his friend snicker and stalk off.

"Hey there," Dante said with a slow grin. The world ground to a slow halt around her.

"Hi," Isabel squeaked after a few gulps. Her heart raced so fast, she worried it was going to fly out of her chest. When he beckoned her closer, she tamped down a hysterical giggle and stepped forward until she was near enough, for the first time, to stare into his eyes. They were vivid green, like the emeralds in her mother's anniversary band.

Maybe his gaze was cloudy with an alcohol haze and he was swaying more than the trees, but Isabel didn't care. If only she could think of something to say.

He reached out and flicked one of her curls, then let his finger trace over her shoulder. Isabel's nipples hardened. Something intense, damp and sticky, tightened deep in her belly. She didn't know what was going on inside her body, but it felt good. In a scary, confusing kind of way. What should she do? Should she touch *him*? Should she say something? Her mind, already fogged with nerves, shut down at his touch.

Which was fine with her body. It had plenty going on.

"As the host of this little get-together," he said, his hand now tangled in her hair, "it's my duty to welcome you to the party. My momma insists I be polite, you know."

His idea of welcome was friendlier than a handshake, Isabel realized, when, with his hand still in her hair, he pulled her against his body.

Her gasp was lost in his mouth. Her hands curled into the smooth delight of his chest as he took advantage of her shock to slip his tongue between her lips. Terrified pleasure filled her. Romantic notions of love-at-first-kiss filled her head, tangled with the incomplete images of dark, forbidden touches.

She'd been kissed before, but never like this. Dante's mouth was pure magic. Soft and sweet, his tongue danced along hers. Something wild, something intense coiled low in her belly. Isabel shifted, trying to find relief, trying to figure out what to do about the power of the feeling.

When his hand cupped her breast, she gasped. Not able to help herself, she pulled back.

He laughed. "You're a sweet little thing, aren't you?"

"That's bad, isn't it?" she asked, her tone as soft as the night air. She'd screwed up. Ruined it. Tears filled her eyes as emotions she didn't understand gripped her.

He flashed a half-smile, then brushed his finger over the strap of her tank top. "It's not bad. I'll bet you taste as sweet as you look…everywhere. Like a ripe, fresh-picked peach."

The image of his mouth on her—licking, tasting—stopped Isabel's breath. Like the scariest ride at the amusement park, she wanted to try it. But at the same time she was terrified. Torn between desire and fear, she stared up at him.

"Dante?"

They both glanced at the redhead standing to the side. Her heavily made-up eyes slid over Isabel in instant dismissal.

"Dance?" she said to Dante, her hand tracing down her throat, over her plump breast, then to her hip.

"Sweet," Dante repeated, giving Isabel a look so hot, she swore she felt her heart melt. He leaned forward again to brush a soft kiss over her cheek. "But I don't do good girls."

A minute later, Isabel blinked back the tears as Dante swayed to "As Long As You Love Me," with the redhead wrapped around him like plastic wrap. From the looks of her, that girl would definitely know how to handle Dante. When the girl's hand slid down the back of his jeans, Isabel clenched her jaw and turned away. She couldn't watch.

She scanned the couples curled up on loungers or lying together on the lawn. She wanted to—*had to*—get out of there, but she didn't see Audra. She hurried inside. As she reached the door, a kid ran through, almost knocking her on her butt.

"Parents! Cops!" he yelled. "Run."

Panic seized her. Couples shot apart and flew left and right. Cops? *Oh, shit.*

A half hour later, she sat in the Luciano's living room, listening to the policeman lecture her and the dozen other kids who hadn't escaped into the woods. This was definitely bad.

Her parents were going to kill her. And worse, be disappointed. She'd never let them down, never given them a single reason to lecture her. Panic flitted, inky black, at the edges of her awareness. The only thing keeping Isabel from sobbing was the fear that if she did, she'd throw up.

Dammit, what had she gotten herself into? She didn't belong here. Her response to Dante proved that. She was just a kid, definitely not ready for the big leagues. Suzi leaned over and nudged her. Apparently, Audra had managed to escape, just like Dante and most of the others.

"Hey, I'd say you made it. Busted like a Wicked Chick, huh?" From the grin on Suzi's face, she wasn't afraid.

Unlike Isabel, who was sure this was her last night on earth.

With a weak smile, Isabel slid down the worn fabric of the couch. Maybe she should have planned this better. Blinking back tears she realized she didn't want to be wicked. The only thing she wanted now was Dante Luciano.

1

"I NEED A REAL MAN," Isabel Santos decided. She shot a bleary look across the table at her best friend, then squinted to take in the rest of the cozy Italian restaurant. Although she and Audra were still seated, there were a few couples on the dance floor, swaying to the soft rock music.

At half past eleven in the evening, the only men left were a pair of waiters who were obviously into each other, a teenaged busboy and the cook. Considering the pasta had been overdone, Isabel crossed him off her potential list.

"I have to admit, a man would have been a more imaginative birthday gift than the nightie I gave you," her friend mused, snagging Isabel's attention back from her useless hunk-search. "But I wasn't sure what size you were in the market for."

Isabel snickered.

"It's not the size that matters, it's the quality," she insisted, careful to enunciate her words through the fog of wine curling through her head. She really should have quit at one glass, but she'd been so bummed over being dumped, turning another year older and discovering she was as desirable as a dried-up prune, she'd ordered a second. Then a third. "I need a real man. A hot, sexy man. The kind that makes a girl squirm, but doesn't require conversation and pampering. You know, a stud."

Audra Walker-Martinez, Isabel's oldest friend, was probably the only person in the world who she'd feel comfortable saying that to. Then again, Audra was an expert on hot, sexy men.

"I'm all for you taking on a hot guy, especially now that you've dumped that pansy boy you were dating. But maybe we should wait until you're—"

"I didn't dump Lance. He dumped me." Isabel sneered, her voice rising as she warmed to the subject. "He was lousy in bed. But no matter how many times I tell myself it's no loss, I still feel like I got ripped off. I'm twenty-six, Audra. The years I should have spent exploring my sexuality, living out my wild fantasies, they've passed me by. I can't afford to wait any longer."

Cringing, her face going flame-red at the cook's disapproving stare and the grins of the waiters, Isabel stopped her rant to suck in a deep breath.

Audra lifted one brow and pursed her lips. "I had been about to suggest we wait till you were sober to make a man plan, but hey, we can start now."

Man plan? Isabel giggled at the absurd idea, then her laughter fell away. *Well why not?* Before taking on any new venture, the first thing she did was sit down and make a plan. Business plans, life plans, weight-loss plans. Damned if most of them hadn't all worked. So why wouldn't a man plan?

"I want the ultimate fantasy plan," she mused as she hauled her suede hobo bag up to the table and started digging through it. "Something with a limited time frame, you know? I mean, I have such a tight schedule trying to get the new store up and running, I can't have a bunch of distractions right now."

Isabel found her ever-present notepad, flipped to a clean page, and chose a pen—red for passion, of course.

"Okay, first step is to define the goal. Sex is a little too broad, don't ya think?" Isabel tapped the pen against her bottom lip. "Hot sex is better, but still not right. What d'ya think? Fling? Affair? Boy toy? Bootie call?"

She glanced up to see Audra grimace. "What?"

"Nothing," Audra denied. At Isabel's pointed look, she shrugged. "It's just…well, this isn't you. I mean, the plan part, that's all you. Goal setting, control, you've got a firm handle on those. But to make a plan specifically targeted at snagging you some emotionless, string-free, temporary sex? That's the wine talking."

"Nope." Isabel shook her head so hard, her curls flew. "I had a fling once. I can totally do it again."

"That fling was a failure, remember? The liar was married and didn't tell you. You were a mess for months afterward."

Isabel wrinkled her nose and tried to shrug like it hadn't mattered. She had been a mess. Not heartbroken, although she'd felt like she should be. But angry and betrayed. The worst of the anger had been aimed at herself, though. She'd given into the romance of being swept off her feet by a sexy guy. She'd been so enamored with all her romantic notions, she'd ignored the warning signs. Separated. And she'd found out from his wife, who thought they were trying to work things out.

The worst part? The jerk had never seen anything wrong with lying to her. To him, as long as he and his wife had different addresses, he was free to do whatever he wanted. It didn't matter that Isabel's idea of free was completely different.

But that had been two years ago, before she'd discovered the power of control. A weekend goal seminar had taught her all about it. Since control was already one of Isabel's favorite things, the seminar had been like finding heaven. All the tools she needed to shift from being a woman who doodled plans and wishes with minimal success to a take-charge business entrepreneur with a solid business plan and a firm handle on her life's direction.

So why not apply the same principles in order to get a rocking sex life?

All she had to do was make this man plan and stick to it. As long as she did that, life couldn't fall apart on her again. Now that she thought about it, that must've been the problem with her relationships in the past, especially with Lance. No plan, no goal. She'd just floated along, letting the guy set the tone for the relationship. Oh, sure, she'd hoped he'd be *the one.* But hoping wasn't planning. It just went to show, the one area of her life she'd left to fate was her love life, and fate kicked her in the ass.

Nope. Outlining her exact wants and needs, then setting specific goals worked pretty well for everything else. She just had to apply it here, to her love life. Or, she corrected with a naughty little smile, what she'd soon make her love life.

"I want *hot sex,*" she insisted, now that she'd made up her mind. The busboy, clearing glasses from a neighboring table, shot them a startled look. Audra gave him a wink. He blushed and scurried away before Isabel could order another glass of wine.

Isabel rolled her eyes. Audra winked and made guys run—to and away from her. Isabel still hadn't quite figured out how to get a guy's undivided attention...or what she'd do with it once she had it.

As usual, watching Audra made her painfully aware

of their differences. Audra could pull off that flirty, spontaneous thing. Isabel worried so much about looking stupid, about failing, that she avoided spontaneity whenever possible.

Not that she had self-esteem issues, really. She knew she was pretty, if in a cutesy way with her shoulder-length, dark curls. Audra, on the other hand, wore her hair short and spiky, the midnight-black tipped in magenta.

Their outer personalities were just as different. Audra being all edgy and wild, where Isabel was known as a good girl.

Inside they were more alike that most people would believe. Not only in their insecurities, but in their drive to have more for themselves than they'd had as kids living next door to each other. Audra'd created a career for herself as a lingerie designer, and Isabel who had started her florist career in her parents' shop was on the brink of kicking off the next phase of her career plan with an innovative new florist shop. Finally, something completely on her own, a venture that would prove to she was a success.

And now she'd apply that planning savvy to the dismal emptiness that was her love life. Between excitement and the wine, it was all Isabel could do not to clap her hands together in excitement. This man plan was going to rock.

"C'mon, quit scaring little boys," she insisted. "Help me here. Consider it my birthday gift."

"I gave you a silk nightgown," Audra reminded her, even as she slid the notebook and pen out of Isabel's hands.

"Yeah, but the rest of the gift can be a guy to wear the

nightgown for. Your designs deserve an audience, right? Help me get one."

A small, sober voice in Isabel's head pointed out that she sounded desperate and needy. It wasn't like she was a troll with no prospects. But she knew she was the kind of gal who drew in *nice guys*. The ones who paid more attention to their stock portfolio and cholesterol levels than they did to mind-blowing physical satisfaction.

Take Lance, for instance. Oh, he was fine on the surface. Good-looking, smart and ambitious. But sex with him was like eating Chinese food. She'd been fulfilled in the moment, but a half hour later she'd felt unsatisfied and puzzled as to why.

"Okay, consider this my gift to you, part two," Audra agreed. She sketched a few words on the page. "Let's start with the basics. You want hot sex. What turns you on? What're your fantasies?"

"Rules first. Before I get to the sex, I need the guidelines firmly established," Isabel insisted.

Never one for rules, Audra just rolled her eyes. But she wrote the numbers one through three on the page anyhow.

"Only three?"

"Too many rules just get in the way. This is it, all you get." She tapped the pen on the page, then raised a brow, as if to ask *well?*

"Okay, number one—I'm in control. I want to call the shots in this relationship instead of being the one following along like an enthusiastic puppy."

Audra nodded and wrote that down.

"Number two—once you're committed to the plan, you can't second-guess yourself," Audra declared. "It's all or nothing. I know you, if you start second-guessing, you'll back out before you even get started."

"Fine," Isabel agreed with a huff. She thought, then poked at the paper. "Number three—no silly ideas about falling in love. It's just sex. Wild, insanely passionate sex."

"That's a given," Audra argued. "Why waste a rule on that?"

"Not that I'm speaking from experience or anything," Isabel said, only half-lying, "but I think with the right guy, if the sex is so excellent and wonderful, it'd be easy to fool yourself into believing it's all romantic. Like love-at-first-kiss."

Audra rolled her eyes, but wrote it down anyway. "Okay, let's get to the fantasies."

"I said I wanted a hot, sexy man," Isabel reminded her meticulously.

"A hot sexy man isn't gonna do you any good if he's not pushing the right buttons. Any dork can be the hottest sex you've ever had if he's tapping into your fantasy."

Isabel considered, then dismissed that theory. She wanted a hot sexy man, not a talented dork. The fantasy angle had potential though.

"How do I make a fantasy list?"

"Think of the hottest guy you've ever seen. Real life, movie, whatever. What guy out there, just by thinking about him, gets you hot?"

She didn't even have to consider it. All she had to do was close her eyes and a face flashed into her mind. Unruly dark hair, vivid green eyes and a body to die for. The hottest, sexiest, guy she'd ever met.

"From the grin on your face, you've got someone in mind?"

"Oh, yeah. Remember Dante Luciano?"

"Nice," Audra said, her tone both appreciative and

amused. "Dante was trouble, through and through. He was so bad, he made me look like a goody-goody."

Which was saying a lot, since back then Audra had one of the wildest reps to ever hit the local high school.

"His father's my contractor, you know?" Isabel said.

When her parents had retired earlier that year, they'd sold the family florist shop and adjoining apartment. Then they'd given her the money to fund her new location. A darling Victorian located on the main street of Santa Vera. The small, tourist haven in Northern California was a few miles from her hometown of Auburn. Close enough to keep some of the existing customer base, far enough away to feel like she was finally striking out on her own.

"Didn't you have to talk to him or something at a party back when we were kids?" Audra frowned, obviously trying to remember.

Isabel just shrugged. She'd never discussed that that night with Audra. At first, because she'd been grounded for three months and hadn't been allowed to go out of the house or to make any phone calls. Later, because she hadn't wanted to hear how bad or how far out of her reach Dante was.

"It's a good thing you didn't hook up with Dante, then," Audra said with a laugh. "He and his dad had major issues. I remember a few times he ended up staying at our place after his old man kicked him out."

Twirling one long black curl around her finger, Isabel frowned. She'd never been jealous of Audra's reputation or lifestyle before. But she'd always been curious.

"Did you and Dante ever, you know…"

Audra gave her trademark wicked grin and winked. When Isabel frowned, she laughed and shook her head.

"Nah, we never did more than flirt. Dante was a couple years ahead of us, remember. He was tight with my brother, Drew. By the time I was up to his standards, he'd left town."

Before Isabel could do more than wonder at the relief surging through her, Audra tapped the notepad with the pen. "Okay, keep your fantasy guy in mind and let your imagination soar. Let's come up a few hot fantasies for him to fulfill."

Isabel eyed her friend, then the notepad. She turned around and called out to the waiter, "Another glass of wine, please."

WHO KNEW BEING A YEAR OLDER would hurt this bad? Isabel pressed the heel of her hands to her forehead to try to keep the pounding from making her eyeballs explode.

She wasn't sure what was worse, the hangover or the sense of impending doom tapping on her shoulder. All these big plans, everything she wanted, was right here, spread out across her desk.

Could she make it happen?

A glance at the color-coded and bulleted spreadsheet told her she was a week behind on the shop renovations. Another week and she stood to lose her contract with the town council for their spring festival. Since she needed that contract to launch her business with enough success to avoid becoming a first-year statistic, she couldn't afford the loss.

Everything she had was invested in this new floral shop. Years of planning, of dreaming and hoping. And she was going to lose it all because her contractor broke his foot? Panic rumbled sickeningly in her stomach. She couldn't fail. Her parents' retirement depended on her success. Their pampered and protected only child—they expected her to excel. They'd sold their store and loaned her the money to open this new floral and gift shop. Sure, they said they wanted to move to the little town in Oregon and retire next to her aunts, but she knew it was because they couldn't both lend her the money and afford to retire in California.

She couldn't let them down. She just couldn't.

Pushing the spreadsheet aside, Isabel grabbed her notebook to outline a possible plan of attack to get the renovations finished on time. Flipping pages, her eyes went wide. She flipped back.

The Man Plan.

Holy shit. She pressed her index finger to the vein throbbing in her right temple. Had she and Audra actually made a plan to catch a guy? A hot sexy guy? Glancing over the pages, a reluctant smile tugged at her mouth. They'd actually created something excellent here.

She ran her finger down the page.

Rules:
1 Take control.
2 No second-guessing or backing out.
3 No falling in love.
Steps:
Find the perfect guy—check credentials.
Feel him out—or up. Make sure the spark is there.
Take the list in order; build up the tension.
Set a time limit. Two weeks is ideal affair length.
Cut him loose. Remember rule three.
Fantasies:
Hot, sexy kiss—make me melt.

Slow, sexy dance. Get a feel for the moves.
Hot, wild and a little rough up against the wall.
Intense passion in a semi-public place.
Pure romance-novel sex. Complete with a ride on
a white horse along the beach.
A smorgasbord of sexual pleasure, complete with
whipped cream, strawberries and lots of decadent
chocolate.
Water play, shower, bath, hot tub. Something with
pulsating heat.
Tied up and crazy—for extra spice, add a dollop
of chocolate.

Isabel snickered. Right. Like she had time for something like this. Maybe after she'd opened the shop. Or later, once *Sweet Scentsations* had wowed the town and made its niche. There wasn't any deadline on the Man Plan.

Regardless, she couldn't worry about it now. She simply had too much to do. Tearing the pages from her notebook, she tossed them on the corner of her desk with a smirk.

Her priority right now was the renovations. With the click of her mouse, she pulled up the phone number and dialed the home of her balance-challenged contractor.

"Mrs. Luciano? Hi, it's Isabel Santos. I'm calling to see how Mr. Luciano is doing and if my job might be back on schedule soon?"

The sweet older lady launched into a description of the extent of the fracture, the extent of Mr. Luciano's displeasure with his confinement, and their worries about losing business.

With a wince, Isabel crossed "get out of contract and hire a new contractor" off her tentative plans.

"Do you have any idea of a timeframe?" she asked, wishing she were the hard-as-nails type who'd insist they meet the original deadlines.

"I found someone to step in," Mrs. Luciano assured her. "He's a wonderful carpenter. Actually one of Frank's best, although lord knows the man won't admit it."

Isabel listened with half an ear while she clicked her mouse, synced her revised to-do list with her task list and updated her renovation plan.

"He said he'd go directly there," Mrs. Luciano continued, "He wanted to look over the job first. Afterwards I'll get him the paperwork."

"I have a copy of the work schedule and renovation outline here," Isabel told her. "Why don't I just print it out for him? That'll save a few steps."

"Wonderful idea. That'll keep Frank from knowing— I mean, from having to wake up and do it himself. The more rest he gets, the better, you know."

Isabel frowned. Had she missed something?

"Mr. Luciano is okay with this substitution, isn't he?"

"This is fine. Perfect, even. Don't you worry. Luciano Construction promises the best, and more important, the best on time. Your renovations will be fabulous and I'm sure we'll be back on track, time-wise, quite soon."

Magic words to Isabel's ears. With a relieved smile, she said her goodbyes and, with the click of the mouse, sent the schedule and outline to her printer.

Two seconds later she cursed. The printer made another loud cracking screech. Paper jam. Again. She tugged the stuck, then ripped paper out of the machine, tossing the bits in the trash. Hit print. Nothing but another grind. She sighed and bent down to find the jam.

A minute later, Isabel jumped back in shock as the

machine started spewing pages before she could get the paper-guide back in place. Grabbing the printed sheets before they hit the floor, she tossed them on the corner of the desk, fit the guide in place, then shoved the stack from her desk under the still-printing pages.

Spying the first page of her Man Plan on the floor, she grabbed the sheet of paper. Before she could find the second page, a loud roaring outside ricocheted in painful volume through the room. Thunder? Isabel pressed a hand to her aching head as the sound throbbed all the way through her body. She moved to the window just in time to see a huge Harley pull up to the curb. With a flick of his wrist, the rider killed the ignition. Silence followed, and she wasn't sure how she knew, but Isabel was sure that in the few seconds he sat there, the guy had taken in every aspect of the house and property.

Wow. Hot, sexy and delivered right to her doorstep? Isabel grinned. Almost like a fantasy? Or better yet, a birthday joke from her best friend. Would Audra send a hot dude to say hi? She snickered. She wouldn't put it past her. After all, Isabel had made a Man Plan. Audra was bound to tease her about it. Too amused not to go check things out, she moved away from the window.

Anxious to see what kind of guy her birthday wish had conjured up, Isabel opened the front door and stepped out into the cool morning air on her wide, wraparound porch.

Even hidden by his helmet and black leather jacket, he was clearly a man used to making grown women drool. Amusement replaced by sudden lust, Isabel swallowed, glad her mouth was too dry to humiliate her.

Eyeing him as he swung his leg over the bike to stand tall on the sidewalk, she descended the front steps.

Lust was fleeting, she assured herself. Man Plan or

not, it had all been a joke. A crazy idea spurred on by too much wine. She'd get over it. Even as she recalled the sexual fantasies she'd concocted, she realized this guy wasn't for her. He was too much. Too sexy, too tough, too damned big. Too everything. Images of just how big he might be flashed through her mind. Isabel's breath shuddered out and she waved a hand over her face to stir some cooling air.

The guy unzipped his jacket, the sound loud in the quiet afternoon street. Isabel watched, mesmerized, as he slid well-muscled arms from the sleek leather.

After tossing the jacket across the seat, he took off his helmet. Isabel's breath whooshed out at the sight.

Black hair curled in damp waves to his collar, surrounding a face meant for sin. A slash of cheekbones and strong chin were the perfect frame for intense green eyes.

She eyed his mouth, the half-assed smirk assuring her he was trouble waiting for an invitation.

An invitation she was tempted to issue. Her list of sexual fantasies played out in Technicolor in her imagination. Each and every one starring the hottest guy she'd ever lusted after.

Dante Luciano, bad boy extraordinaire.

Isabel's heart stopped. Impossible, yet there he was. There was no way Audra could have pulled this off as a joke. At least, not this quickly.

She took a visual inventory. Long, hard and sexy. Drool-worthy, as a matter of fact. A pierced ear, tribal tattoo on his bicep, and a black T-shirt molded over a chest that looked like it was carved from stone. Amazing! He'd actually improved with age. She hadn't thought it possible.

"How're you doing?" he asked. Even his words were

sexy. Low and husky, there was an underlying some-thing in his voice that made her stomach clench. It was like teetering at the top of a roller coaster, knowing one tiny push and you'd plummet. Dark, dangerous but oh-so-tempting.

She swallowed, trying to find her own voice.

"Fine, thanks," she answered after clearing her throat.

Irritated with herself when her pulse wouldn't steady, Isabel lifted her chin and pulled back her shoulders to look taller. His gaze held hers for a brief second, then dropped to her breasts. Her breath caught. Isabel knew she was modestly covered. Her silk T draped more than hugged, barely showing any cleavage. Even so, his gaze felt like a caress. Soft, knowing, purely sexual. Heat curled deep in her belly.

"Two-eighty-five Main Street. Sweet Scentsations, right? I'm Dante Luciano. Luciano Construction." His gaze slid back up her features, appreciation clear in those hypnotic eyes as he met her wide-eyed stare. "I hope I didn't keep you waiting. I hear you've got a list for me to take care of?"

2

DANTE LUCIANO SLID a long look over the woman staring up at him. Dark curls, a delicate face and curvy little body. *Not bad.* Even better was the look of appreciation in her eyes. Nothing like watching a woman enjoy the view.

The clothes, long flowy skirt and simple top in a muted shade of purple, were a little mellow for his tastes, but he had a good enough imagination to figure what was beneath the yards of material. Between his imagination and the look in her eyes, working with her might turn out to be a very sweet distraction. One he wouldn't mind tasting a few times while here in town.

Who knew Santa Vera had gained such a nice view in the years he'd been gone? His shoulders twitched under the weak morning sunlight. He tried to shake off the feeling of claustrophobia that had engulfed him the minute he'd crossed the city limits into town. A man who prided himself in making life a pleasure, Dante made a point to avoid discomfort whenever possible. And Santa Vera always lived up to its promise of discomforting him. In spades.

As soon as he helped his mom with this guilt-induced favor, he'd say his good-byes and get the hell out of town. He was sure Santa Vera would be glad to see him go.

"Isabel Santos?" he asked, remembering the contact name his mom gave him.

"I'm Isabel," she murmured. "How'd you know about my list?"

Dante frowned. Was he missing something? "Sylvia Luciano's my mother. She told me you had some changes to the scheduled renovations."

Sharply arched black brows drew together over eyes the same color as a stormy sky. She looked like she was taking a mental step backward, then gave him another once-over. This time it wasn't nearly as hot. He figured his name finally registered.

He didn't know if he should sneer or sigh. Almost a decade later and he was still the bad boy of Santa Vera? You'd think they'd have found something else to gossip about after all this time. Then again, he hadn't changed his wild ways much, so why would he expect the town to quit being a pain in his ass?

"I didn't realize you worked for your father," she said with a frown.

"I don't." He wasn't about to admit that his mother blackmailed him, though, so he just shrugged. "I'm helping out on a couple jobs. It's just temporary."

"Right, short-term. Sounds like the perfect plan…" Her voice trailed off, and an intriguing look crossing her face. He suddenly felt like a one-pound box of rich, creamy chocolates sitting in front of a starving woman. And damned if he wouldn't enjoy her diving in for a taste.

Maybe this stint in purgatory wouldn't be too bad with the help of the sweet Ms. Santos.

Then, like she'd given herself a mental shake, her face cleared. "So in a roundabout way, you're working for me, hmm?"

At his shrug her face went smooth, a professional mask falling over her porcelain features. Dante grimaced. He hated masks.

But unlike his typical reaction—to sneer and turn away—Isabel's mask made him want to coax it off her. Odd, since he was a man who definitely preferred the easy route. And coaxing anything from a woman, no matter how sexy, always ended up with him wrapped in strings. And strings were never easy.

With that in mind, Dante wasn't sure why he gave Isabel his most charming smile. The kind that usually made women melt and go all soft and agreeable. He leaned close, just enough make her eyes widen. Her perfume, the scent of spicy sensuality, swirled around him.

"I'd say we're working together, if you know what I mean." Grin in place, he watched for her reaction. Sweet thing like her, he figured she'd go all outraged and uptight.

Instead, her full lips twitched and Isabel's eyes twinkled with humor. A soft gust of wind sent her curls bouncing around her shoulders.

"If you think I'm going to do you any good when it comes to hammering drywall, you're going to be sadly disappointed," she informed him. "I have many talents—" her pause sent a shaft of heat straight through Dante's body as he imagined two or three he'd like to try out "—but construction isn't on the list."

"No?" He cast another look over her body, then met her eyes and winked. "What *is* on that list of yours?"

"You'd be surprised," she said with a laugh that hinted at nerves. "For now, let's focus on the renovations, hmm?"

Dante glanced around the tidy commercial neighborhood. Quaint and picturesque brick sidewalks flanked cute buildings. The whole street screamed uptight, upright and closed-minded. Dante was willing to admit he might be a little bitter, given his history here. In truth, he'd earned the wild reputation they tagged him with, but that still didn't make this his kind of place. He wondered how soon he could finish and go home to the beach. He missed Southern California already.

"The details were a little vague when I got the call to come help. Just that you'd paid your money and had a deadline. Want to fill me in?"

"Sure. Your father's already finished the basic renovations. The apartment upstairs is done and the storefront has been framed, but not completed. Before your father broke his foot, we'd discussed making a few changes to the initial plans."

She reeled off a grocery list of jobs still to be done. Two refrigerators, the small kitchen, finish work, floor, bathroom tiles and fixtures. Among other things.

"Damn, that's a lot of work. And you want it all done by the original date?" Dante paused, wondering how that was going to translate, time-wise. He wanted to be on the road by the end of the month. Could he finish this job in twenty-six days? "I've got a tight schedule myself. I hope you're okay with me being here a lot."

Her eyes had heated to a smoky haze. Dante didn't know what had inspired the change, but the sexy look was doing wild things to his body. Watching those heavily fringed gray eyes blur made him want to see if he could make them go even darker with a little loving.

He'd bet his Harley he could.

"C'mon in, I'll show you around," was all she said. "After you've seen what's what, I'll get you the list."

He gestured for her to go ahead. After a long look, she

nodded and turned to lead the way up the wooden steps to the house. He noted the outside was in good shape. An ode to its time period, the gingerbread trim and spindled porch seemed to say "c'mon in and check us out." He wondered what she'd be selling inside.

Dante slid his gaze down her body, letting himself linger on the way the silky fabric of the skirt molded itself to her legs and butt as she walked ahead of him up the stairs. She had amazingly long legs for a woman of less-than-average height.

Long enough to wrap around a man and hold tight. He'd imagine they were silky smooth, too. His fingers warmed at the thought of sliding them down her leg. He'd start at the calf, there just below her skirt. He'd smooth a path over the delicate curve of her ankle and down to her toes. Then he'd give himself the pleasure of a return trip, only this time he'd keep heading north.

"You *do* work in construction, right?" Isabel asked, pulling him out of his sexy little detour. She shot him a sidelong look as she opened one side of the double door. "I don't remember your father saying anything about this being a family business. I'm not questioning your abilities or anything, but it'd definitely be a plus if you're experienced enough to handle this job."

"I don't work for Luciano Construction, no." According to his old man, Dante was the end of three generations of tradition. Not because he wasn't any good at construction, he was making his living at it, after all. But because he sucked at taking orders. And Frank Luciano was big on orders. The old man was probably dancing in fury, cast and all, over the fact that his worthless son was bailing his ass out. If his wife had even told him. Sylvia Luciano was big on keeping the peace.

"Don't worry about it, though. I'm sure I'm experienced enough to handle just about anything you come up with," he assured her.

ISABEL'S PULSE SKIPPED at the image of how Dante could handle *things*. She'd bet he could handle them just fine—and then some.

It was all she could do not to pinch herself. *Dante Luciano, bad boy extraordinaire* and hunk of her fantasies…here, in front of her. It was almost too much to accept. Was it a dream? A hangover-induced birthday fantasy in 3-D? Her mind whirled with possibilities, but it felt real. Her body's reaction was definitely real.

But she'd already done her idiot impression for Dante, ten years before. Holding tight to the image of her humiliation, she vowed to keep it cool this round. If fate had brought him back into her life, she'd make the most of it. Lucky for her, she'd never even registered on his radar, so he didn't remember her.

Excited—if deluded—triumph surged through her. This was her chance to meet him on even ground. Or as close as possible, all things considered. Sure, she might peek at the man while he worked, but she'd be damned if she'd blush and stammer when caught. After all, she was all grown up now, hardly an inexperienced sixteen-year-old good-girl.

"Yeah, but I'm talking about construction," she corrected, proud of her offhand tone. He grinned in response. "I don't suppose you have references or anything?"

"No references, but I've never had a single complaint."

She slid an appreciative look over his body and gave a little hum. Years of hot, wet dreams flashed through her mind, all starring the man in front of her. She was sure complaints were the last thing he heard the morning after. Then, realizing what she'd done, her gaze flew back to his as color flooded her cheeks.

So much for not blushing.

Dante's grin widened.

He moved through the open area that took up the front half of the house. Still under construction, it was one big, raw space. She watched as he inspected the wiring and plumbing.

"What're you aiming for when this is done?" he asked.

"Sweet Scentsations will be one-stop gift shop," she replied, glad to focus on her project instead of her wayward body's reactions. "I'll not only offer fresh cut flowers, bouquets and plants, but handmade candies made by a local chocolatier. There will be a small selection of gifts, cards and balloons."

"Clever." Dante quirked a brow. "Is Santa Vera big enough to support such a specialty shop? I've seen plenty of clever ideas fail in larger cities."

"I've done the research. Santa Vera caters to its tourist population and over the last three years has created a solid niche as a wedding town. I wouldn't have invested my entire capital into this shop if I didn't have a plan to make it work."

His eyes widened at the vehemence of her tone, but Isabel barely noticed. She was too busy tamping down the demons his question had stirred. Failure wasn't a consideration. She had too much to prove, after all.

"That'd explain the plumbing," was all he said, though. "What's back that way?"

Still putting out the last embers of panic at the idea of failure, she followed him toward the storage rooms. Her gaze locked on the tight planes of his butt, highlighted in loving perfection by his worn jeans. Her fingers itched to reach out and touch the soft denim, just there where it curved over his left cheek.

Focus, she reminded herself. Be professional. She pulled in a breath and folded her fingers together. She'd have plenty of time to pant after he left.

"This is where I want the storeroom and a small kitchen to make candies on site. I also want to add another cooler for the flowers, as well as a small greenhouse on the back of the building. Those are on the list of changes."

She went on to describe the details of the job, when the walk-in refrigerator and appliances would be delivered and her timeline. At least, that's what she hoped was coming out of her mouth. Because when Dante shoved his hands into the front pockets of his jeans, she lost focus. She slid a quick glance over his clenched biceps, her eyes narrowing in heated desire.

Realizing she'd stopped mid-sentence, her gaze flew to his. Under the amusement dancing in his green eyes was a burning flame of interest. Oh, God. She was making a complete ass of herself. Again. This was completely unacceptable. He had to go so she could get control of her thoughts. There was no hope of controlling the lust that surged through her body, but she could at least keep it from being so obvious.

"I have the list in the office," she finally said. "We can go over it now."

Dante shook his head.

"I've been on the bike for a couple hours. I need to settle in and get a shower. How about you give me the list now, I'll read it. I'm good at reading. If I have any questions, I'll let you know."

Good, he'd be gone sooner. The short trip to her office was used to lecture herself on the value of control and how stupid she'd feel if he knew how badly he affected her. Not even bothering with a file folder, she snagged the pages from the printer and clipped them together.

She stood there, her future clutched in her fists, her past looming like a testosterone-flexing reminder of how easy it was to lose one's brain cells at the sight of the ultimate fantasy.

A taunting little voice in her head reminded her of the Man Plan she and Audra had created. Oh, sure, she'd wanted a man. Not just a man, but a man who could make all her hot, sexual fantasies a reality. And now one—not just any man but her ultimate fantasy man—was at her front door and what did she do?

Blush, stutter and hide in her office. Not okay. After all, number one on her list was control. Number two was not looking stupid. Isabel pressed her hand against her stomach, trying to calm her edgy nerves. He was just a man. Albeit her ideal man, but that was beside the point.

The question was, would she pursue the man?

Or hide?

She didn't know yet. But for now, he was technically her employee. So she needed to get over her girly nerves and act like the professional she prided herself in being.

Pep talk in mind, she returned to the shop. Stopping a safe distance away, she thrust the handful of documents at him.

"I was starting to wonder if you were coming back," he commented, taking the papers. His eyes widened at the thickness of the stack. "Damn, how many changes do you plan to make? And Frank had approved all these for your timeframe?"

"They're all approved," she said. She needed him to go. Now. Before the pep talk faded and she tried to lick him.

He glanced at the top sheet, his lower lip dropping a little at the bulleted list, prioritized and color-coded.

"Scary," he breathed.

"They were already printed out and on my desk," she said, ignoring his comment. "I'd intended to put them in a file folder and all, but you seem like you're in a hurry and I don't want to keep you waiting."

He seemed to get her unspoken message, loud and clear. He winked. Then he tried to kill her.

He took her hand in his, smoothing his thumb over the sensitive flesh. One second turned to five as he held her gaze. Ten seconds and her smile dropped away. Her vision blurred and her body stiffened, but she didn't pull away. Dante's smile quirked.

It was that smile—almost a smirk, but not quite—that brought her back to sanity. She suddenly wanted to take his cocky self down a peg or two.

"Maybe I should let you in on a little secret," she murmured, her words low and breathy. She was proud of that tone. Like she was about to tell him her deepest fantasies.

"I'd like to hear all your secrets," he said as he lifted her hand to his lips. He pressed a kiss to her knuckles, then rubbed them against his cheek.

Since they mostly featured him, she was sure he'd get a kick out of them. One thing about Dante Luciano, he wasn't hurting in the ego department. He never had been.

"Let's settle for just this one, hmm?" She turned her hand in his, then patted his cheek. "I'm the boss here, and I don't think mixing business and pleasure is a good idea. But I'm sure if you take your hot and horny self down to the east side of town, you're bound to meet up with some old friends. Or make new ones even. You'll have no trouble finding yourself a good time."

Apparently unoffended, Dante flashed a delighted grin. "I'm much more interested in a challenge," he told her. "Like I said, we'll be spending a lot of time together. Why not make the most of it?"

"Thanks for the offer. But no thanks." She laughed, actually amused. "Besides, I doubt we'll be spending that much time together."

"Why not? Scared?" He stepped closer. Close enough for her to smell the warm sunshine on his skin and the musky spice of his cologne. Close enough to see the tiny flecks of gold in his bottle-green eyes. Desire blurred her vision as flames of edgy wet heat flickered deep in her belly.

When Dante reached out and wrapped one of her inky curls around his index finger, it was all she could do not to whimper.

But she didn't pull away. Hell, no, she wasn't giving in like a namby-pamby good girl. Instead, she rolled her eyes and gave what she hoped was an amused sneer.

"Oh, please? Is that supposed to be a dare? Now what? I prove I'm not afraid to have you within lusting distance without throwing myself at you?"

"Lusting distance, huh? Why don't we talk about that?"

"Why don't we not."

Dante laughed. "You know, I was looking forward to coming back to Santa Vera as much as I'd anticipate a prostate exam. But I have to admit, now I'm actually looking forward to my four-week stay in hell."

TWENTY MINUTES later, Dante pulled out his key and unlocked the door to the motel. He hadn't bothered to go by his parents' house. He had, though, taken a quick trip around the property his boss wanted. Nice way to kill a few birds with one stone—help out his mom, piss off his dad and do his regular job at the same time.

Dante snickered and tossed the room key on the cheap dresser. Maybe he was still trouble? Hell, even the desk clerk had recognized him. And charged an extra two-hundred bucks deposit. Apparently she remembered his going-away party. Back in high school, he and some of his buddies had trashed three of the rooms, she'd been quick to remind him.

He shrugged off the irritation. He'd known he'd be judged if he came back. That's how small towns were. Quick to blame, long to forget. And it wasn't as if his reputation hadn't been earned. He'd been hell on wheels as a teen and he hadn't changed a whole lot since.

Sure, he had a steady job now. Ironically, despite his issues with his father, he'd taken the old man's profession to heart. A troubleshooter for one of the largest construction firms on the West Coast, he didn't lift a hammer much these days, but he was sure he hadn't lost this touch. Instead, he spent his time traveling from site to site, handling everything from zoning to personnel issues.

Travelling thirty weeks out of the year kept him from boredom, as well as entanglement-free. Buddies to party with in the various towns he visited on Tremaine business, ladies satisfied with a few weeks here and there. It should be perfect. But lately, it'd been bugging him. He shrugged off the idea that his life was lonely; it was exactly how he wanted it.

Free, easy and unencumbered.

Every once in a while, his boss had him scout out properties to take over, since the guy had a weird desire to own pieces of the entire world. While the job gave Dante enough freedom to keep him from going crazy, the challenge was wearing off.

But other than a cushy bank account, a house on the beach and the Harley, he was still pretty much the same hell-raising no-good he'd been ten years before when his father told the sheriff to escort him out of town.

Dante sighed and looked around the plain motel room. Same ol', same ol'. Living on the road was definitely losing its appeal. He unpacked his MP3 player and docking station, needing some unwind music. Before he could drop to the bed to see if it was as lumpy as it looked, his cell phone rang.

"Luciano," he answered.

"Did you check out the property?" his boss asked on the other end. Luke Tremaine wasn't a man to waste time with pleasantries.

"Yeah, I saw it. As luck would have it, it's right across the street from the place I'm working on. Good location, nice lot. I'll get inside in the next couple days, see what kind of shape it's in."

"Doesn't matter." Luke dismissed his comment. "We'll raze it. From the reports, it's one of those old-fashioned monstrosities. That won't suit my purposes."

Dante pulled a face. He could just imagine one of Tremaine's signature, sleek chrome-and-glass dance clubs on Main Street. It'd stick out like a sore thumb. And piss off the townspeople like nobody's business. Not his problem. His job was to scout, assess and report to Tremaine Construction.

"Don't forget you're still technically on the clock," Tremaine reminded him. "Confirm the lot size and stats, then get me a report."

With that, the phone went dead. Dante was about to toss it on the bed when it rang again.

A quick glance told him it was his mother. Dante grimaced, but didn't answer this time. He needed to unwind before dealing with her questions and unspoken expectations. He'd take her to dinner, of course. Otherwise she'd be hurt. And not hurting his mother was one of the few rules Dante followed religiously.

But for now, he'd settle in. A quick shower, a nap, then he'd be ready to deal with the coming weeks.

The Santos job was the only major thing on his father's schedule. A few other little jobs here and there, but nothing big. Dante's focus would be on the intriguing Isabel's renovations. Get those done, then he could leave, free and clear.

What was it about her that tugged at him? Other than her looks, she really wasn't his type. Not that he liked to think of himself as being so predictable that he *had* a type. To him, all women were simply fascinating. But a man didn't hover on the edge of thirty without learning a little caution around serious, sweet women.

And the vibe the woman in front of him put off was seriously sweet. Not uptight, but not on par with the hit-and-run sexual satisfaction he made his benchmark for involvement with a woman.

Dante grabbed the papers she'd given him, scanning her list. Damn, it was gonna be a lot of work. And the sweet Miss Santos was obviously planning on tracking him with a stopwatch.

Pacing off the irritated energy, Dante flipped to the last

page. Hand written, numbered, with notes in the margins. Great, directions.

He focused on the words.

Oh, yeah baby.

Hot, wild and a little rough up against the wall.
Intense passion in a semi-public place.
A smorgasbord of sexual pleasure, complete with
whipped cream, strawberries and lots of decadent
chocolate.

Dante's mouth went dry and the words blurred on the page as he pictured he and Isabel in each of those scenarios. Especially that last one. Fast, intense and a little rough got his juices flowing like nothing else. The idea of taking Isabel against a wall sent a bolt of heat straight to his dick.

Rock hard, Dante wondered how long it would take to get back to her house. Less than five minutes, he figured. Then again, given his present condition, he probably couldn't even straddle the Harley without breaking a vital part of his anatomy.

He blinked and scanned the rest of the list. Any woman who could come up with fantasies this hot was a woman he wanted to get to know. Really, really well.

Looked like the lovely Miss Santos wasn't so sweet after all.

3

"AT FIRST, I THOUGHT you were pulling some kind of prank," Isabel said into her cell phone. She automatically glanced both ways before crossing the empty cobblestone street to the old-fashioned, brick-fronted town hall. "I mean, what're the chances that we're talking about Dante Luciano and the next morning he shows up at my doorstep on a Harley?"

"Definitely slim," Audra agreed. "It's kinda funny, though. And I'm sure he wasn't nearly as hot as you remembered, right?"

Isabel didn't bother to correct her. After all, admitting that actually talking to Dante Luciano in person was better than almost every sexual fantasy she'd ever had was a little pitiful.

"Did he remember you?" Audra asked.

"Hardly. I wasn't the type to even register on his radar. I doubt Dante Luciano even remembers the night we met." After all, he hadn't done sweet girls. With a sigh, she realized he still probably didn't. The question was, did she want to be sweet or not? Ten years ago, he'd scared the hell out of her.

Isabel recalled the way his eyes had slid over her body the day before. The delicious, welcoming heat of his appreciation had been blatantly clear. She shivered at the memory. Apparently she'd registered on his radar this time. And she definitely wasn't scared.

"So I guess he's not, you know, like a birthday wish come true, huh?" she asked, only half joking.

"No no, baby," Audra said with a laugh. "You need training wheels first and a guy like that is bound to be as bad as that mean machine he rides. Way out of your league."

Insulted, Isabel was tempted to defend herself. Hey, she wore big-girl panties; she could do the Man Plan. Then again, a guy like Dante was probably used to women who didn't wear *any* panties. Who knew she'd reach the point of envying pantiless women and their experience? Just went to show what obsessing about sex could do to a gal. Not pretty, not pretty at all.

She sighed as she pulled open the door to the town hall. "I've got to go, I've got a business-association meeting in a few minutes."

"Why? You're not volunteering again, are you?"

Isabel winced.

"You are, aren't you? Why do you do that? Don't you have enough on your plate with starting a new business and trying to settle into a new town? C'mon, Isabel, quit with the do-gooder stuff and give yourself a break."

Isabel puffed out a breath and tried to think of a way to defend herself. She wasn't a do-gooder. She just wanted to fit in. To be a part of things. And since nobody ever invited her in, she volunteered.

"It's not really volunteering," she excused. "It's the town planning council. They're focused on controlled expansion, keeping the main street image intact, stuff like that. A lot of it is in preparation for the Sweetheart Festival in February."

"What's that?"

"To have a business on Main Street, you have to sign a contract agreeing to participate in the festival. They have a whole slew of requirements, but the promotion for the business is going to be phenomenal."

It was all Isabel could do not to rub her hands together at the prospect. She'd been dreaming of this for years. She'd be an integral part of the town, the go-to girl for flowers and gifts.

"I want to make sure Sweet Scentsations' placement in the festival is front and center. If I can, I'd like to provide the flowers for all the events, possibly even the gift baskets for the dignitaries. It'll be a huge step for the business if I can pull it off. From what I understand, prime positioning like that is snapped up fast. Usually by council members."

"Still sounds like volunteering to me," Audra muttered. "But, whatever. Just don't get crazy, okay? I've gotta go. Hey, check for hot-dude business owners while you're in there. I'll bet someone like that would work just fine for the Man Plan," she advised with a laugh before she hung up.

Isabel wrinkled her nose at the phone, then tossed it into her bag. Settle for just some guy? After seeing Dante, feeling her body go into sexual overdrive, she didn't want to settle. But Audra was the expert on all things sexual, and she obviously didn't think Isabel could handle Dante.

Of course, a guy as hot, as gorgeous as Dante probably had his own list, or only got involved with women at his experience level. Which meant she was nowhere in the vicinity. Didn't it figure, even within touching distance, he was still out of her reach.

TWO HOURS LATER, ISABEL stomped out of the hall, shoving her notepad into her purse. One of the reasons she'd been so excited to become involved with the business association was to take her place among the town's business leaders. To prove herself and her main claim to fame—her planning skills. There had been ten leadership positions available, and conveniently, the association had ten attending members. But had they given one to each member? Hell, no. One guy was so special he'd be leading two committees. And her? She'd got diddly squat. Oh sure, her skills would be appreciated on any committee but they still didn't trust her to lead.

She wanted to kick the lush fichus tree on her way out of the hall. The only reason she didn't was the fact that the ceramic vase would probably break her toe. She should have thought of that when she'd delivered it the previous week as a show of appreciation and camaraderie for her new associates.

Associates, hell. She shoved the door open. Next time she'd deliver a cactus in a wicker pot. That way she could kick it as hard as she wanted, and hopefully it'd land on the council leader's head.

"Isabel," someone called out. "Wait up."

She turned and bit back a sigh. Just what she needed, Mr. Perfect.

"Lance," she said in greeting. His short blond hair ruffled, but didn't muss in the brisk breeze. Even his haircut was perfect. Isabel swallowed her snarky attitude. It wasn't Lance's fault he was so together. She figured years of PR work as a real-estate agent had honed his persona until he was the epitome of together.

He gave her his patented smile, all friendly confidence. "I wanted to see if you were okay," he said in a low tone. Ever the multitasker, he kept his gaze on her face at the same time he nodded his greeting to a passerby.

Maybe that was why things hadn't worked out between them. He'd never managed to focus solely on *her.* And he'd definitely never understood her. That had been obvious back in the meeting. Oh, sure, she knew he'd been trying to talk her up, give her support. But all that talk about new ideas, time for change and new blood had clearly put people's backs up.

Isabel told herself it wasn't Lance's fault. Tension shifted across her shoulders, but she forced a pleasant look on her face. No point in getting upset or taking him to task. She'd done that once or twice before, but he was oblivious. To Lance, his way was the only way and anyone who didn't agree simply needed his friendship and advice even more.

Being mad at him was like trying to be pissed at Mary Poppins. Pointless and frustrating. Because inevitably, he always felt he knew best.

"I wanted to talk with you about the meeting. You seemed a little disappointed." He pulled a face and rubbed his hand on her shoulder. Isabel pulled away. For some reason his touch gave her the creeps now that they'd split up. Besides, it drove her nuts when people patted her like she was a little kid who needed placating. Small didn't mean stupid, she wanted to yell. Of course, since that urge came with the urge to stick her tongue out at him, she didn't figure he'd believe her.

"I didn't realize, of course, that you might volunteer for any of the positions or I would have warned you," he continued reasonably. "Santa Vera is growing rapidly, but at heart, it's still a small town, and there are a lot of small-town attitudes that come with that. It's not that you don't fit in," he said. Isabel supposed his tone was supposed to be soothing, but the way it grated down her spine made her want to scream. "It's just a matter of time. People have to get used to you. To see what you have to offer. Give it time."

Time? She'd been here for six months. How much time did they need, for crying out loud? Back in Auburn, she'd have led any committee she wanted. But of course, her parents had been well-known business owners.

She tried to shake off her irritation, knowing it was pointless. Too many times to count, she'd been frustrated in the face of his implacable fortitude.

"I think I'd be fine with the council's expectations," she said, trying to keep the pout off her lower lip. "I'm a successful businesswoman, after all. You could have mentioned that back there, you know. Your respect for my qualifications probably would have gone a long way with them."

"Give yourself time. I'd advise you to volunteer to serve on one of the committees. You know, observe, learn the ins and outs of how we operate here. Give people a chance to see how efficient you are and to appreciate what you have to offer. In a couple years, they'll be welcoming you as a committee leader."

Isabel ground her teeth. It was like he was talking to a little kid. Was there not one person who believed she could jump in and excel? No wonder she had hang-ups with everyone who doubted her.

He reached over to pat her shoulder again, this time giving it a brief squeeze. "You'll catch on. If you need help, feel free to give me a call."

Isabel's eyes narrowed as Lance turned and walked away, his gray pinstripe suit a vivid contrast to the other more casually dressed businesspeople milling around the hall. That was the second time today someone had intimated that she was in over her head. What was up with that? Was she really so incompetent that she couldn't handle a simple committee role? Or a man like Dante Luciano?

She pursed her lips and sighed. Well…maybe Dante was a bit more than she'd thought she could handle before. But wasn't that the purpose of the Man Plan? To push out of her comfort zone and have mind-blowing, awesome sex.

Not an easy thing to do when everyone seemed to have so little faith in her abilities on any level—be it business or sex.

LATE THAT AFTERNOON, Isabel arranged a winter bouquet of hothouse lilies.

Was it her? Did she come across as incapable of running with the big dogs? *Sweet little Isabel, why don't you go read a book instead of trying to ride that skateboard? Oh, Isabel, don't be silly, you don't know enough people to win as class president; you'd just be hurt if you tried. Sweetheart, quit daydreaming. Pull your head out of the clouds and set goals, instead.*

All her life, she'd been pigeonholed. Protected. Because everyone expected it—hell, demanded it—she'd played it safe, in life and with her goals. Even this business, as much as she had emotionally invested in it, was a well-calculated risk. And now that she wanted to break out of the box? Expand herself, reach for the stars? What did she get? Naysayers and doubt.

Just once, she'd like have someone expect huge things from her, that she be better than *good enough*. She wanted to be an integral part of something. Always, she was the outsider looking in, the quiet one in the back of the room. Ignored. God, she was sick of being ignored.

Her movements sharp and abrupt, she snapped the stem completely off one flower. With a little growl, she tossed it at the garbage can. It hit the rim, bounced off and slid back across the floor to land at her feet.

"Damn," she muttered.

"You don't seem like a happy camper," a voice said over Nickelback's "Photograph."

Isabel gave a little shriek worthy of any horror-film starlet, breaking yet another of the fragile flowers and sending the vase tottering at the edge of her worktable.

"Hey," Dante said, suddenly at her side. "I didn't mean to startle you."

Before her mind could acknowledge who had scared the crap out of her, he reached around her to steady the wobbly vase. With the push of two fingers, he moved it to the center of the table, then gave her a long, questioning look from those deep green eyes. Her body tensed as excitement swirled through her system. Her fingers shook. Ignoring the part of her yelling *liar liar,* she blamed the nerves fluttering in her stomach on the scare.

"You okay? I didn't take you for the high-strung type or I would have announced myself."

Isabel's heart skittered. She wasn't sure if it was from surprise, or from Dante's proximity. But when it didn't settle, she figured the credit went to him.

Because if anyone deserved it, he definitely did. Making a show of straightening the flowers she'd scattered, she cast a glance over him. From the tips of his beat-up work boots to the strong expanse of his shoulders, he was even sexier today than he'd been swinging off the Harley the day before.

His green eyes had that same slumberous look that made her insides melt. But instead of damp waves like the other day, his hair was a sexy, just-out-of-bed tumble to the collar of his forest-green T-shirt. Her fingers slid along the smooth stem of the flowers, imagining how that silky hair would feel in her hands. On her belly. Brushing along the sensitive skin of her thighs.

Isabel caught her breath at the image. Oh, God, he was gorgeous. She was too aroused to even be embarrassed at her thoughts.

"I'm fine," she belatedly answered on a puff of breath. "I didn't hear you come in, is all. I'm so used to working alone back here, I didn't think to turn down the music to listen for the door."

His slow grin assured her that yes, indeed, she was babbling. Isabel sucked in a deep breath and set the last flower in its space, then faced him, chin held high.

"I'm not high-strung, but I was startled. Thanks for saving the vase." She gestured to the large glass urn. "It's the last one I have in inventory and I'd hate to disappoint my client."

"Since I hate being disappointed, I can definitely understand that," he said, a wicked light twinkling in his eyes. It guaranteed he never left a woman disappointed, either. A flickering spark of desire flamed deep in her belly.

A man who guaranteed satisfaction? One who'd spend as much time as she liked, do all those deliciously wild things she dreamed of? In the past, all her fantasies of Dante had been of the things she wanted to do to him. The way she wanted to worship his body, to see it poised under hers. But now…his words spurred a whole new fantasy and in it, *he* was the one doing all the work.

"I wanted to get started tomorrow morning," he continued, oblivious to the mental pleasure he was giving her. "I figured I'd check to see what supplies were on hand. We should go over some stuff, too. Schedules, the list…that kind of thing."

The way his voice deepened, his eyes growing dark and sleepy, when he said that last part, sent Isabel's system into overdrive. Her nipples beaded painfully beneath the light sweater she wore as the damp heat moved from her belly to her panties.

It'd been a long six weeks since she and Lance had split. Not that she couldn't go without sex for a long time, but the sex she'd been getting prior to the split hadn't been anything to celebrate. She was sure that was why her body went crazy over the innocent statement. Dante obviously wasn't implying anything sexual.

Now if she could just get her body to believe that.

"It must be nice to visit home," she babbled, trying to distract her body. "I grew up over in Auburn, only ten miles away, but it's like a different world here. The people have been really welcoming. Since you're from here, if you have any ideas for the renovations please feel free to share. I'm all for using whatever I can to make the business better."

"I doubt any of my insight into the town will improve your business," he said. Isabel frowned at the tension, almost an underlying anger, in his tone. She gave him a searching look, but he just returned a long, blank stare. It didn't answer any questions, but it did stir her juices again. Holy cow, even with that stoic look on his face, the guy was hot.

"I didn't realize you were already open for business," he commented with a gesture to the floral arrangement.

"I'm not, really. At least, not to the general public. I

do have a clientele from my previous floral shop I'm still serving. It seemed smart to hold on to as many existing customers as I could, you know? A lot easier than trying to tackle the goal of making this new business fly high immediately. Baby steps, small goals, all that."

Dante shrugged, the muscles in his biceps rippling in a way that made Isabel want to nibble on him. Just there, on the arm, to see if he was as hard as he looked. If he tasted as good as she imagined.

"Why bother with little steps?" He narrowed his eyes, a wicked glint flashing in the green depths. He took one step, then two, closer. Close enough for her to smell the spicy scent of his cologne, to feel the heady heat of his body. Her own body reacted instantly, heartbeat racing as nerves battled desire in her belly. A distant memory flashed through her mind, clouded by time, wine and fear. She'd been this close to him once, that night at his party. This time, though, she knew what to do.

His voice dropped to a husky tone suited to dark nights and silk sheets. "If you want something, go for it. You might not get it the first time, but it beats pussyfooting around—playing it safe."

"You don't think it's smarter to take the big steps in areas you're good at, and smaller ones in the unknown?" she asked in a breathless tone.

"How do you get to be any good if you don't take a chance?" Dante shrugged again, so close she could almost feel the movement of his body. "If you want something, make it happen. Otherwise, while you're sitting there wishing, someone else will grab the ball and run with it." He looked around the storeroom, then gestured to the photo display of her floral arrangements and the healthy houseplants thriving in the windowsill.

"You're clearly good at what you do. You seem like a smart woman…" His gaze drifted down her body, a sensual caress of appreciation. "And definitely a beautiful one. Why wouldn't you go for whatever you want?"

It was like he'd ripped the lock off her inhibitions, giving her permission to ask for anything she wanted. He clearly believed she could reach for the stars. Power, indelibly combined with deep swirls of desire, simmered in her belly.

"Did you ever make a birthday wish?" she asked, her gaze locked on his lips. They were so close, and she'd bet anything they tasted fabulous. She wanted to taste them, test their texture. To run her tongue over the pouty fullness of his lower lip and tempt him into wild desire.

Isabel's breath shuddered at the image.

"Like blow out a candle and think about something you want? Sure," he said, his voice a low murmur. The sexy purr washed over her, wrapping her in a shivery kind of excitement. "Why?"

"My birthday was last Saturday," she murmured.

"What'd you wish for?"

Isabel licked her lips, then with a deep breath, looked up to meet his eyes. She could drown in those rich green depths. It wasn't the sensual promise there that gave her courage, although that was mighty tempting. It was the absolute acceptance. As if he saw right through her, all the way to her fears, insecurities and body hang-ups. And he wanted her anyway. His desire for her was a tangible thing, clear and tempting.

"I wished for a birthday kiss. A really hot, really special birthday kiss," she hedged, not ready to admit her entire fantasy wish. *Ha, baby steps be damned.*

A slow, sensual smile curved his lips.

Dante took one more step closer, bringing his body within caressing distance of hers. Isabel's fingers burned with the need to run them through his hair, then down his arms. When he slid a hand behind her neck, angling her face toward his, she couldn't stop her breathy moan.

"Happy birthday," he murmured right before his mouth took hers.

At the touch of his lips against hers, years of dreams shattered into a million pieces. Nothing in her deepest fantasies had prepared her for the dark, rich delight he invoked through that simple caress. One brush, two. Then, his sleepy green gaze holding hers prisoner, he ran his tongue along Isabel's bottom lip. Her breath shuddered to a halt, then whooshed out as he closed his eyes and got down to the serious seduction of her mouth.

Like the roller coaster she'd once likened him to, he took her on a terrifyingly wild ride with his mouth alone. The thrust of his tongue didn't invite, it demanded her participation. Lights, shimmering and sparkly, flashed against Isabel's closed lids as she gave over to the parry and thrust of his kiss. The feel of his body, deliciously hard, against her thigh, made her groan.

The sound seemed to be his signal to halt, since he slowed the slide of his tongue. One final caress, a butterfly kiss against her lips, then he gently pulled back.

Well, well. If the passion zinging through her body was any indication, he had actually improved with age. She sighed in delight.

"Hope it lived up to your wish," he whispered.

She sighed.

"I wanted to talk to you about this list of yours," he murmured against her hair. "There are quite few items there I really liked. I want to make sure I get them right."

So tuned in to her body's sighs of pleasure, Isabel barely caught his words.

"List?" she murmured.

"Right. The list of sexual scenarios. You hit on all but one of my absolute top fantasies."

What? Isabel pulled back so fast, Dante's arms slipped from her waist. Her skin chilled, whether it was from the loss of his body heat or his words, she didn't care.

"List of…?"

"Sexual scenarios. Fantasies," he expanded helpfully. Without asking, he pulled her back into his arms. She was too shocked to move again.

"You have my…" Oh God. Isabel's mind ran in a million directions, none of them good. Part of her noted how odd it was that she wasn't embarrassed to have had the hottest man she'd ever met read her deepest sexual fantasies. But that part was pretty well drowned out by the other parts all screaming *holy shit, how'd he get the list?* She'd had it on her desk, hadn't she? When had she last seen it?

"How?" she mumbled.

"It was with the renovation instructions you handed me yesterday."

Isabel closed her eyes and nodded. Of course it was. Anything else might be less embarrassing.

"Hey," he said, his tone soft and sweet. "You have nothing to be ashamed of. Sexual fantasies are normal, you know? It's the people who deny their fantasy life who have problems."

Why was she sure that meant he was completely problem-free? Then the rest of his words sunk in. Had he expected her to act like some virginal maiden shocked to have anyone realize she had a thing for sex outdoors?

"I'm not ashamed," she said honestly. "Embarrassed, yes. I can't believe I didn't notice that list was missing."

"I'll be happy to return it," he said with a slow grin. "Of course, I'd be happier to fulfill it with you."

Isabel almost came then and there. She crossed her arms over her chest to hide her rigid nipples and tried not to moan at even that minute contact.

She nibbled on her bottom lip, trying to figure out what to say. Oh, she knew what she *wanted* to say. Let's go, was the obvious reply. Then she'd suggest numbers three, four and seven. She managed to control herself, though. After all, hot and wild string-free sex was one thing. Having it with a man who was *essentially* working for her was another.

Besides, as much as Dante turned her on, a million doubts flew through her head. He was way out of her league, fantasy hottie or not. Hell, she'd almost come from a kiss alone. Could she keep up with a guy like that? Sure, she wanted to go for her goals—especially her fantasy ones. But she needed to think about this. Number one on her list, she had to be in control. Who knew having a wish staring you right in the face could be so scary?

So instead of dragging him into her office, shoving him down on her desk and running her tongue over his body, she gave a casual shrug.

"Thanks for the offer, but I'll have to pass."

"You sure?" He flashed an amused look and winked. "Because I'm betting with only a few changes, that list is the outline for the best sex possible."

Isabel gaped. "Changes?"

"Yeah, just a couple here and there." Dante gave her that slow, sexy smile. Rubbing his finger up and down her arm in a slow, steady caress, he leaned in to brush his lips over her ear. The warmth of his breath seared through Isabel, heating her all the way to her core and making her squirm. "Change that horse to a Harley, the forest to the beach."

The images flashed through her mind, her and Dante, both naked, on that huge black Harley of his. The rumbling power of the engine as it purred beneath them adding to the sensation as she rode him in the moonlight. Licking her lips, Isabel pressed her thighs together.

"Let me get this straight," she said, unable to hold back a baffled laugh. "You're trying to revise my fantasy list? Why don't you just go make one of your own?"

"Because yours is already almost perfect. It just needs a few minor adjustments."

"And you're the man to make them for me?" She posed it as a question, but she already knew the answer.

"Babe, I'm the perfect man for your fantasy list."

Even though her body agreed with him, Isabel struggled to grab control of her reactions and the conversation. "What an ego. Does that work for you often?"

"I've been called an expert by more than one lady," he offered. Despite the humor dancing in his eyes, Isabel didn't think he was teasing her.

"I'll just bet you have."

"I'd be happy to show you," he promised, his breath warming her temple. "We can work our way up to the Harley ride."

The wispy tendril of desire unfurled, low in her belly. Isabel realized this was a man who could bring her to orgasm with his voice alone. She'd bet he could do it without even using dirty words.

"I'll have to pass," she said faintly.

Dante let her pull away without protest. But the laser-sharp look in his eyes told her he was likely aware of her every fear and knew exactly which moves would alleviate the apprehension. And which would shift it over that blurry line into the realm of dark, edgy sexual craving.

She hurried from the room before she begged him to do just that.

DANTE SHIFTED UNCOMFORTABLY as he watched Isabel walk away. Damned if she didn't have a sweet sway to her hips in another one of those silky skirts. After tasting her, feeling the luscious pressure of her lips under his, all he could think of was holding those hips as she rode him. Dante wanted to chase her down and haul her back into his arms.

He could still taste her, sweet as a peach, on his tongue. The feel of her small body against him, her flowery scent filled his senses. God, she'd turned him on.

Down, boy. It wasn't gonna happen. As interested as she might be—and he'd tasted plenty of interest as her tongue had wrapped around his—she was holding back. He didn't know why, but she obviously didn't want to give in to the attraction.

Maybe because he'd seen her list? She really didn't seem embarrassed, but who knew with women? All he knew for sure was that Isabel obviously liked control. And Dante was the kind of man who thrived on making women lose control.

And it was only fair. That list of hers had kept him awake half the night, imagining her, them, living out each of those fantasies. Dante shifted, his jeans still uncomfortably tight.

He battled down the frustration. Tasting heaven, then being told he couldn't have more just didn't sit well. It was all he could do not to go after her and see if he couldn't seduce her into changing her mind.

But he wouldn't. He was here for less than a month, and while some women would be fine with that, Isabel didn't seem the type. He almost groaned as he remembered the way she'd sucked his tongue into her mouth. Damn shame, but probably just as well. As much as he'd hoped she'd jump at his offer to make her list a reality, he wasn't the kind of guy who chased a woman down when she'd put up the red light.

Trying to distract himself from the frustrated desire still stiff in his system, Dante shuffled through the supplies, checking them against the inventory list. It was probably just as well he was putting his sex life on hold while here. After his talk with his mother the previous night, he was sure if she caught the slightest whiff of interest on his part in a woman in town, she'd climb on the nagging wagon. Not just for the grandbabies she claimed to want. But for him to grow up, get over his issues with his father and come back to Northern California.

As if. The old man had never understood him, never appreciated that just because Dante didn't do things his father's way, that he had anything worthwhile to contribute. To Frank Luciano, his word was law. And his son, having broken that law, belonged in hell.

Dante threw a box back in its bin so hard, the cardboard burst and metal clips flew everywhere.

His mother didn't accept that, though. She figured time and distance should heal soul-deep wounds. She wasn't willing to accept that the two men in her life were too proud, both of them, to give in. She'd already tried to con Dante into coming to the house for a family dinner. Considering the last family dinner he'd had at his father's table had ended in the words, 'you're never welcome here again,' Dante didn't have much interest.

So, there you had it. A lot of good reasons to stay away from Isabel Santos, when he wasn't working. One: she wasn't the quickie type, even though her eyes had promised she'd like to try. Two: unless they kept it to sex in the storeroom during work hours, there was no way his mother wouldn't clue in. And three, four and five: the woman's fantasy list rivaled his own. She had the gumption to take on the closed ranks of a small town like Santa Vera and expect to succeed. And he'd dreamed of her last night. Dante never dreamed of women. She was already too intriguing. Getting involved with someone who invaded his subconscious, who might be his perfect match in bed was pure idiocy. At least, it was if she was attached to reasons one and two.

He recalled Isabel's eyes, their smoky hue, when he'd flirted with her. Damned if she wasn't the sweetest thing he'd ever met. As a rule, Dante didn't have a taste for sweets, but he was pretty sure he could become addicted to Isabel.

With that in mind, he didn't bother to stick his head in her office to let her know he was leaving. Instead he headed straight for the door.

He stepped out onto the front porch, his gaze landing on the property across the street. It would definitely shift the quaint feel of Main Street once Tremaine planted his chrome building there. And Tremaine wasn't the type to take into consideration surrounding aesthetics. The guy had something to prove. Whether it was a coffeehouse, a store, or in this case a dance club, he branded them all the same. As if there were a giant, chrome *Tremaine was here* sign.

It wasn't Dante's job to question why. It was his job to assess the property and scope out the local zoning issues. He had no idea how the businesses fared after Tremaine took over; that wasn't his problem.

Dante glanced down at the plans in his hand and puffed out a breath. Isabel's renovation completely centered around the charming antiquity of Main Street's current businesses. She sure wasn't going to be a happy camper when she saw her new view.

Not his problem, Dante assured himself as he straddled the Harley. Why, then, did it make him feel guilty?

4

"GUESS SOME THINGS DON'T improve with age," Dante muttered to himself as he stepped into his past. Downtown Diner looked exactly the same as the last time he'd been thrown out of it. Kitschy, a little run-down, smelling like onions and fried meat. He automatically seated himself in the booth to the left of the door, not even realizing why until he saw his own initials scratched into the aged Formica.

He puffed out a breath. Weird. It was just weird being here. The town, the diner. All of it.

A plastic menu slapped down on the table in front of him with a loud smack. "Wanna start with coffee?"

Dante lifted his gaze from the yellowed menu to the craggy creases of Lorna Bostrom's face. Like the diner, she hadn't changed much. Graying, grumpy and ungracious. He met her shrewd blue eyes, not surprised to see them widen, then narrow.

"You're back, huh? I must have missed the weather forecast."

"Hell's ice storm? I'd have thought you'd be the first to know."

"Right, because Satan and I are on a first-name basis."

"I'd heard that," Dante agreed, giving his most pleasant smile.

On anyone else, he'd have called the light in her eyes humor. But since he was pretty sure Lorna had been on the lynching committee that had run him out of town, it was probably just a manic gleam.

"What're you doing here?"

"I'm hungry."

Lorna just stared, her beady eyes narrowed under those bushy brows, until Dante shifted in his seat. Shifted, dammit, like a busted fifteen-year-old. This town was definitely bad for him.

"My mom needed help," he muttered.

"Good boy. One thing nobody could ever deny, you were always good to Sylvia." She planted her meaty hands on her hips, giving him a frowning once-over. Like she was considering how he'd managed that one decent trait in his lifetime of flaws.

Dante shrugged. So he was good to his mother. It wasn't a crime, was it? Needing to change the subject before he did something insane, like blush, he asked, "Can I get a burger, hold the chitchat?"

"You taking on your daddy's jobs, what with him laid up and hurt like he is?" Lorna asked, ignoring his request.

"I'll have the onion rings on the side."

"Bet he's fit to be tied, knowing how he hates asking for help. You came by that honest enough, I suppose."

"Cola, lots of ice."

"What job are you here to do? Your dad was juggling quite a few things," Lorna rambled on, "more than he shoulda been, if you ask me. After all, a man with heart problems is supposed to be slowing down."

Heart problems? Dante hid his shock. Why hadn't his mother mentioned it? It couldn't be that bad if nobody told him, right? Dante shifted, trying to ease the tension from his shoulders. But he knew it wouldn't go away till he checked on the old man's health. Not that he cared. But, well, his mom didn't need any more stress.

Fortunately, Lorna was too absorbed with her interrogation to check for a reaction.

"Bet you're working on the new girl's place." She frowned, taking her pencil from behind her ear and tapping it on the table. "Pretty little thing, you better watch it around her. She's a sweetie, if you ask me. And one of those good girls. Definitely doesn't need a wild boy like you dragging her down the wrong path."

His jaw clenched. Nothing ever changed in Santa Vera. Dante would have commented, but it wasn't worth the effort. It never did him any good to protest. People thought the worst of him despite anything he said or did to the contrary.

He remembered Isabel's fantasy list and realized the worst probably wasn't far off. Just the thought of her and that list made his body heat. Hot hadn't begun to describe his reaction to Isabel. He'd been turned on just meeting her, but could have blown that off. Nice wasn't his thing. But the insight into her fantasies, the images they invoked... damn. She'd become *his* all-time hottest fantasy. The ancient plastic seat creaked as Dante shifted. He'd reached a new low—horny and hot in the Downtown Diner.

Like a bloodhound catching scent of something juicy, Lorna gave him a narrow look. She knew something was up, but Dante didn't figure she'd have a clue what. He still felt like a little boy caught with his hand down his pants.

"I'll take a piece of apple pie to go, too," Dante added to his ignored order. He fixed a hard stare on her face, hoping she'd get the hint.

Lorna gave him a lethal glare, but at least she'd stopped gabbing. With a sniff, she turned and stomped away. Dante ignored her slow return to the kitchen, refusing to watch as she stopped at each occupied table to whisper and point at him. Instead, he leaned back in his seat and stared out the plate-glass window.

He felt the stares, even as the hiss of whispered conversation filled the air. Nothing changed.

Seven minutes later—he knew because he'd timed it—Lorna stomped back and slapped his plate on the table with a dull thud. His soda followed, the brown liquid sloshing to the edges. It was a testament to her thrifty nature that not a drop slopped over the side.

"That'll be seventy-eight-fifty," Lois grunted.

Dante glared. "For a burger? Prices a little steep these days, ya think?"

"You still owed me for the destruction of property from your last visit, boyo. Didn't think I'd let you get away with that, did you?"

He sneered. He'd worked off that debt when he'd built the brick barbeque out back of the diner for Lon. Typical of the residents here, Lorna only remembered what served her. Reality had little purpose in this damned town.

Arguing was useless. He tossed his Visa on the table, his gaze daring her to ask for ID or validation.

Instead, she swept the card up, gave him a look he couldn't decipher and waltzed off with a head-toss worthy of a queen.

Too hungry to do more than growl, Dante bit into his burger. The taste exploded on his tongue, rich and delicious. Just the way he liked it. Medium rare, grilled onions and a hint of mustard.

He'd been served one of the best burgers in the world and been screwed over. All in one meal. Yup, he was home, all right.

SATISFACTION FILLED Dante as he let the hammer swing, the second nature of his rhythmic pounding relaxing the knots of stress across his shoulders.

Two days back in Santa Vera and already he wasn't sleeping. He wasn't sure if it was irritation at being forced back to his old stomping grounds, or if it was the sexual frustration brought on by the hot little florist he couldn't get out of his head. Since he spent most of the night imagining how it'd feel to make each fantasy on her list come true, he figured she got the lion's share of the blame for his exhaustion.

The irritation, he had to admit, was all Santa Vera. Not that he'd given the town's reaction to his return any thought before. After all, returning hadn't ever been an actual option in the past. But if he'd wasted the energy wondering, he'd have figured he'd pass through pretty much unnoticed. It'd been ten years, why would anyone care to remember him? Or his past transgressions?

Apparently, plenty cared and they remembered in fine detail.

Did they have any interest in the fact that he'd made a success of his life? Had one person asked him what he was doing now? For all they cared, he made his living stealing hubcaps, or worse, breaking kneecaps. He wanted to rub his successful career in their faces. To tell them all he worked for one of the top dogs in Southern California. But then he'd have to confess who that top dog was. Not a good thing. Especially since Tremaine's plans would legitimately put Dante right back at the top of Santa Vera's most hated list.

Instead of merely starring in the top ten.

Dante put a little too much power behind his swing, the hammer smashing both the nail and the beam. He glared at the gashed four-by-four. *Refocus.*

After two days of practice, his thoughts shifted easily to Isabel and that fascinating list of hers.

He hadn't seen much of her. Usually he'd be fine with that. After all, who needed a distraction, even one as pretty as Isabel, hanging around while he worked? Not Dante. But if he couldn't get the woman out of his head, she might as well be there in the flesh.

His mouth watered at the images flashing through his mind. Isabel's sweet little body laid out on his Harley in the moonlight. He'd bet she had lily-white curves under those loose clothes of hers. He knew he wanted to find out. Maybe it was that buffet fantasy, but he'd swear he'd been starving for her ever since he'd read it.

A smorgasbord of sexual pleasure, complete with whipped cream, strawberries and lots of decadent chocolate.

A flash of color caught the corner of his eye. His body knew she was there before he even shifted his gaze from the four-by-four to the doorway.

Isabel, framed by the smooth rose tones of the doorframe, looked around. She looked good enough to eat. *Snack time.*

Black curls were gathered high on her head, adding inches to her small frame but leaving nothing to distract from the porcelain beauty of her face. The faint color of her cheeks was echoed in her silky pink blouse. His gaze trailed over her soft curves, appreciating the journey. His hands had held that waist. His fingers itched to feel the delicate curves again. To roam up and down her spine, making her shiver in reaction.

A skirt covered her legs, its brown material hitting the top of her ankle boots. Not an inch of skin showed. Damn. He wanted to see those legs. After two days of dreaming of them draped over his shoulders, he wanted to *feel* those legs.

It was all he could do not to stride over and grab her in his arms. So much for not chasing her down.

"Wow, check out the progress," she exclaimed, a hesitant smile lighting her face. "You've really got a lot done in here. And so fast."

"No point in wasting time," he told her. He ignored the pleasure that surged through him at her praise. He was good at what he did; it was stupid to get excited over her appreciation. That's what she was paying for. Now if she'd praise him for other things…well, that'd be exciting.

"I didn't even hear you come in," she continued, wandering through the room, stepping over piles of wood. He liked that, despite her fancy clothes, she seemed oblivious to the sawdust and construction mess. No diva here.

"I was up. I had the key, figured I might as well get to work."

"You're a morning person?" she asked. At his nod, she smiled. "Me too. I don't understand how anyone can sleep through the sunrise. If I'm not out of bed by seven, I feel like I'm playing catch-up all day."

He thought about watching the dawn with her after a long night in bed. The soft morning light on her bare skin, stretched out on his sheets, her arms reaching for him, her mouth moving over his body. Dante shoved his hands in his pockets. The sun wasn't the only thing rising.

Focus, Luciano. It was one thing to be all hot for her

at night when he was on his own time. But this was work and she was, for all intents and purposes, his boss. At least during work hours.

Maybe it was break time?

"I need to get the framing done for the refrigerators, then I'll get back to work on the front room. But don't worry, it will be done before the refrigerators are delivered," he said, forcing himself to stay on topic. "That way you can worry about decorating and crap while I install them and finish the back rooms."

Her laugh was low and husky. She shot him a teasing look and raised one brow. "Crap?"

"You know, wall color, fabric, decorating. I build things. I can make them solid, but I don't have a clue what makes them pretty for customers."

"I can't wait to start." She gave a little laugh. "I take my time getting plans in place, you know? Making sure everything is just right, giving it time to gel in my head to be sure I don't want to change anything. But once I'm sure of what I want, I'm a little impatient. I hope I don't drive you crazy."

Too late.

"I'm the same," Dante admitted. "Once I've got something designed or planned, I figure why wait?"

They shared a look of understanding. Dante held her gaze. Other than drink preferences and sexual positions, he rarely learned this much about a woman. It was an odd feeling. After a few moments, she bit her lip and glanced away.

"I really like how you've curved the counter," she said absently. Then she frowned. "That's exactly how I'd envisioned it, but I didn't tell you, did I? I know I'd made a list for you last night, but I haven't given it to you yet."

She stopped, obviously remembering the other list she'd made. He could tell by the way her face flushed. But then she gave a little grin and shrugged.

"You know what I mean," she said. "Instructions for the work in here. I figured that way, if I wasn't around, you'd know exactly how I wanted everything."

"I didn't need to wait for instructions. I know exactly what you like."

Isabel stopped in front of him, her eyes going smoky as she caught his double entendre. Gaze narrowed, he waited to see how she'd take it. Desire spiked when she put her hands on her hips and gave him a slow grin.

"Oh, really? A little cocky, there, aren't you?"

Cocky was right. He grinned, pleasure spiking hard and fast. Knowingly or not, sweet Isabel had issued a doozy of a challenge. And given him the perfect excuse to toss aside that heroic crap about giving her space. He never backed down from a challenge. Dante wasn't sure what turned him on more: the idea of tasting Isabel's mouth again, or the thrill of the chase.

"Not cocky. Assured. I know what you want done in here, just like I know you'll like this," Dante promised her as he meshed his fingers with hers. He stepped forward. Close enough to be enveloped in the heat of her. He let the sweet spice of her perfume wash over him. He wanted to smell it there, at the delicate curve of her neck exposed by her upswept hair. First a nuzzle, then a taste. Maybe even a bite or two.

"More?" he asked.

Her eyes huge, she arched a brow in question.

"If you want more, you have to tell me. I want you to detail exactly what you want. I've seen your list. I've spent a couple long, sweaty sleepless nights because I couldn't stop thinking about it. Thinking about you." He brought her fingers to his mouth, rubbing his lips over the soft flesh. He watched her breath shudder, power twining with desire in his system. "I'm sure I know exactly what turns you on, exactly how to make you scream with pleasure."

Her gray eyes went even darker as those lips, glistening in the morning light, parted. He felt her swift intake of breath and wanted to groan as the move pressed her breasts against his chest.

"But using that knowledge to seduce you would be wrong." A small smile played at the corner of his mouth as Dante watched disappointment war with denial in Isabel's eyes. "You wrote the list. That puts you in the driver's seat. The power position. That might scare the hell out of some guys, they might try and overpower you, push your buttons so they can regain power."

He moved, just the slightest bit, and put more pressure against her breasts.

"Me?" He continued, "I know I'm man enough to handle that list and anything else you want to bring to the table. So, you have to ask. To tell me exactly what you want."

As her gasp pressed the pointed tips of her lush breasts against his chest again, Dante hoped like hell she'd hurry up and ask. For something. Anything. As long as it was soon, before he made a liar out of himself and begged for a taste of her mouth.

IT WAS LIKE SOMETHING out of one her hottest dreams. Isabel couldn't breathe. That had to be the reason she felt so lightheaded. Or it could have been the heat radiating off Dante's chest, the way it warmed her breasts, beaded her nipples, turned her body into a molten pool of desire.

This was it, the most amazing moment in her life…at least, her love life. And damned if she wasn't going to make the most of it. All she had to do was breathe.

As if.

She looked up into Dante's eyes, more relieved than she wanted to admit at the hot desire she saw flaming in those intense green depths. At least she wasn't alone this time. What use was a Man Plan if she was the only one hot and bothered? The basis for that plan was hot, intense sexual exploration. Which required both parties' total involvement.

So maybe she should take that breath and do something about his obvious interest. After all, he was her Man Plan personified.

He was still the baddest of the bad boys. And—Isabel batted away the panic whispering around the edges of her mind—maybe she was still too much of a good girl to keep his attention. But if the fantasy gods were going to grant her greatest wish, who was she to run from it? And best of all, he was only there short-term, so she didn't have to worry about breaking her rules. Just here-and-now passion. The less time he was here, the less chance she had to do anything stupid. *Rule number three: no falling for him during their affair.*

This was her chance with Dante Luciano. The reality felt even more amazing than she'd dreamed. A once-in-a-lifetime shot to live out her wildest desires with the guy who'd fueled her every single sexual fantasy.

Dante ran the back of his hand over her cheek. The rough texture against her smooth flesh sent a shiver of delight through her.

"What's up?" he asked softly. "I can almost see your mind spinning like a tornado. Something wrong?"

The memory of that first kiss, ten years before, played in her mind. Incredible, worthy of years of fantasies. But… she hadn't been enough, then. The fear that'd made Isabel walk away from Dante's kiss two days before hadn't faded. He was prime fantasy material. But was she? Could she handle her own list?

Her fear must have shown in her eyes, because Dante shifted. Just the tiniest shift, but enough to let her know she still had control.

That sense of power was all she needed. Giddy excitement surged through her system, so strong that Isabel had to force herself not to giggle. Whether she could handle it or not, she'd be an idiot to let such an incredible man— to say nothing of a once-in-a-lifetime opportunity—go. *Rule number two: no second-guessing.* She shoved aside her doubts. She could worry later. Right now, she had more important things to do.

"No, nothing's wrong. I was trying to decide exactly where I wanted you to start," she murmured before she wrapped her hands around the thick warmth of his neck and pulled his mouth down to hers.

She felt his grin against her lips before his mouth took hers. Dante obviously didn't believe in taking it slow and easy. Excitement whipped through her at the feel of his tongue pressing for entry. Dark, heady and wild, she gave herself over to the ride.

Dante didn't disappoint. His mouth enticed; his hands electrified. With the softest brush of his fingers, he made her shiver. She could feel the heat of his hands where the palms hovered over her breasts, but he didn't touch. Just his fingertips, gentle and soft, tracing her collarbone.

Anticipation curled in her belly as Isabel waited for

him to touch her breasts. Her body strained, needing the pressure of those large, warm palms on her skin.

But while Dante's tongue entwined with hers, his kiss hot and deep, he didn't touch her. Not the way she wanted.

Impatience surged. It wasn't enough. She wiggled and gave a low moan, trying to send him a telepathic demand that he touch her. She wanted to scream when he ignored all her signals, obviously holding strong to his demand that she tell him what she wanted.

"More," she finally murmured against his mouth.

"More what?" he asked in a low, husky tone. Isabel's eyes fluttered open to meet his hypnotic gaze. A wicked grin played over his mouth, swollen and wet from their kisses. "Tell me, Isabel. Tell me exactly what you want."

She licked her lips. Dante's gaze followed the movement, his green eyes dark with desire. She'd never told a man what she wanted. What did she say? How? Did she use the technical terms for body parts? Dirty words? Flowery euphemisms? Frustration and desire warred in her, even as her excitement spiked at the idea of telling him what she wanted. And just exactly how she wanted it.

"I want you to touch me," she finally said. "I want to feel your hands, your mouth, on my skin."

He didn't move, his eyes challenging her to take that last step. Isabel swallowed.

"I want to feel you against my breasts," she said quickly, getting the words out before fear closed up her throat. "I want you to touch me like you'd go crazy if you didn't."

"I *am* going crazy with the need to touch you, to taste you," he assured her.

Dante reached out, his long fingers brushing her skin

as he slowly, deliberately, unbuttoned her blouse. The silk slid smoothly away, revealing her satin and lace demi-bra. Isabel watched, unable to look away, as his eyes dropped to her chest. Her hands pressed against him, curling into the soft cotton of his inky black T-shirt. She felt as much as heard his groan of delight.

"Will you taste as good as I've been imagining?" he asked as he curved his hand over one breast. Heat flamed low in her belly as her nipple hardened, pressing against his palm.

Dante kissed her again, reaching with both hands now to cup, caress and squeeze her breasts. He rubbed the tips of his fingers over her pebbled nipples, peeking out over the top of her bra.

With a soft press of his mouth against hers, he slid his lips over the curve of her jaw, then nibbled his way down her neck. When he rasped his tongue over one straining peak, Isabel cried out in delight. She clenched the fabric of his shirt tight. Dante released her breasts, not stopping the magic of his tongue, and grabbed both her hands, pulling them over her head. He bracketed both wrists in one large hand and pressed his lower body against hers, holding her captive, the long, hard evidence of his pleasure pressed to her belly.

Her head fell back against the sheetrock, her breath shuddering out.

Hot and a little rough against the wall. Check one fantasy off the list.

Somewhere in the periphery of her awareness, a door slammed. An all-too-familiar male voice called out.

"Isabel? Are you in here? We need to talk."

5

IT WAS LIKE STANDING between two boxers seconds before the bell rang. Still rumpled, her blouse rebuttoned but hanging loose, Isabel tried to focus through the foggy remnants of passion clouding her brain. As the tension wrapped around her, she shot a look between the two men. Could they be any more different? Other than being male, it was like they were two different species.

Lance stood, arms akimbo, with his navy slacks and dress shirt pressed and tidy, every blond hair rigidly in place. The stubborn look on his choirboy face was one she'd never seen before.

Dante, on the other hand, was tousled and tough. Even though it wasn't yet noon, a hint of shadow darkened his chin. His hair fell loose around the face of a fallen angel. Dusty jeans, a skintight black tee and…Oh my, those were some big boots on his feet.

Distracted from her comparison, Isabel eyed the beat-up leather and wondered at the size. At least a twelve. She gave a low hum. The delicious hard male length she'd felt pressed against her earlier supported that old size-of-the-feet story.

"Isabel?"

"Hmm?" she murmured, wondering how different it would be to make love with a guy with…*feet* that big.

She glanced up and met Dante's eyes. The icy chill in his gaze slowly melted as he responded to the heated appreciation in her look.

"Isabel," Lance repeated, anger giving his usually smooth tone a nasty edge. "I asked you a question."

She pulled her gaze away from Dante and the promised pleasure in his eyes and glanced at Lance.

"Sorry, what'd you say?" she asked. Isabel drew in a deep breath, trying to get a handle on the out-of-control lust surging through her system. Wow! Dante definitely packed a wallop. But as good as it felt, it probably wasn't smart to be so hot for a guy that she couldn't even follow a simple conversation. He was like a potent liqueur—one shot was all it took to muddle her brain.

"I asked what he is doing here," Lance repeated. "Do you know who this is?"

Dante's sneer almost hid his wince, but Isabel was so sensitized to him, she caught it. Her brows shot up. How did he and Lance know each other? And more important, why was Dante uncomfortable?

"Dante is finishing the job for his father," Isabel answered carefully. She gestured to the half-finished store and shrugged. "Mr. Luciano broke his foot, remember?"

"Frank and I are on numerous committees together. I saw him last week. He didn't say anything about—" Lance gestured to Dante like he was a rabid dog, disdain overlaying what looked like trepidation on his face "—his return."

"Guess you didn't get all the dirt then, huh? And here you probably figured you had the old man dialed in." Dante made a tsking noise, shaking his head in mock sorrow. "Sucks to be wrong, doesn't it?"

Lance's jaw worked, but he didn't answer. Isabel gave Dante a questioning look. He shrugged and gestured with the hammer still clenched in his fist. "I've got work to do. You need me, I'll be in the back."

"You might take someone else into consideration, for once," Lance snapped at Dante's retreating back. "Oh wait, I forgot. Life's all about you, isn't it? You never did care how you hurt anyone else."

Isabel gasped, her gaze flying to Dante. His shoulders squared, but he didn't say anything. Without even looking back, he strode through the arched opening. She looked back at Lance, who stood in silence, fixated on the archway. The only sound in the room was Dante's footsteps, then after a few seconds, the heavy pounding of his hammer.

What was that all about? The only thing the two men had in common was the aura of anger emanating from both. And while Isabel would love to think she was so hot two guys would face off over her, she wasn't that deluded.

She waited expectantly, but Lance didn't say anything. He just glared at the newly cut boards on the sawhorse. She wanted to know what had inspired the anger-fest. Given the two men involved, she had a much better shot of getting it out of Lance than she did Dante. She wouldn't to let him leave her until she'd found out. Isabel set her jaw, crossing her arms over her chest.

Finally, she couldn't stand it anymore.

"I take it you've met Dante before?" she asked. Lance shrugged, but didn't answer. Her curiosity, already aroused by the edgy antagonism cutting through the room, spiked. Lance usually went on and on about anyone he knew, from the bank teller to the kid at the drive-through to the mayor. Isabel pursed her lips. Interesting.

"How do you know him? Through his father or something?"

Lance got a closed, stubborn look on his face. Finally he met her gaze. "It doesn't matter. What matters is that we find someone else to do this job for you. I'm sure Frank Luciano will understand."

Her brows flew up. Replace Dante? Her body screamed a silent protest. But she'd just got him. The man was perfect, in every way. His mouth should be registered a lethal weapon. And those hands. She'd just started living out her fantasy. Hell, no, she wasn't replacing him.

"He's doing a great job," was all she said, though. "I'm very satisfied so far." Liar. Her body was still humming with sexual energy, desperate for release. "And we're on a tight schedule. Replacing him would be crazy. But feel free to fill me in on how you two know each other."

"If I do, will you ask him to leave?"

"Is he an ax murderer?"

"Of course not."

"Wanted by the FBI?"

"Isabel—"

"A threat to women, children or small animals?"

Ruddy color flushed Lance's cheeks. "There's no reason to mock me."

"I'm not mocking you, Lance. I'm just trying to make it clear how silly this is. I don't understand why you have a problem with Dante. Unless you can tell me, and I agree with your reasoning, I won't ask Dante to leave."

"You're new here, Isabel," Lance started. Her jaw worked and Isabel could actually feel her defenses rising at his words. *New.* Like it was a crime or something. What did new have to do with her ability to listen, reason and think?

"So there's no way you'd have heard of the man's reputation," Lance continued. "He's bad news. He always has been, always will be. That's all you need to know. You're too smart a woman to invite trouble. Contact Frank. He'll find another way to finish the job. I don't know what his son is doing back in town, but I guarantee you, it's not out of any altruistic gesture of helping his father."

Was that supposed to convince her? Isabel frowned and shook her head. "Based on a reputation that's…what? Almost a decade old? You want me to kick a guy off a job that, so far, he's doing excellent at, just because he was a wild teenager?"

"Look, we're friends, right?" Lance asked in that same soft, sweet tone that had hooked Isabel into their first date. "Even though things didn't work out between us, we're friends. I want you to be happy. I'm only warning you because I care."

Some of the tension melted out of Isabel's shoulders and she gave Lance a tentative half-smile. When they'd broken up, he'd said he wanted to stay friends. She'd figured that was just a polite brush-off, though. Maybe she'd been wrong?

"Okay," she demurred. His smile was almost enough to make her forget how pissed she'd been when he'd ended their relationship. *Almost.* "I appreciate the warning. But I'm sure you appreciate my position. Luciano Construction is contracted to do this job. With Frank laid up, he had to make arrangements as he saw fit. He's the one who sent his son to finish it for him. Obviously Dante's almost decade-old reputation isn't an issue for him. Why should it be an issue for me?"

"Just watch him," Lance warned. He shot a look at the door Dante had gone through, then set his chin. He leaned close, his voice dropping to a low whisper. "He was run out of town for stealing. People don't change that much."

Despite the way the words grated down her good-girl spine, Isabel tried to shrug them off. She'd seen herself the kind of things Dante stole. Liquor from his father's cabinet; dad's truck borrowed for a joyride. Nothing a lot of teens hadn't done.

When she didn't respond with anything but a stare, Lance frowned and reached out, but let his hand drop before he touched her.

"Look, you're important to me." Lance gave a deep sigh and shook his head, his blue eyes filled with over-the-top concern. Isabel felt horrible brushing him off. "I know we ended things, but, well…it's not like my feelings just disappeared, you know?"

Isabel didn't realize her mouth had dropped open until he glared. With a snap she closed it, but couldn't find any words. He had feelings for her? But he'd dumped her, not the other way around.

"Lance—" She didn't know what to say.

"Don't say anything now," he commanded. He flicked back the starched cuff of his shirt and checked the time. "I've got appointments in ten minutes, so I'll go now. But think about what I said, okay?"

"Sure, I'll think about it," Isabel agreed. She didn't know if he meant the part about having feelings for her, or the part about getting rid of Dante. Either way, how could she not? He'd sent her head spinning.

"I'll be in touch," he promised as he headed for the door.

"Why?"

Lance stopped, his hand on the brass doorknob. He shot her a slightly impatient look. "To make sure you're thinking about things, of course."

Right. She'd forgotten what a nag he was.

Relieved, she watched him walk out, the heavy cherry wood and glass door closing with a creak. She'd need to get Dante to fix that. She glanced around the bones of her future. Three walls were plastered and trimmed but unpainted. One was still bare wood with a tangle of electrical wires winding through it. The dust-covered floors were still the original, yellowed linoleum, and there were boxes and building materials stacked in the corners.

Despite the disarray, she could imagine the completed store in her mind. Soft rose-toned walls, the cherrywood trim and service counters with their sparkling glass fronts. The air scented with the sweet tang of flowers and the delicious aroma of chocolate. Cascading green plants, flowering bushes and posies of every color filling the new cooler Dante was going to install. Wall-to-wall customers, online sales, *success*. It would be perfect.

Her head fell back against the wall, Lance's words ringing in her ears. Here she was with two dreams she'd waited for…well, what felt like forever. Her store and the Dante fantasy. She wanted both so bad she could taste them. Especially Dante. The memory of the rich, delicious flavor of his kisses filled her senses. He'd gotten her more turned on with just those kisses than Lance had ever done, completely naked.

And she was supposed to toss away both plans? Just because Dante had been a little wild as a teenager? Hardly. Isabel sucked in a deep breath and squared her shoulders.

Her wishes were right here, waiting to come true. She was grabbing on with both hands and making them happen.

Ready to handle Dante or not, she wanted him.

Isabel swallowed hard, firmed her shoulders and lifted her chin. Maybe it was time to quit second-guessing and put the Man Plan into action.

DANTE SWUNG THE HAMMER with a satisfyingly loud thud. Damned pretty boy, Anderson. The asshole had been the bane of Dante's high-school existence. Half the trouble he'd been accused of had come from Anderson. And it had only gotten worse after Dante had been elected homecoming king over pretty boy. Not that Dante had even shown up; he'd been out partying and found out the next day.

Why the hell did that guy still have to be around? If anyone should have left town by now, it should have been that weasel. Dante snorted. Of course Lance had stayed. He was a big self-inflated fish in an easily impressed pond here. Anywhere else he'd be shown up for the loser he was.

"Hey," said a soft voice..

Dante halted his swing and glanced over his shoulder.

"What the hell are you doing with that loser?" he demanded before he could stop himself. Then he mentally shrugged. So what if he sounded jealous. The thought of that loser and Isabel was enough to make his stomach turn.

Her mouth, those plump lips glossy and tempting, dropped open. Smoky eyes signaled a storm front and her chin lifted.

"I beg your pardon?"

Dante faced her with a bad-tempered sneer, ignoring the way his body jumped to attention at the sight of her sweet curves.

"You heard me. What's with you and pretty boy? You two hooked up or something?"

Isabel planted her fists on her hips. He almost grinned at the outrage on her face. She was so small she looked like a seriously pissed-off pixie. He couldn't wait to see her explode.

But instead of sending sparks flying, Isabel took a deep breath. Dante squinted as her lips moved silently. It looked like she was counting. He snorted. Weird. This woman was seriously hooked on keeping control. What was up with that hot fantasy list, then? To say nothing of the sexy vibes she kept sending his way.

It was like there were two chicks: one all about control, the other dancing on the edge of wild. He knew which one he wanted to spend some one-on-one time with.

"It's obvious you and Lance have some kind of problem," she said quietly, obviously gripping that control again. "Since neither of you has seen fit to fill me in on the details of your hate-fest, I'm going to ignore you both on this issue."

"Oh, really?"

"Yes, really," she shot back. "Unless, of course, you'd care to fill in those details? I'm guessing it has something to do with your history here? I know Lance is a native to Santa Vera, and you used to live here…"

Dante let her trail off, but didn't pick up the thread. Instead, he shrugged and turned back to the drywall.

"That's fine," she said. The quirk of her brow made it clear she hadn't expected anything else. "Just so we're clear then. You don't fill me in, I don't listen to your posturing bullshit. Same goes for Lance."

This time Dante couldn't hold back his laugh.

"Posturing bullshit?" He snickered.

She gave a dainty lift of one shoulder and stepped closer. Near enough to fill his senses with the rich spice of her perfume. Dante could taste her on his tongue; his head filled with that scent. He wanted to feel her under his mouth again. At the image, his dick stirred. His gaze locked on the sweet curve of her lips.

Eh, who cared about Anderson? He wasn't worth wasting the brain cells to worry about. Dante'd much rather focus on Isabel.

"Deal," he agreed. "You're a smart woman. You don't need grief just because I've got a history with your boyfriend."

"He's not my boyfriend."

Dante grinned, relieved. He winked. "Thanks, I was wondering."

She gave a little growl, then shook her head. "Change of subject. What are you working on here?"

"Finishing off this drywall. I wanted to get it plastered so you can paint and move all that crap back here from your storefront. So I called up a buddy, got the building inspector out this morning so we could get the electrical signed off."

"So you do still have ties to Santa Vera," Isabel teased. "I was starting to think you'd cut all connections except your parents."

Dante snorted, but didn't comment. His ties to his parents weren't strong enough to count. And he was fine with that. At least, he was when he wasn't in Santa Vera. Now, though, he kept remembering family events. The big dinners on Sunday. The holiday hoopla, and even the simple things like the smell of his mom's cinnamon rolls and his dad's... As he always did when thoughts of his dad sneaked into his head, Dante slammed that door shut. Didn't hurt if you didn't have to look at it.

Instead he thought of the inspection. The buddy was one of Tremaine's connections. One of the most costly and irritating delays in construction was waiting for inspections. Since Dante planned to get the job done and get the hell out of town, he had no compunction pulling strings to hurry the job along.

"What made you move to Santa Vera?" he asked instead. "This hole-in-the-wall is hardly the ideal destination for the up-and-coming entrepreneur."

Isabel laughed, the sound low and husky. "You don't think highly of the town, do you?"

"Gee, is it obvious?"

"Just a bit," she agreed. She shrugged, glancing over her shoulder to the window view of Main Street visible through the arched opening. "I like Santa Vera. It has a cozy feel and warmth I never felt growing up. When I had a chance to move, I made a list of what I wanted. Here my business can grow and thrive, but still not get so big I lose control of it. Big cities might offer more opportunities, but a small town like this offers a sense of community that was my top priority."

Big thrill, that. Dante grimaced, but let it go. "So you chose, on purpose, to move and start your business in a town so small it doesn't even have its own high school."

Not that he'd minded that aspect when he'd been here. The relief of mixing with the larger population of the neighboring town's high school had probably been what kept him sane as a teenager. And out of jail.

"But that's one of the things that appealed to me. The tight-knit community and small size. There isn't much chance of being overlooked in a town this small."

No shit. Back when he'd lived here, Dante hadn't been able to scratch his butt without it being reported back to his parents within a half hour and broadcast through the rest of the town before sundown. His list of crimes, both real and imagined, had been so extensive that, by the time he'd actually landed in jail accused of burglary, nobody had thought twice of his guilt.

"No," he agreed aloud. "Not much is ever overlooked here."

The look she gave him, soft-eyed and sweet, was pure understanding. Which didn't make sense, because for all Isabel's sparks of wildness, she had good girl written all over her. He raised his brows in question.

"My best friend and I grew up in a small town. Oh, not nearly as small or as tight as Santa Vera, but nosey all the same. She was always the subject of gossip, speculation or nasty talk."

"Trouble?"

"Always." Her smile was filled with fond amusement.

"What about you?" He tried to picture her as a wild teen. It didn't quite click. It was possible she'd reformed over the years, tucking away the wildness. But he didn't think so. "Did you do the parties, cut school, push boundaries?"

Isabel gave him an odd look, then she shrugged. "Hardly. Private girls' school. Honor roll, never broke curfew and was too...well, too repressed, I guess, to push too many boundaries."

"Sorry babe, I've read your fantasy list. You might not be wild, but you're definitely not repressed. Just the opposite, in fact."

Even as pink washed her cheeks, Isabel's gray eyes lit with a spark that set Dante's body aflame.

"Really?" she said, sounding a little breathless. "What's the opposite of repressed? I'd have thought it was wild?"

"Nah," he told her, setting the hammer on the sawhorse and stepping closer to her. Not touching, just close. He liked that—even though her breath hitched and her eyes flashed caution signs—she didn't back away. Instead she lifted her chin, almost daring him to bring it on.

Oh, yeah, baby.

"Repressed is uptight. You know, all impulses tightly locked up and hidden away in case something nasty or naughty gets out. Since the nasty-naughty stuff is where the fun's at, that tends to make repressed people pretty boring." Dante laughed at the face she pulled. "Exactly."

"So what's the opposite?" she asked again.

"The opposite of repressed is sensual." Never one to deny his impulses, Dante reached out to wrap one of her inky black curls around his fingers. Someday—soon— he wanted to feel those silky curls spread over his belly, sliding down his body.

"Sensual is someone who takes pleasure in the physical, all levels of physical from sex to food to what her clothes are made of. But she chooses her pleasures carefully. Makes sure they're worthwhile."

He watched her breath catch. Her gaze slid away from his for a moment, but before he could even register disappointment that she wasn't going to play, her smoky eyes met his again. From the heat there, she was not only willing to play, but she'd already thought up a few games herself.

She licked her lips and tilted her head to one side, so her cheek brushed against his hand.

"And wild?" she asked.

"Wild is out of control." He nodded when her brows lifted in surprise. "Believe me, I'm an expert. Wild is all about letting loose and not giving a damn about the results."

Her lips pursed and she gave him a long, slow look through her lashes. Then she took that last step, closing the gap between them. She reached up to press her hands to his chest, spreading her fingers over his T-shirt. Heat flamed through the fabric, tattooing the shape of her long, elegant fingers to his chest. Eyes narrowed, Dante watched to see what she'd do next. His body, primed and ready, strained to feel her pressed tight against him, but he liked the way she handled control. He couldn't wait to see how she handled out of control.

"Didn't you think my list was a little…you know, wild?" she asked in a near-whisper.

Dante's own breath was a little shaky as he recalled her list. He hadn't got to finish his wild-against-the-wall move earlier. It was all he could do to keep from grabbing her wrists, swinging her around and finishing it now.

"Your list was hot," he assured her. "Hot enough that I haven't thought of much else since I read it. But even as sexy as it is, I wouldn't call it wild."

She blinked a couple times, her brows furrowed. "Why not?"

Dante grinned at her offended tone.

"I told you, you're sensual. Sexy, hot and, you know… sensual." He gave in to the desire and curved his fingers over her hips. In a slow caress, he slid his hands from hips to waist, then back, loving the feel of her body.

"But?"

"Like I said, wild means you don't give a damn. That

you're ready to do anything for the simple—or not so simple—pleasure you'll get from it. Without giving a thought or a damn about anyone or anything else but that pleasure. Wild is all about total self-gratification."

One hand left her hip to rub at the frown between her eyes. Dante gave her a half-smile and leaned down to brush his lips over her forehead.

"To be wild, you'd be willing to risk it all to make that list happen," he said softly. "Doing all the things you had on that list with *me,* that'd be wild. Because doing so means you'd be risking everything you've built here. Everything you're trying to build here. And baby, I'm damned good, but even I think that is too high a price for the best sex of your life."

He hadn't thought so when he'd had her pinned half-naked to the wall. But then Anderson had shown up. Him and his reminders of exactly how judgmental this town was.

Isabel smiled, though, as he'd hope she would. But her eyes were troubled, like a stormy sea. Dante leaned down again, this time brushing his lips over the soft cushion of hers. An easy, almost-friendly gesture to let her know he wouldn't hold it against her. After all, she was a smart woman, one who was obviously careful and painstaking in her planning. Why would she risk her goals for hot sex?

"So you think my making that list into a reality with you as my co-star would be wild?" she asked.

He nodded.

"Why? Because of your reputation here in Santa Vera? A reputation that's, what? Ten years old, at least?" At Dante's nod, she pursed her lips and sighed. "Were you really that bad? Or do you simply have that much resentment toward the town?"

"Sweetie, I was definitely that bad and worse. And I've already had in-your-face proof of how Santa Vera feels about me. I promise you, get involved with me and you'll end up regretting it. In this town, I'm like the kiss of death, reputation-wise. If you doubt me, check with Anderson. I'm sure he'll be happy to fill you in."

Isabel nodded and slowly slid her hand from his chest. She took a step back, forcing Dante to release his hold of her hips.

"You know what? I think you're afraid."

His jaw dropped.

She nodded, a short jerk of her chin.

"I think my list is so hot, so sexy, you're afraid to take it on. That's okay," she said with a little shrug. "You go ahead and hide behind the excuse of an almost-decade-old reputation. If you get over it before you leave town, though, let me know. I'm sure I can teach you a thing or two about *really* being wild."

6

ISABEL PUSHED OPEN the door to her favorite Sacramento lingerie boutique, Simply Sensual, her mind on much more than lunch.

"Hey," Audra called from behind the counter. "Give me five, okay? Natasha isn't back yet."

"No problem. I wanted to shop anyway." Isabel set her purse on the counter and made a beeline to the silk nighties. Peach, pale pink, soft gold. She flipped impatiently through the sweet offerings, not sure why they bugged her so much.

At Isabel's comment and her rough handling of the wares, Audra's brows rose to meet her spiky black bangs. She leaned forward, elbows on the counter, her wedding ring glinting as brightly as the glittery Sex Kitten declaration on her black T-shirt.

"Shopping, huh? Planning to get lucky?"

"It's not like it's so freaking impossible, you know," Isabel snapped. She slapped the hangers so hard, a flurry of pastel silk puddled to the floor in protest.

"Whoa there, bad girl," Audra said, hurrying around the counter. Isabel knew it was a testament to their friendship that Audra's complete focus was on her and not the disrespect to her merchandise. She pulled in a shaky breath, trying to tamp down her temper.

"Sorry," she muttered, bending down to pick up the nighties.

Audra grabbed her arm and pulled her back up. "Leave them for now. What's wrong?"

Isabel shrugged. "I'm just moody, I guess. That's no excuse to be obnoxious."

"Guy crap, huh?"

"Why would you think my moods are related to guy trouble?" Isabel stuck her nose in the air. "My life is fuller than that, Audra. I could be having trouble with the business, PMSing, anything."

"Right. Except business troubles challenge you and PMS makes you mopey, not pissy." Audra, irritatingly stronger than her petite body indicated, pulled at Isabel until she followed her to the seating area. Isabel dropped to the plush gold chair with a pout.

"Only guys get you pissy," Audra continued, "when you ditched the cheating dirtbag you were ready to build a bonfire and roast him—and any other man unlucky enough to cross your path. You and Lance broke up and I found you with piles of his business materials and full length photos of himself. You were drawing red circles with lines through them…over his crotch."

Isabel snickered. "Then you offered to go to the chamber of commerce and get the ones he had on display."

"Hey, I'm a firm believer in honest advertising. The dickless wonder deserves to be exposed."

"You'd be interested to find he and you are actually both on the same page on certain subjects," Isabel informed her.

Audra gasped, her face turning as pink as the tips of her spiked black hair. Isabel laughed.

"Not possible," Audra sneered, recovering her dignity. "The only thing I can imagine he and I agree on is the fact that air is necessary to breathing."

"Nope. Dickless or not, he also feels I'm way out of Dante's league. And not in a higher up, superior way. More like an oh, you-poor-deluded-thing way."

"What a jerk." Audra sneered. "He had the nerve to say that?"

"Not in those words," Isabel said, with a twitch of her shoulders. "But he made it clear that I'm not Dante's type."

"Type-schmype. If you wanted Dante, you'd get him."

"That's not what you said before," Isabel muttered. She rolled her eyes, irritated with the whininess in her voice.

Audra grimaced. She dropped into the other chair, kicked off her spiked heels and tucked her feet under her.

"Okay, well maybe I think Dante's a tough mark. And maybe, based on how well I know you and your sexual history, I might worry about you going after Dante. But not because I don't think you're good enough to hook up with him."

Yeah, right. Isabel folded her arms over her chest, gave Audra a long look and waited.

"Look, we both know you can do anything you set your mind to. So it's not like he's out of your reach. It's a matter of, you know, experience. Not experience in the act of sex, but in the process. You haven't put in a lot of time with the free and easy, emotionless do-me deals."

Isabel raised both brows and sighed.

Audra growled. "Okay fine. Your experience level isn't even close to Dante's. Hell, I'm willing to bet *my* experience level isn't, either."

Isabel snorted.

"But enthusiasm beats out experience nine times out of ten. You've got a vivid imagination, a solid grasp on what it is you want to… Well, what you want to *do*."

Audra gave a moody shrug and blew out a puff of air so hard it fluffed her bangs.

"The emotional factor can't be blown off, though," she advised finally.

"What emotional factor? Remember rule three? Besides, he's leaving in less than a month. Only a crazy woman would let herself think it could be more than sex. Do I look crazy?"

Audra gave her a contemplative, up-and-down look that made them both laugh.

"I'd worry about you," Audra admitted, after the giggles trailed off.

"Okay," Isabel conceded. "But I spent years worrying about you."

"Touché."

They both sat in silence for a solid minute. Then Audra leaned over and grabbed a pair of fur-lined handcuffs from the basket on the table. She tossed them in Isabel's lap.

"Could you use those?"

Isabel fingered the cuffs, the soft fur an erotic contrast to the cold metal. She imagined using them to anchor Dante to her four-poster. The visual of him, lean muscles naked against the pristine white of her Egyptian cotton sheets made her mouth water.

"Oh yeah, I'd use these."

"Then go for it," Audra encouraged. "Like I said, you can do anything you set your mind to. Sex isn't like brain surgery or major-league sports. You don't need years of training and conditioning to be good. You're imaginative, your fantasy list is hotter than I could have come up with. Use that as your guide. Blow the guy's mind."

Now that she had permission, so to speak, Isabel was afraid. It'd been a lot easier having Audra's doubts holding her back. But with that excuse gone, Isabel was stuck facing the truth.

"I think I'm scared," she admitted with a self-deprecating grimace. Her fingers curled around the handcuffs. "I mean, not of the sex. I can't stop thinking about how great that would be. But of, I don't know…" She reached out to fiddle with the cardboard backing on a pair of sex dice displayed on the little café table next to her. Games. Risks. Losing. "Of not being good enough."

"Screw that."

"C'mon, you said it yourself. I'm sadly lacking major sexual experience. A high-school fumble, college gropes and a couple of failed affairs don't add up to much. Unless you count experience by osmosis and what I picked up from you."

Audra laughed, then got a serious look on her face. Leaning forward, she tapped Isabel's knee. "That's not what counts. Experience doesn't make good sex. It makes jaded sex."

"It adds confidence."

"Maybe. But ask yourself this. Why did you make that Man Plan?"

"Because I wanted hot sex." She thought of Dante and the way he'd pressed her up against the wall. The feel of his tongue on her skin, the hard length of him throbbing against her body. He definitely qualified as hot sex.

"Because you were tired of your rut. Ready to break free and push your own boundaries," Audra claimed.

"Don't forget horny."

"That's a given," Audra laughed. "So what did you do any time you've wanted to push your boundaries in the past? You made a plan."

"We've already covered that, remember?"

"When you set goals, do you stop with writing down what you want?"

"Of course not, I break them down into steps, see what I need to do or learn or acquire to achieve each step…" Isabel trailed off, seeing what Audra meant.

"Okay," she agreed. "So I need to break the list down?"

"Not so much the list itself. I mean, it was pretty self-explanatory. And your timeline is a given, since Dante's only here for… What? A month?"

Isabel nodded. Her heart did a little flip at the idea of Dante being gone. Stupid, it wasn't like this was an emotional thing. She had to keep that in the forefront of her mind.

Keep it all about the physical. She could do that.

"Want paper and a pen?" Audra asked with a husky laugh, obviously realizing Isabel was already working up a plan in her mind.

"Nah, I've got my own." A gentle chime filled the air, indicating that someone had come into the lingerie boutique. Isabel nodded her chin toward the door. "You go ahead and help them. I'll be busy for a bit."

She followed Audra to the counter, grabbing her purse as her friend greeted her customers.

Thirty seconds later, she curled up in the chair, her feet tucked under her, paper and pen in hand. Lost in thought, she outlined everything she could think of.

Research. She'd need books. She'd skip learning intensive subjects like Tantra and the Kama Sutra and concentrate on *The Joy of Sex,* how-to manuals and erotic romances.

Confidence. She gulped. Not something she'd find in a book, that was for sure. But she could do other things. A massage, maybe one of those body-facial types that included buffing and polishing. Mani-pedi, possibly even waxing. She winced, putting two question marks next to that one. New lingerie was mandatory, of course. She glanced around the boutique, wondering if she needed a more daring style than her usual slip-style nightie. Probably. This wasn't going to be her usual sex.

Implementation. She tapped the pen against the paper, stumped. She didn't know what to do there. Seduce him? How? It wasn't as if he'd run the other way, he was obviously interested. Her list had piqued his interest. Even if he did think it needed minor revision. There was his whole holding-back-for-her-own-good crap. But maybe her challenge had taken care of that?

Despite her misgivings, she decided not to worry about implementation right now. As long as she did her research and buoyed up her confidence, she'd be able to wing it. Hopefully Dante would help.

She looked over her outline, making a few notes here and there, adding ideas as they came to her.

She ignored the fluttering terror in her stomach, screaming that this was so far out of her league she should be put on medication for her delusions.

Nope. She swallowed. She wanted this. The Man Plan itself had been serious enough. But the chance to live out years of fantasies, to achieve her sexual goals with the guy who'd inspired them?

No way was she chickening out.

She tossed the paper and pen back in her bag and got to her feet. With a determined jut of her chin, she grabbed one of the wicker shopping baskets and set out to find her hot new lingerie. No sweet pastels or safe styles this time.

Nope, she wanted black lace, red satin and sheer sensuality.

Ten minutes later, after a quick greeting for Natasha, Audra's partner and sister-in-law, Isabel set a second basket next to her first on the checkout counter.

"You're giving me a discount, right?" she asked with a nervous laugh. She'd never bought this much clothing, let alone lingerie, at a single time.

With a nod, Audra rang up the expensive little bits of nothing. Isabel pulled out her credit card.

"Here, charge it and don't tell me the total, okay?"

"That'a girl."

Isabel sucked in a deep breath and pressed a hand to her roiling stomach. This sexual overhaul was definitely not for sissies.

"Hungry?" Audra asked, misinterpreting the gesture.

"Sure," she hedged. Then glancing over her new list, she asked, "Do you know of a good, classy adult bookstore nearby?"

Audra's brows shot up. "Sure, a couple. Why?"

"Maybe if you have time, we can do some shopping after lunch."

"Toys?" Audra frowned as she ran Isabel's credit card through the machine. "You're giving up on the doing Dante angle? Or are you adding an extra element to it?"

"Research. They'd have books, how-to's, that kind of thing."

"You're kidding, right? If you need directions, you

already have your Man Plan. Those were plenty wild-enough ideas there." Audra paused while wrapping tissue around the delicate lacy lingerie and frowned. "This isn't a test, you know."

"Of course it is," Isabel insisted. "Even if Dante won't be offering a grade, it's a personal test. I don't want to fail or do it wrong. Or worse, embarrass myself."

Isabel shuddered at the idea. No. Embarrassment was out of the question. Dante'd turned her away once before. *Too sweet. A good girl.* Not this time.

"I need to grab onto my once-in-a-lifetime fantasy," she declared. Even as she said it aloud, she knew she was trying to convince herself more than her friend. "It's not like I'll ever have this chance again."

"Don't worry so much. You're hot, Isabel. From what you've told me, the guy is already into you. Added to that, you have a natural sensuality that, as soon as you let it loose, will guarantee you both an incredible experience."

"That's not enough."

Isabel slid her credit card into her wallet and grabbed the burgundy-and-gold bags filled with her new wardrobe of sexy little bits of nothing. She'd been blown off as too sweet once before. There was no way she wanted to waste all this energy, this work, only to be blown off again. She met her friend's gaze with a determined stare.

"I'll be damned if I'm going to ruin my fantasy with the possibility—however remote you, in your obviously biased view, think it might be—that I'm a lousy lay."

ISABEL SANTOS HAD TO BE the sexiest woman alive. Dante couldn't get the taste of her out of his head. The woman filled his dreams, his waking thoughts. It was baffling. It was also pissing him off.

Dante stomped down the steps of Sweet Scentsations, hoping distance from her shop would give him a break. He hit the sidewalk and took a deep breath, the quaint charm of the town soothing him. Cobblestone streets, brick-lined sidewalks and pristine storefronts all lent themselves to the warm feel of welcome. A welcome he'd never actually felt before, but that was crystal clear now..

He didn't know when Santa Vera had gone from being a miserable prison sentence to a source of peace. Another thing to blame Isabel for, he figured. She must be softening him.

"Watch it, dude."

Dante jumped back just in time to save his toes from being skewered. A surly teen, probably sixteen or so, glared at him through the tangle of hair hanging in his face.

"You're in the way," the kid said. He stabbed his nail-tipped stick at Dante's work boot. That's when Dante noticed the wrapper under his foot. Trash duty. Santa Vera's town punishment for teen infractions. Dante couldn't count the number of times he'd had that stick in his hands.

"What'd you do?" he queried, keeping his sympathy to himself.

"Redecorated the park."

"Graffiti?"

"Art."

Dante snickered. Sure it was. Probably complete with anatomical suggestions for the school principal.

Dante spent a few minutes BSing with the kid, amused to see the sullen anger he'd once perfected on someone else's face.

Before he could comment, though, his cell phone

rang. The kid shuffled past, his bag over one shoulder, stick in hand.

"Luciano," Dante answered.

"Tremaine here. I've got some extra work for you."

Dante averted his gaze from the house Tremaine had the hots for and headed toward the diner.

"I'm tied up here another couple weeks," he informed his boss. "Is it something I can take care of after the first of the month? Otherwise you'll need to get someone else."

"You can do it there," Tremaine insisted. As usual, the guy was implacable. He never showed much emotion one way or another. Tremaine reacted the same whether it was a huge real-estate coup or a crashing loss.

"Seriously, I'm up to my ass in work here. Unless it's something I can do in my sleep, you're out of luck."

"I've purchased the Main Street property this week under the Tennyson umbrella," his boss said.

Dante glanced back at the aged Victorian in question and grimaced. *Damn.* Tremaine didn't need to fill in the details. The guy used dummy corporations, like Tennyson, when he was planning an aggressive real-estate strike. Most sellers didn't care, but Tremaine, or one of his flunkies, had obviously done their homework and realized that nobody in Santa Vera would sell to a man of his reputation. Never one to take no for an answer, he simply hid his identity, swooped in, bought up the property and had his way with it.

Guilt, rarely felt, tugged at Dante's guts.

"Why are you so hot for this property?" he asked. "It's not like a club here is going to bring you in much income, especially after the town council and business leaders realize who you are."

"My reasons are just that…mine."

"Fine." Dante shrugged. "I've got things to do. I'll check in when I get back to work the first of the month, okay?"

"Apparently there is some ridiculous zoning requirement for liquor service in that town. A bit paranoid, aren't they?"

"Not so paranoid if it's got you on edge."

"Touché." Tremaine laughed. "I need details."

"About Santa Vera's liquor laws? They should be easy enough to find, put your lawyers on it."

"I'd prefer inside information."

Now didn't that sound dirty? Dante frowned. No matter what issues he had with the town, it had been his home. Was still his parents' home.

"Like I said, I'm busy."

"This is your specialty, isn't it? Troubleshooting?"

"When I'm on the clock, sure." Dante shivered in the cold afternoon air. Enough already, he didn't need this kind of conflict. "If you want, I'll check into it when I'm back to work."

"You're salaried, remember? You're on a working vacation. I thought you hated your hometown. And yet you're balking at something as simple as sharing information. Why?"

"My reasons are mine," Dante returned, throwing his boss' words back at him. "Like I said, I'm busy. Gotta go."

Without waiting for a reply, he hit the off button. Clipping the phone to his belt again, he shoved his hands in the front pocket of his jeans and considered his newly discovered loyalty to Santa Vera.

His thoughts were interrupted by the sight of Lorna stomping across the cobblestone street. That she didn't even bother to look for traffic was a testament to the slow pace of the town. That would change once Tremaine got his way. For good or ill, the guy never left anything the same.

"You were late," Lorna groused once she was in speaking distance. She held up a foil-covered plate. No Styrofoam takeout in Santa Vera. "I brought your lunch."

"I was on my way to get it," he told her with a frown as he took the warm plate and wrapped utensils. Which was the bigger shock? That he was in a lunchtime rut in less than a week? Or that Lorna, Queen of the Grumps, cared enough to make sure he ate?

"Does this mean you're falling for me?" he teased to hide his reaction.

"Hardly. That'd require Satan ice skating in a tutu." Lorna harrumphed. "You're momma needs you here, so I'm doing my part to give her support, that's all."

Dante believed her. Not just because of his faith in her rock-solid dislike of him. But because that's how Santa Vera was, the people here supported each other. That edgy bite of guilt nipped at his conscious again. Dante slapped it back. After all, their support toward his getting the hell out of town had been unanimous, too.

"You're all she talked about at bridge yesterday," Lorna informed him. "She's proud. Better yet, she's looking happier than I've seen her in years."

Uncomfortable, Dante just shrugged.

"You're doing a good thing," Lorna admitted, her hands shoved into the pockets of her eye-watering lime-green quilted jacket. "Maybe Frank will use this downtime to make some changes. He needs to take on a foreman, get somebody he can rely on. But the stubborn old cuss thinks he has to do it all. Look where that got him. Begging his son for help."

With a look of stupefaction, Dante gave a snorting laugh. "Begging? My old man? Not likely."

"You came back out of the kindness of your heart?"

"I don't have a heart, remember?"

Lorna reached up and patted his cheek, her work-roughed hand icy in the cold afternoon air. Dante's mouth dropped open in shock. He couldn't help it.

"You've grown up. Not enough, but you're getting there. Mend your fences, your parents need you," she instructed.

Dante just stared.

"Look, I know you had a bad rep as a boy. And I know I held a lot against you. But Sylvia is a good woman. A good friend. She's got enough on her hands with your daddy's health. It does her good to have you here. Besides, I know how gossip is. You probably weren't nearly as bad as the chatter made you out to be."

Hadn't he been? That was probably debatable. Dante'd always figured for every exaggeration flying around him, there were at least three transgressions unreported. It all balanced out in the end.

"So… What?" he asked with a baffled laugh. "Hell did freeze over?"

"Not yet," Lorna said with a sniff. She turned to leave, then shot over her shoulder, "but it's getting a mite chilly."

7

TWO DAYS AFTER HER lingerie spree Isabel was ready to scream. Apparently all her soul searching and ego boosting had been for nothing. Her challenge to Dante had been enough to send him into oblivion.

She didn't think he was avoiding her, per se. He'd been working. At least, the work was getting done somehow. Although for all she knew, it was carpenter elves in the dead of night.

She sighed. Teach him to be really wild, her ass. As if she had a clue. She couldn't figure out what'd come over her. One minute she'd been all turned on and excited, thinking he was going to finish the delicious pleasure that'd been so rudely interrupted. The next, he'd been warning her off.

Just like Lance had, as a matter of fact. Isabel growled low in her throat as she rolled primer over the newly finished wall. And she'd thought Dante was so much smarter than Lance.

Fortunately for her sanity and the state of her walls, her cell phone rang. With a quick swipe of a cloth to clean the splattered primer off her hand, Isabel reached into the back pocket of her jeans for her phone.

A glance at the screen released the remaining tension in her shoulders.

"Hey, Audra," she said.

"Hey, when are you getting here?"

From the sound of music and voices in the background, here was a party of some sort. Isabel frowned.

"Isabel? You didn't forget, did you?" Audra gave a rueful laugh. "Wait, I forgot who I'm talking to. You never forget anything. After all, I'm sure it's all written down in that organizer thing of yours."

Forget what? Isabel frowned, trying to picture her calendar, but it was all blank. Great, she was so busy freaking out over Dante and wondering if she'd scared him off just when she was ready to have her wild way with him, she was losing her super-organizational powers.

"Of course I didn't forget," Isabel lied as she hurried through the storeroom doorway and into her office.

With a wince at the sight of her fingers still speckled with primer, she flipped open her organizer. Her stomach pitched when she saw, right there in big red letters, Drew's birthday. What was wrong with her? Sex on the brain, she supposed. It'd obviously fried her ability to think normally.

She'd promised she'd stop by and wish Audra's older brother a happy birthday and spend the evening celebrating with the siblings and their spouses. Since they were the closest thing Isabel had to family in the area now, she always tried to join them.

"Isabel?" Audra's voice was pure suspicion. "You forgot, didn't you?"

"I didn't forget Drew's birthday," she denied. Proof positive was there on the credenza, wrapped in shiny blue foil with a fluffy, yet masculine, bow. "I've got his card, his gift is wrapped, everything."

"You'd have had that done a week ago," Audra dismissed. "I know you. Even though I said stop by any time after five, you'd have been here at four-fifty if you'd remembered."

True. Isabel winced but didn't bother denying it. Instead she rushed to the bathroom to try and scrub the mess off her skin. It was all she could do to not scream at the sight of her reflection. Dull, white dots freckled her face, chest and throat. Even the oversized denim work shirt she'd tossed over a tank top was a mess. She tossed it aside, sneering at the lacey bra visible under the thin straps of her top. Oh yeah, she was sure putting that fancy lingerie investment to good use.

"Give me an hour," she said at the sight. It'd take her at least that long to clean up.

"Take your time," Audra said smoothly. "While you're getting ready you can tell me all about the hottie and how the seduction is going."

Isabel sighed at her reflection. There was nothing to tell.

"What's wrong with me, Audra? Do I have some kind of internal compass that automatically points to the man most likely to treat me like I'm a brainless idiot who can't make decisions for myself?"

"Whoa? Dante tried to push you around? What'd he do, put the rush on you? Try to get you naked too fast? Want me to kick his ass?"

Isabel snorted. She'd do it, too.

"Well?" Audra demanded. "Should I come over?"

"Chill your jets, hot shot. Actually it was the opposite," Isabel admitted. "He's avoiding me. Totally. He shows up for work in the wee hours of the morning before I get here, or… I swear, if it were any other guy I'd think he was waiting down the block for me to leave before he comes in."

Isabel faced her reflection. Remembering her seduction outline, she squared her shoulders. What was she, a woman or a mouse? Chin high, she clenched her teeth.

"He's not getting away with this hiding crap," she declared. "He had me up against a wall and got me crazy-hot. That's tantamount to the promise of an orgasm. He owes me and I'll be damned if he's going to get away with not following through."

Audra snorted so loud, Isabel had to hold the phone away from her ear. While the tinny laughter filled the air, she used a wash cloth to rub the specks from her skin, then flipped open the medicine cabinet door to grab her moisturizer. She had it all rubbed in before Audra regained control.

"You can stop snickering," Isabel said as she returned the phone to her ear. "It's not that far-fetched, you know."

"Right. You, chasing big, bad Dante Luciano around, trying to haul his scared ass into bed for some wild monkey sex. Yup, that's not far fetched at all."

Isabel pulled a face and started applying makeup from the emergency bag she kept stashed in the drawer.

"So he's avoiding you, huh? I wonder what's up with that. Maybe he lost the mojo over the years?"

Isabel thought back to the feel of him, hard and throbbing against her belly. "Nope, he's got plenty of mojo. He used the same stupid excuse Lance did. You know, how he'd be bad for me, his reputation would rub off on me, blah blah blah."

"No way. You didn't tell me that before," Audra said with a growl. "What a tired line of bullshit."

"That's what I said. I told him I figured he was afraid he couldn't handle my list."

"Well that is one sweet list," Audra snorted. "I can't

believe ol' starched shorts had the nerve to warn you off, though. What right does he have to comment on your sex life?"

Sex life. Not love life. The distinction, minute though it was, made Isabel pause in the act of swirling blush over her cheek. She swallowed, meeting her own gaze in the mirror. *So what?* She'd made a Man Plan—for sex. Not love. She didn't need to fluff it up and make it all pretty. She wanted hot, wild, once-in-a-lifetime sex.

"He's just being a friend," Isabel excused Lance. "I do think he and Dante have a history, although neither will admit anything."

"Hmm," Audra contemplated. "You know, Drew could answer that. Tell you what, ask him when you get here. He was tight with Dante—he's got dirt. Better yet, if you see the hottie, grab him and bring him along."

Before Isabel could scoff, the bells on the front door rang. She frowned and tossed her makeup bag into the drawer before hurrying out to see who was there.

A vaguely familiar woman stood inside the entry looking around. Blonde, Isabel's age or maybe a few years older. Jeans and a blazer gave her an air of casual business chic. Isabel smiled and told her friend she'd see her later.

"Don't forget to bring the hottie," Audra reminded before she hung up.

It was only the stranger's presence that kept Isabel from rolling her eyes.

"Hi," she said. "Can I help you?"

"Isabel, right? I'm Eileen. Chairwoman of Santa Vera's business council. We met briefly, but I haven't had a chance to visit with you, yet. Since I missed the last meeting, I figured I'd stop in and say hello."

"That's nice of you," Isabel said as she crossed the room, hand outstretched. "It's a pleasure to see you again."

"I hate missing meetings, but I had a doctor appointment. I'm sure Lance filled in just fine, though."

"Lance? I thought Mr. Karcher led the meeting." The old fart. Isabel swore, she could have stripped naked, danced on the podium, waving her bare butt in his face, and the guy still would have ignored her.

"Oh sure, Old Man Karcher is officially the second-in-command," Eileen said, wrinkling her nose in distaste. Isabel's grin was automatic. "But everyone knows Lance is really in charge. After all, we all turn to him for advice, guidance, you know, everything."

From the way Eileen's blue eyes went wide and sparkly, Isabel suspected she wanted a little of his everything.

"I didn't realize Lance was so integral to the business council." Did that mean he was to blame for her lack of a committee to chair? Isabel mentally rolled her eyes. She needed to get over this crappy resentment. It wasn't like he sat around thinking up ways to screw up her life. After all, he could have done that by staying involved with her.

"Actually, it was Lance himself who suggested I stop in. I'd realized we had a new committee opening and while you're listed as volunteering to serve on a number of them, you aren't leading any." Eileen grimaced, her look making it clear she realized Isabel had been stonewalled. "I ran it by Lance over dinner last night," she added with a look that let Isabel know that the woman considered Lance hers now. "We both think you'd be the perfect chair of the new zoning committee."

"I'd love to," Isabel exclaimed. Yes! Here it was, her chance to wow the people of Santa Vera and snag those business contracts. "Do I have a committee? Is it in place already or shall I call for volunteers?"

"Well, there isn't enough involved to require a whole committee, actually," Eileen explained. "It's a one-person job. Set up the zoning charter, make sure all the businesses, especially those here on Main Street, are in keeping with our town's bylaws. Most of the businesses should have current contracts, but you'll need to check that. You know, get anyone who hasn't already done so to sign, hook up with the zoning commissioner and make sure anyone buying new property signs the contract. That kind of thing."

So much for Isabel's dreams of spearheading major committees and being the go-to gal of Santa Vera. Her lack of excitement must have been clear on her face, because Eileen came forward and laid her hand on Isabel's arm. With a friendly look, she said in a low tone, "Boring sounding, I know. But it will add to your résumé with the business committee. We all have to start somewhere, right?"

And somewhere was obviously the bottom. Isabel thought of her goal list and reminded herself of how important the in with the business council was.

"Of course. I'd be happy to chair the zoning committee."

"Wonderful," Eileen exclaimed with a clap of her hands. "In addition to saying hi and the request, I wanted to look around your shop to see how it's progressing. I'm in charge of the Sweetheart Festival, you know. We're going to press with it in two weeks and I can't include a business that won't be prepared, now can I? After all, can you imagine how much it would cost to reprint all of our programs? A pretty penny, let me tell you."

The implicit threat was clear. Isabel wasn't worried, though. Her place would be ready.

She showed Eileen through Sweet Scentsations, spending the time pitching her floral skills and subtly working in ideas for the festival. It wasn't easy, though, since all the other woman wanted to talk about was Lance. Isabel realized five minutes into the tour that Eileen was pumping her for inside info on her ex-boyfriend. Warning the blonde that he was boring as hell in bed probably wouldn't snag her the festival's flower contract, though, so Isabel kept her mouth shut.

They'd returned to the main room when the door opened again.

Isabel's body went on full alert, a flush of awareness heating her cheeks when she saw Dante. A cool, crisp gust of wind rushed through, carrying his scent, rich, clean and all male.

He stopped short on his way through the door at the sight of the two women staring at him. His gaze met Isabel's, heat flashing in his green eyes as they skimmed her body. She folded her arms over her chest to hide the way her nipples perked up at the sight of him. Leave it to Dante to turn her on simply by walking through a door.

"Ladies," he murmured, setting his toolbox down, then letting the door swing shut behind him. He frowned when it creaked, but didn't say anything.

"Dante?" Eileen squealed. "Dante Luciano? Is that you?" She made a big show of looking out the window and shaking her head. "I hadn't realized hell had frozen over."

Isabel snickered at Dante's expression when Eileen threw herself at him, her blonde curls smothering his face. His face was priceless. Shock and dismay were quickly hidden by manners his momma had obviously drummed into him. Probably with a stick, judging from how fast he grabbed Eileen's shoulders and set her away from him. Of course, that could have been the quick grope the blonde made of his butt.

Who could blame her? Isabel wouldn't mind a handful of that sweet manflesh herself. Of course, that was her best option to grab Dante, seeing as he seemed to be running from her.

"The freeze is only temporary," he assured her. He shot a look at Isabel, horror, puzzlement and a hint of pleading in his green eyes. She realized he didn't have a clue who'd just felt him up.

"Dante, you remember Eileen…" she trailed off, her own laughter dying as she realized she didn't know who'd just felt him up, either. *Damn.* Isabel racked her brain trying to recall the woman's last name, but she came up blank.

"It's Johnson," Eileen slipped in graciously. "Dante and I know each other from school. Remember, Dante? Spring Ball, our junior year?"

Other than a slight squint, Dante's blank expression didn't change.

"You went to the ball together?" Isabel asked.

"Oh, no," Eileen exclaimed. "Dante didn't do dances. I went with David Benton, but Dante was out in the fields, you know, partying. I slipped out to cool off between songs and Dante and I had a…" she trailed off, giggling. "Well, a little thing."

"Between songs, huh?" Isabel pressed her lips together to keep from laughing. That didn't bode well for his staying power. She hoped he'd improved with time.

Dante's mouth twitched. Obviously reading her mind, he cocked a brow as if challenging her to doubt his prowess. She tilted her chin in response, letting him know she'd not only take him up in that challenge, she dared him to prove it.

From the heated look he gave her, she thought he was going to take the dare. Then Eileen giggled again and his eyes went blank.

"I'd heard you were back, of course. We haven't spent time together in forever. Remember when you won homecoming king on a write in? I did that, I voted for you," she told him, twirling a lock of hair around her index finger. "How long are you here? I'd love to get together and visit about old times."

"Yeah, that's an idea," Dante said.

Isabel stared. A bad idea, she hoped he meant. Not that she was jealous or anything. The sick ball of anger in her stomach had nothing to do with the image flashing through her mind of Dante, spread out on a football field, with a naked and giggling blonde climbing all over him.

Wasn't Lance enough for the woman?

"So Eileen, you'll get me the information on the zoning committee, right? I'd love to get started on it right away. Maybe you can e-mail me the particulars this evening, and I'll come by your office and pick up the files first thing in the morning."

"Oh, no rush," Eileen said, not even glancing at her.

Isabel ground her teeth together, but managed to keep the smile on her face. "Sure there is, remember? We've got a lot to do and you want to make sure those programs look good."

"Programs?" Eileen tore her gaze from Dante and glanced at Isabel. "Oh, right. Dante? Are you planning to be here for the annual Sweetheart Festival? We have so much planned. Booths, entertainment. A dance."

Isabel didn't even try to keep from rolling her eyes this time. Before she could suggest the woman strip naked here and now and get it over with, Dante shook his head.

"I'm only here a couple weeks. I'll be busy finishing some jobs for Luciano Construction, then I'll hit the road."

"Oh." Disappointment dripped from her words as Eileen sighed. "Well, that's too bad. Maybe we'll still find a chance to catch up?"

When Dante shrugged, Eileen pasted a smile on her face and turned to Isabel.

"I'll get that information to you this evening, okay?" She slid a glance back at Dante, then, eyes huge, made a small fanning motion that he couldn't see. "You have a good time, okay? And don't worry if you get, you know, busy or something. The job is an easy one, there's plenty of time to catch up after your…um, you know, renovations are done."

Isabel managed to thank her without snickering. She didn't meet Dante's eyes until the door squeaked shut behind Eileen.

"Well, that was interesting," she said with a laugh. "I didn't realize you were into, you know, dances."

Dante frowned. "I don't even remember her."

"You did so many girls between songs that they all blur in your memory, hmm?" Isabel teased.

"Hardly," Dante scoffed. "I might have been wild, but I wasn't a man-slut. I remember the girls I did. And I don't remember her."

"Maybe she dreamed it."

"Ha ha. She probably got wasted at the dance and

hooked up with one of my buddies. We all looked alike to her kind."

The bitterness in his words surprised Isabel. "Her kind?"

"You know, the ones out to notch their belt. They'd do as many different guys as they could. A jock, a geek…"

"A bad boy?"

"Sure. It wasn't personal, it was a game."

"But you didn't play?"

"Nah. Even then, I wanted the women I had sex with to be doing it for the right reason."

The fact that he fulfilled the ultimate sexual fantasy might not qualify, she realized with a guilty twinge.

"You were homecoming king?" she asked, changing the subject.

"Not on purpose. I didn't even go to the dance. Like she said, it was a write-in thing. It wasn't like I actually ran for it or anything."

His discomfort was cute. Isabel held back a giggle and dropped the subject.

"You're here awfully late for work," she commented. Not quite ready to accuse him of avoiding her, especially since he was acting as if nothing was wrong, she took the roundabout route to finding out where he'd been.

"I was across the street taking a look at the old Victorian and I got a phone call. Your job's been delayed. I figured I'd stop by and let you know."

The panic whispering in Isabel's ear distracted her from wondering about his interest in the Victorian. "Delay? We're on a really tight schedule. There isn't room for delays."

"Can't help it," Dante shot back. "There was some kind of mix up at the lumber supplier. Someone picked up your supplies by mistake. They have to reorder, it'll take a day or two."

"Does that kind of thing happen often?"

"Never to me. But this is Santa Vera, so who knows how they prioritize things. Some local might have wanted the lumber for a dog house and they went ahead and gave him yours. You know, 'cause he's one of their own."

Isabel rolled her eyes. "A little paranoid, are we?"

Dante shrugged. "No matter. We're delayed. I can't do much but busywork until that lumber is replaced, so I'm going to finish up some of the other jobs on Luciano's list early. As soon as the order is in, I'll get back here full time."

Isabel pursed her lips. What could she do? Not only was this delay jeopardizing her opening date, but it was denying her the thrill of Dante's company. Cheap thrill though it might be, seeing as he was so intent on keeping his hands off her. But she'd been figuring enforced company might change that. This wasn't working in her favour.

"Are you done for the day?" she asked absently.

"Yeah, I was on my way to the motel."

Images of motels, beds and clandestine sex flashed through her mind. Since she doubted he'd let her follow him back to make good on the vision, she held up a hand in a "wait here" gesture.

Thirty seconds later, she was back with a clean shirt over her tank top and her leather jacket, purse and Drew's gift in hand.

"Let's go," she said as she reached Dante.

"Go?"

"Yeah, c'mon. We can take my car."

Dante frowned and gave a shake of his head.

"C'mon," Isabel insisted. "You don't have anything better to do, and this will be fun."

"I already told you, *we're* not a good idea."

"Get over yourself, Luciano. Not every woman is panting to do you between songs. I'm holding out for a concert's worth of music, okay?"

He still hesitated, so Isabel grabbed his hand.

"Your virtue is safe with me. There's someone who wants to see you."

"Who?"

"It's a surprise." She tugged at his hand. "C'mon."

He held back another few seconds, then curled his fingers around hers.

"Fine, but we'll take my bike."

Excitement shot through her at the idea of straddling that huge, powerful machine. But Isabel shook her head. "How can it be a surprise if you're driving?"

"You figure that out. You want me, we do it on my bike."

Her mouth went dry at the same time other parts got wet. Isabel sucked in a shuddering breath, glaring at Dante's naughty grin. He knew exactly what he was doing and figured she'd back down.

"Fine," she said, tucking her arm in his and leading him out the front door. She shivered a little at the contrast of the cold outside air and the sensual heat of his body against her side. "Let's see how well you follow directions."

8

DANTE STRUGGLED TO KEEP his attention on the road. It was damned hard, though, with Isabel's sweet little body wrapped around him all snug and tight. He puffed out a breath, the icy-cold air turning to a white cloud of vapor, then disappearing instantly as he sped down the freeway.

He didn't bother asking her if they were heading the right way. She'd refused to tell him where they were going, instead she gave him that mellow smile of hers and a jut of her chin indicating he climb on and drive. So he had, figuring they'd get lost, or she'd give in soon enough.

He'd been wrong. With just a squeeze of her hand around his waist, the press of her thigh to the outside of his, she'd let him know exactly where to go.

What would they be like in bed with this level of unspoken communication? They way she effortlessly let him know exactly where to go, how fast, how slow. Dante sucked in a breath, wishing the icy air would cool off his body.

It'd be the best sex ever. No words, just physical pleasure to the sensual sounds of a pounding surf. Or better yet, to the heavy beat of hard rock pounding around them. Dante liked nothing better than sex to music.

He recalled the blonde at Isabel's place and her insistence that they'd got it on back in high school. Not likely. Sure, he'd known he and his buddies were worth points to do. They'd all laughed about it, and hell yeah, taken full advantage. What teenage boy wouldn't? But he hadn't done the blonde. It wasn't so much that he remembered all the women he'd been with as it was the fact that she'd done some guy *between* songs. If it'd been Dante, they'd have done it behind the stage curtains, the music blaring around them.

Isabel pressed her thigh against his and nudged her chin against his right shoulder. With a slight nod, he took the indicated off-ramp. Auburn, huh? His old stomping grounds.

As they slowed to a stop at the end of the exit, he asked over his shoulder, "Do you like music?"

"Love it."

Excellent. Even the cool air couldn't cool his body off now. His iPod was in his saddlebag, fully loaded with his favorite hot and heavy playlist. He could hear the beat in his head—both heads—his body throbbing in unison at the temptation.

A very wide, very wicked grin spread over Dante's face. He'd be damned if he could remember why he'd told himself to stay away from her.

He hoped wherever they were going, it was a short visit. Lookout Point, his favorite high-school makeout spot, was nearby.

And Dante was feeling a little nostalgic.

A few more squeeze and presses and he pulled the Harley to a stop in front of Good Times Sports Bar. A huge grin on his face, he pulled off his helmet. Dante swung his leg off the bike and took Isabel's hand to help her off.

"Now this is a surprise," he told her. "One of my buddies used to live here."

"Really?" she asked as she pulled the spare helmet off her head. A quick shake fluffed her ink-black curls around her face in a temptingly messy style. "I come for the appetizers. Nobody does nachos like Good Times."

"The nachos? Really?"

Isabel smirked and took his hand again, pulling him toward the door. Dante didn't let himself think about how good, or how natural, it felt to wrap his own, much larger hand around hers.

It wasn't until they were well into the bar and he recognized one of the voices yelling out for Isabel that Dante realized his buddy hadn't only lived there once, he still did.

"Drew," he called out gruffly. "Dude, how are you doing?"

His best buddy from his teen years, and the only regret Dante had over leaving Santa Vera so abruptly, grabbed him in a bear hug and laughed.

"Audra said Isabel might bring me a birthday surprise, but this kicks ass. I had no idea you were in town."

Dante just grinned. Drew looked the same. Oh sure, a little less scruffy than he'd been ten years before, but his reddish hair still waved over his forehead, his brown eyes held the same challenge that had always dared Dante to push the limits, his smile was wide and infectious.

"Your dad still run the place?" Dante asked after he'd been reintroduced to Audra—Drew's not-so-little-anymore sister—and met her husband and Drew's wife.

"Nah, he died right after you left town. Cancer."

Dante frowned and clapped his hand on Drew's shoulder in sympathy. "Sorry."

"So, what'd Isabel have to do to get you here?" Audra

asked, a wicked grin curving her dark red lips. Her lipstick matched the tips of her spiked black hair. Dressed in purple lace over some kind of silky dress, the woman was hot. Surprised, Dante realized she didn't do it for him, though. Not because she was his buddy's sister, or because of the hulking dude who'd obviously staked his claim. No, somehow his tastes had shifted from hot, obviously sexy to subtle and sensual.

Audra's snicker caught his attention again. "I don't see any rope," she said, "so I guess she didn't tie you up."

"Nah, we're saving the rope for later," he said. She gave an appreciative laugh and Dante met Isabel's eyes. Humor, and a tempting hint of interest, danced in the gray depths.

"All she had to do was take my hand and lead the way," he admitted. "I was pretty much willing to follow her anywhere."

"Nice switch," Drew said with a laugh as he pulled up a pair of chairs for Isabel and Dante. "Used to be it was the chicks following you around."

Dante laughed and let his friend catch him up. A waitress brought a tray of drinks and the group settled into chatting. He was surprised at how comfortable he felt. Not so much with Drew, hanging with him was like sliding into a well-worn pair of jeans. Comfortable, easy and right. But everyone else. Dante wasn't big on socializing. His job kept him on the road a lot, and his few friendships were one-on-one rather than group things.

This group, though, put him instantly at ease with its welcoming friendliness. Drew's pretty blonde wife, Natasha, despite her sedate appearance, was quick with the jokes. Audra's husband, Jesse, was kicked-back and mellow, his hand never leaving his wife and his eyes seeming to take in everything at once. Dante wasn't surprised to find out the guy was a cop. He had that look.

But it was Audra and Isabel who fascinated him. He barely remembered Drew's little sister, except the impression that she'd been trouble through and through. But here she and Isabel acted like lifetime friends. When had they met? How?

Then he recalled Isabel's comment about her best friend. She'd obviously been referring to Audra. His gaze bounced between the two women, trying to see how they'd clicked for so long. The contrast—naughty versus nice—only made Isabel that much more intriguing. And him that much more determined to figure her out.

"Drew's spoken of you often," Natasha told him. "After all his stories, I'm surprised the two of you turned out to be such fine, upstanding citizens."

"I don't know about the upstanding part, but there is an entire town filled with people shocked we didn't end up in jail, or worse," Dante said with a laugh. His laugh died as he remembered that one of them *had* ended up behind bars.

"They must be thrilled to see how well you're doing then," Natasha continued, unaware of the undercurrents. "Drew said you work for one of the biggest construction companies on the West Coast now?"

Dante frowned. How'd word of that got out? It'd be hard to finish Isabel's renovations with the townspeople trying to stake him through the heart when they found out he worked for Tremaine.

"I don't think I'd say they're thrilled, exactly," Dante responded.

"Horrified? Appalled? Paranoid?" Audra summed up with a roll of her eyes.

"You've talked to them, huh?" he shot back with a laugh.

"Don't have to," she said. "I'm a card-carrying Wicked Chick, so I know how hard it is to get people to look past their prejudices and see me for who I am now, rather than judging me by a decade-old reputation."

"That's stupid," Isabel broke in. "People should be judged in the present, not the past."

"It's not like she's changed that much," Jesse pointed out quietly. "Audra is still just as bad as she ever was. That's what makes her special."

"And you're as much a good girl as you've always been," Audra teased. "At least, you were until that plan."

Plan? Dante's eyes narrowed. Did they mean the sexual-fantasy list? Meeting Audra, he could see how she'd be involved with something like that. How much was Isabel, then? He thought about her kiss, the heat of her body. The way she'd writhed against his tongue and begged for more.

No worries, that list was all hers.

"But, still," Isabel protested, "it's stupid to stick a label on someone when they are eighteen and expect it to still fit now."

Dante and Audra both shrugged.

"Drew was as bad as Dante in school," Isabel pointed out in obvious frustration that they weren't offended by other people's perceptions of them. "But nobody holds that against him."

"That's because he's morphed into a goody-goody over the years," Audra joked. "Everyone around here got to watch him go from wild to mature. You know, all responsible and upright. Because they saw it with their own eyes, proof positive, they're willing to cut him slack."

BUSINESS REPLY MAIL

FIRST-CLASS MAIL   PERMIT NO. 717   BUFFALO, NY

POSTAGE WILL BE PAID BY ADDRESSEE

HARLEQUIN READER SERVICE
3010 WALDEN AVE
PO BOX 1867
BUFFALO NY 14240-9952

NO POSTAGE
NECESSARY
IF MAILED
IN THE
UNITED STATES

"Kiss my ass," Drew muttered to his sister. "Besides, Dante always had a wilder rep than I did. He was trouble. I was just along for the ride."

Everyone laughed and talk turned to Drew's youthful escapades.

"Were you really all that bad?" Isabel murmured next to him.

"I told you…. Wild."

"Aren't reputations often based on rumors? You know, exaggerations and stuff? Like dance stories and mistaken identities?"

Dante grinned at her reference and shrugged. He thought of Anderson and the golden reputation he'd crafted for himself.

"Sure, sometimes. But mine wasn't." He didn't want her thinking he'd been some poor, misunderstood kid. He'd earned that reputation, fair and square. And, really, he hadn't changed much since. "Like I said, some people are just wild. Smart people avoid them if they know what's good for them."

"I'm smart," Isabel assured him.

"Yeah. I know."

"But I'm also not a wussy girl who runs at the prospect of what someone else might think about my actions."

Dante stayed silent. After all, she really didn't know what she was talking about.

Obviously reading his thoughts, Isabel raised a brow and jerked her chin toward Audra. "You don't think I have a clue? That I haven't been advised to step away from the bad influence? Berated for my questionable taste and bad judgment?"

He glanced at Audra with her spiked hair, leather choker and wicked smile. Dante recognized a kindred spirit. But the guy she was feeling up under the table was a *cop*. Maybe he was wrong. Maybe Isabel *did* know what she'd be getting into with him.

"How'd you stay so good?" he asked with a baffled laugh.

"A stubborn streak a mile wide, only child to elderly parents and an overwhelming need for their approval," she reeled off. "But my lack of prudishness and loyalty to my friends balanced those things out."

"Not a prude, huh?"

"Nope. I'm virtually unshockable," she assured him.

"Is that a fact? I'll bet I could shock you."

One black brow winged up as Isabel considered his challenge.

"I'll bet I could shock you first," she dared back.

Dante's smile was slow and wicked. She might be *virtually* unshockable, but he was completely unshockable.

"You're on," he agreed.

"Drew," she said, interrupting the other's discussion. "We're going in the game room, okay? Don't cut the cake until we get back."

"You want to keep it private, don't forget to lock the door," Drew said, his face expressionless. But the glance he shot Dante said volumes. *Watch your ass.* Isabel might consider herself a big girl, but Drew's look was pure warning.

WHEN ISABEL REACHED OUT, Dante automatically put his hand in hers, their fingers intertwining. A chorus of dirty jokes and sexual advice flew around them. She laughed at the look of confusion on his face. It was sweet. For such a bad boy, he came across awfully innocent in the face of teasing.

"Don't worry, guys," she assured them. "I'm more than capable of handling anything Dante comes up with."

Dante gaped. Everyone else laughed.

With a nod to the others, she led him away from the relative quiet of the booths up front, through the milling patrons circling the bar and its bank of wide-screen televisions, toward an arched opening labeled Game Room.

There was a dartboard, a few pool tables and even an air-hockey table. All were surrounded by bodies. Despite her frequent visits to the Good Times, Isabel rarely came back to the game room. The unfamiliar setting added to the surreal, dreamlike feeling she'd had since taking Dante's hand.

A tall, leggy waitress, her red hair a wild tangle of curls under her baseball cap, waved. "Hey, Isabel. Ya going to the back?"

Isabel nodded, but as the redhead was busy scoping out Dante's package, she doubted she noticed. Isabel stifled her giggle, sure it was too sweet sounding for what she had in mind. Already nervous enough, no way did she want to give Dante the impression she was anything but ready to handle anything he could dish up.

"Drew knows we're in the back," she said, catching the waitress' eye. "We'll yell if we need anything."

"Did you want to start it off with a drink? An order from the kitchen?" The redhead's voice trailed off as she eyed Dante. She licked her lips and gave him a slow, predatory smile. "Anything you want, I'll be happy to give it to you."

Isabel glared. She'd just bet she would. The woman was looking at him like Dante was a juicy slab of beefcake she wanted to gulp down.

Isabel wanted to snarl, but realized she wasn't much

better. Except her plans involved slow, nibbling bites. For the first time, she wondered if the Man Plan was a bad thing. Not the sex part, that would be excellent. But...was she treating Dante like a piece of meat?

His hand curved around her waist, the warm heat of it making it clear to the waitress and anyone else just exactly where his interests were.

That was all she needed to shove aside the worry and focus on the task at hand. *The Man Plan, fantasy number four.*

"We don't need drinks," she told the waitress with a dismissive look before she tugged Dante around the barracuda.

"You need any help back there," the redhead called, "you be sure to give me a yell."

"I can definitely handle it myself," Isabel returned dryly.

"So, how good are you with the stick and balls?" she asked as they entered a dimly lit room. She flicked a switch, lighting the stained glass fixture over a regulation pool table.

"I can hold my own," he said.

She turned to face him for the first time since she'd told Drew they were heading back here. Nerves simmered beneath the surface. But more than anything, she wanted this fantasy. Her chance to make years of hot, sexy dreams come true.

"I'll bet you can," she said with a smirk. "Sorry about Barracuda Barb. She's voracious, but basically harmless."

"No biggie," Dante dismissed with a shrug. "So we're back here to play...pool?"

"Right. Pool." She stepped around him, close

enough to feel the heat of his body, to let the scent of him fill her senses. She flicked the lock on the door. "Are you any good?"

"Like I said…."

"You can hold your own."

"Right. What about you?"

"I've watched the game a few times. Audra and I used to hang out back here when we were kids. I figured it would be fun to play a game or two." Of more than one sort, if she had her way. Her heart beat so loudly, she was surprised it didn't echo in the room. She'd seen Audra use the pool table as foreplay many a time, but she'd never tried it herself. First step, relax. "Besides, it seemed like you might need a break from all that companionship."

Dante stopped his perusal of the cue rack to give her a surprised look. "It showed?"

"Not really, but I was sitting next to you. I felt you grow more and more tense as time went on."

"They're nice people," he assured her. "And Drew's a great guy."

"But you're not used to hanging with groups?" she hazarded.

"Right."

"Well, it's just the two of us now," she assured him.

"So we're here to, what? Give me a break from socializing?"

"Nope." She reached past him, her hand wrapping around the smooth wood shaft of one of the pool cues. "We're here to play."

That way, even if she chickened out on the rest of the plans, at least they'd get in a few games.

Being a nice guy, he let her break. She was too stiff to

play with her normal style, nerves sending the cue ball into the corner pocket on her fourth shot.

He snagged the cue ball and set it behind the break line and ran three of his balls off the table in quick succession. Isabel stepped forward, just inside his line of vision, and traced her finger over her collar bone. Not nearly as suggestive as she'd seen her friend do, but it worked anyway. He missed. Chalking his cue, he watched her set up for the next shot.

Time to up the stakes. She took a deep breath, and gauging the view, bent over the table. Watching out of the corner of her eye, she gave a little wiggle of her hips, gratified when his eyes glazed over. His eyes stayed on her butt as she pocketed two more solid balls.

"You're good," he realized with a laugh.

"I lived next door growing up. Like I said, Audra and I used to come back here a lot." She pointed at the corner pocket in front of her. Then, blowing him a kiss, she leaned over the table and made a full table bank with ease.

Dante shook his head. "Talk about a con. You set me up."

"We used to play after school while we did homework," she told him over her shoulder. With an exaggerated swing of her hips, she moved around the table to line up her next shot. "After we were good enough to beat Drew, we realized what a gold mine we had. We had it all worked out. I mean, Audra obviously looked like she could kick butt at pool, you know?"

At her questioning look, Dante nodded.

"But nobody looking at me would figure I even knew what the game was," she continued as she cut the eight ball into the corner pocket to win the game. "So Audra would haul in players, we'd do this little shtick, then the two of us would fleece the suckers." Isabel gave a wicked little laugh. "It was great while it lasted. It kept me in chocolate."

"Chocolate?"

She leaned her hip against the pool table, running the cue between her fingers in a sensual gesture that made Dante's eyes go molten-hot. As her fingers stroked the length of the polished shaft, she imagined it was him. The long, hard length of him under her hand. Up, down, back up again. Her breath shuddered out.

"I wasn't allowed sweets at home," she told him, trying to stay on topic. "And my parents weren't big on spending money. So I used my winnings to buy chocolate."

Dante grinned. "I take it you have a sweet tooth?"

"I'd do anything…" she paused suggestively "…for really good chocolate."

He carefully set his pool cue on the table, then planted his hands on the rosewood frame on either side of her hips. She licked her lips, heat swirling like a whirlwind in her belly.

"Tell me more," he said as he leaned in, nuzzling her hair. She breathed in his scent. It reminded her of winter. Cool, fresh, tangy.

"Chocolate, someone once told me, could be compared to good sex." Time to put up or shut up, she realized. With a lift of her chin, she gripped his hips, one hand on either side, and pulled him closer before sliding her hands around to cup his butt. The delicious strength of his muscled rear was obvious even through the fabric of his jeans.

She gave a giddy laugh at his growl of approval.

"How do they compare?"

"Both are necessary for mental and physical health. If they are good enough, they satisfy like nothing else. And there are so many delicious ways to have them, you want to try them all."

"You're making me hungry," he said before he gave a groan of surrender and took her mouth. Tongues danced in a quick, wild pace, setting the tone for their lovemaking. Fast, hard, intense. Just the way she'd dreamed it'd be.

Isabel rode the wave of desire, loving the way he slid his palm over her waist. She wanted to feel those fingers under the fabric of her shirt. She wanted to feel his mouth *everywhere*. The image, the idea of it sent her sliding down that slow, slippery slope of desire.

Determined to show him she wasn't a good girl, she slid her hands between their bodies and cupped the hard length of his dick.

With a growl, he lifted her tight against him. She grabbed his hips again and gasped at the sweet pressure of his dick against her damp, aching center. She gave a swift mewling intake of breath. He ground himself against her in a slow, undulating motion. One step was all it took to anchor her against the pool table, freeing his hands for other delights.

Keeping the rhythm, he slid his hands up the curve of her hips until he reached her breasts. Isabel's breath shuddered, her mind turning to mush. Dante cupped her tender breasts through her shirt, making her moan again. He tested the weight, his fingers unerringly finding the hardening nipples through the layers of fabric.

In a move made all the more exciting for his obvious desperation, Dante yanked the shirt from her shoulders. The loud ping of buttons bouncing against the walls, ricocheting off the floor, was almost drowned out by her gasp.

Isabel pulled her mouth from his, staring up at him in dazed pleasure. Grabbing her hands, he pressed her back against the table. He loomed over her, his lower body holding her tight, her arms anchored over her head. Bracketing her wrists in one of his hands, he used the other to tug her tank top down until the neckline curved under her breasts, framing them for his voracious gaze.

She'd lost all control of both herself and the fantasy. Even in her dreams, she hadn't imagined anything this primal, this intense. She was on the edge of an orgasm already, feeling the intense power building low in her belly.

He smiled, a slow, wicked curve of his lips, when he saw her bra had a front clasp. Holding her gaze as long as he could, Dante leaned down to unhook it with his teeth. She watched, taking in his hooded eyes, the desire tightening his face.

"You're going to come," he promised before he nuzzled her bra aside. Isabel let her head fall back, her eyes closed. She gave over to the sensations as he swirled his tongue around her aureole, circling tighter and tighter, then rasping over the nub. She clamped her legs around his thigh, pressing close to try to relieve the building pressure. He sucked her nipple deep into his mouth. With his free hand, he tweaked her other, groaning as her rhythmic gyrations against his thigh intensified.

It was straight out of her dreams. A wild, wet, incredible dream. Isabel's body strained, her every thought focused on Dante and what he was doing to her body. Fingers clenched in the silky length of his hair, she wanted—needed—to feel him inside her. Delicious anticipation spiraled as she imagined her body closing around him, gripping the length of him as he set a fast, intense rhythm that would drive them both over the edge.

With an eager growl, he tugged her nipple between his teeth, biting with enough intensity to send a shocked gasp through her body. Her moan of delight filled the air as she wrapped one leg around his back to pull him closer.

Her hands strained, trying to escape his hold. But Dante didn't let go. Instead he shifted to the other breast, using his tongue and teeth to make her squirm even more. At the same time, he reached down and unsnapped her jeans. The zipper hissed as he slid it down.

He released her hands then so he could push her jeans down from her hips. Before she could even lower her arms, he slid down her body, using his tongue to trace a heated trail over her belly until he reached the core. Her musky perfume filled the air. With the same fast, intense rhythm he'd used in his feast of her breasts, he spread her knees wider to devour her.

Soft whimpers grew to panting cries as he used his tongue, fingers, and then his teeth, to drive her wild. Dante's own breath was labored. Isabel lost herself in the powerful sensations flying through her body.

With a swirl of his tongue, he used one finger, then two to increase the tempo. Isabel met his thrusts, her fingers gripping his hair. One thrust, two, then her body arched. The orgasm grabbed her so fast, so strong, she saw stars. Dante sucked the swollen flesh between his teeth, growling at the sound of her keening moan. Pleasure rippled through her, aftershocks of a mind-bending climax. He shifted his attentions to a soothing, gentle rhythm, his hands tracing her waist, up, down, in soft, calming strokes.

So much for control. Isabel shuddered and told herself it didn't matter. After all, the pleasure had been beyond anything she'd ever felt before.

Oh, God. Even her dreams hadn't been this good.

IT TOOK DANTE A FEW seconds to realize the pounding he heard wasn't his heartbeat, but the door.

"Ya'll want a drink or anything, I'm just outside," a voice called. Dante recognized it as the pushy redhead. He wanted to yell out just where she could shove her drinks, but he figured she'd probably done that once or twice and would take it as an invitation.

The mood, the wild sexual haze, was broken, though. Reality, the fact that they were not only in public, but a public place owned by one of his few friends, slapped him upside the head.

In a strange fit of chivalry, Dante pulled back. He wanted Isabel like crazy. Looking down at her sweet body spread out there on the table, hot and ready for him, the idea of stepping back was pure insanity. But if he did her here, there was no way it wouldn't be public knowledge. Even if the public was made up of her friends, that wasn't cool. For the first time in his life, Dante wanted more than pleasured satisfaction from a woman. He wanted her respect.

A little weirded out by the idea, he shoved it aside and forced himself to recite building codes until he regained control of his body.

Tugging the denim back over her silky smooth thighs was enough to make a grown man whimper, but Dante sucked it up and did the right thing.

"Why?" she asked, her voice still husky with pleasure.

"No protection," he improvised, sure if he said he was

stopping for her own good, she'd do something crazy. Like strip off his clothes, shove him back on the green felt to screw his brains out.

His hands stilled on her jeans as he considered. A quick shake of his head banished the image, but unfortunately, not the vicious bite of desire.

"I'll bet the birthday cake is chocolate," he said, hoping to make her smile.

Her lips twitched. "Yum. At least one of us is getting plenty to enjoy tonight."

"Believe me," he took her face in his hands and tilted it up to look deep into her misty gray eyes, "I completely enjoyed you."

Her brow quirked.

"I can still taste you on my tongue," he said, his voice low and husky. "I can still hear the sounds of your soft cries in my head. Maybe I didn't get off myself, but I got one hell of a charge out of your pleasure."

Her breasts rose and fell with her shallow intake of breath.

"Think of it like that chocolate you love so much. It's delicious and you want as much as you can get, right? But sometimes, it's as good to be the chef, cooking it up for someone else. There is a lot of pleasure in watching them lose themselves in the delicious enjoyment of it."

She gave a low hum as she considered. It was all Dante could do not to lean down and take her pursed lips with his own.

Then she shrugged and gave him a naughty little smile.

"Well, then, who am I to deprive you of showing off your chefly expertise?"

He laughed, relief easing the knots in his shoulders.

He gave in to temptation and brushed a soft, easy kiss over her swollen lips, then released her. It was pure hell to watch her stand, snap and zip her jeans, then reach under her tank top to hook her bra.

She slipped her long-sleeved shirt over those milky-white shoulders and, as she was buttoning what few buttons were left, met his eyes. Her face was flushed, and nerves danced in the gray depths of her gaze. But she lifted her chin and smiled anyway.

"But I expect you to return the favor, hmm? Next round, I'll be the chef and you'll be my very own chocolate dessert. Delicious, rich and creamy."

Dante's dick, still hard from their pool-table encounter, jumped in anticipation. Down, boy.

"I'll enjoy you until we've both had enough," she told him. "Then I'm going to do it all over again."

With that, she flicked the lock and sauntered out, leaving Dante painfully wishing it was payback time.

9

ISABEL TIGHTENED HER ARMS around Dante's waist and, eyes closed, laid her head on the hard expanse of his back. Thanks to the warm protection of his body, she barely felt the cool night air as it rushed past them. Between his warmth, and the soothing rumble of the Harley between her thighs, she was in a nice state of mellow, relaxed dreaminess.

Oh. My. God. Dante Luciano. Her. Pool Table. It just baffled the mind. She gave a deep sigh and shifted, her body singing with remembered pleasure.

All thanks to Dante. *Yum.* The man was as decadent and delicious as Drew's double-chocolate mousse birthday cake.

She gave a tired smile as she remembered her friends' reactions when she and Dante returned from the game room. Poor guy, he obviously wasn't used to being teased.

Of course, she wasn't used to taking a guy into the back room and being brought to a whimpering orgasm as he pleasured her on a pool table, either.

She got wet all over again remembering the intense power of her climax. He'd been so…well, incredible. Demanding, powerful, as if he was half-crazy with wanting her and refused to accept anything less in return. She'd gone completely mad.

Isabel's cheeks burned in the cool night air. Where was her modesty? Her sense of decorum and pride? They'd all disappeared with that Man Plan of hers, apparently. And thanks to Dante, she could now check two items off, moving them from the fantasy wish list to the fantasy fulfilled list. Up against a wall, and wild semi-public pleasure. Check and check again.

Wasn't it great when a plan came together? Isabel giggled against Dante's back. When he shifted his shoulder as if to see what she wanted, she lifted her head to look around.

Ooh. She realized they were close to the legendary Lookout Point. She'd never actually been there, but like anyone from the area, she knew where it was.

She gave Dante's waist a squeeze to indicate he should take the next exit. His body went stiff. She held her breath. Would he refuse? After a few heart-pounding seconds, he finally changed lanes and took the exit.

She didn't have to give him any further directions. After all, he knew the way better than she did. He probably had his own entrance.

Despite his acquiescence, tension ratcheted through Isabel's shoulders. This fantasy thing was hard work. She'd never chased a guy before. Usually she did the good girl thing. When she met someone, she'd wait for the guy to express interest and decide if she wanted to reciprocate or not. Which was probably why her relationship list was so dismally small.

Dante was the first guy she'd wanted enough to pursue. She'd written an entire fantasy list around him. Not that she'd ever tell him that. It was like he was into her, but he didn't want to be. Why? Because she wasn't his type? Was it the good-girl thing? Did he think she'd get all serious, or worse, that in her lack of experience, she wouldn't be as hot as he was used to? That she'd be— once again—too much of a good girl for him?

A part of her—the please everyone, don't make waves for crying out loud part—wanted to let it go. To accept the thoroughly delicious panting orgasm he'd given her on the pool table and consider herself lucky. She was sure there were plenty of women who never experienced that exquisite pleasure, especially from their ultimate fantasy guy.

Isabel's bottom lip poked out. She didn't want to be grateful and let it go, though. She wanted her fantasies— all of them, dammit. It wasn't like she was asking Dante to suffer miserably, was she?

She considered his reaction on the pool table. She might not have oodles of experience, but she knew a turned on, rock-hard man when she felt him going down on her. No, he'd been totally into her. Or at least part of him had. Unfortunately, not the part she was craving.

Isabel's body clenched at the memory of how hard, how big he'd felt against her thigh. Her breath shuddered as she imagined how he'd feel sliding into her. That long, heated length of him moving in the same wild, intense tempo his tongue had used.

Why was he hesitating? If it wasn't chemistry, what was it?

Isabel's internal debate came to a halt as Dante pulled onto a narrow dirt road. Brows furrowed, she tried to make out their location in the dark. Cool evening air swirled around them. She shivered inside her jacket. Moonlight weaved a soft white glow through the lacy black overhang of bare tree branches. She heard the faint sound of water in the distance and realized they must be by the lake.

Despite the cold and the nagging, nervous voice sending doubts through her head, a low flame of desire sparked deep in her belly. Lookout Point. Make-out central, if the rumors were true. This would be where Dante had cemented his bad-boy reputation as the hottest lover this side of the Rockies.

Resolving to ignore the nerves, Isabel firmed her shoulders and lifted her chin. And this would be the place she made him beg to costar in the rest of her fantasy list.

"So this is it?" she asked as he helped her off the bike. "The infamous Lookout Point. Would you classify a visit here as wild or as sensual?"

"Depends."

"On?"

"On exactly what you do here."

Isabel laughed. "I thought everyone did the same thing here."

"That's like saying all chocolate is the same," he said, referring to her earlier chocolate comparison.

Isabel recalled Audra once comparing sex to chocolate, claiming that it's all about the degree of satisfaction. That even M&M's satisfied. Isabel realized that until tonight, all she'd ever had were M&Ms.

"Besides," he said, taking her hand, "I don't think too many people ever came to this particular spot."

"No?" She glanced around, but unlike her teenage imaginings of orgies around a bonfire, it didn't look like an outdoor den of iniquity.

"Nah, there is a lower entrance that everyone hits. But I wasn't ever much into public performances."

He started down a narrow path, brush and bushes growing thick and wild on either side. The dirt trail was so narrow, Isabel had to walk behind him. Night sounds filled the air, including a sudden howl. She shivered. She was so not an outdoor kind of gal. She'd never even camped out. This little adventure was definitely surreal. She took comfort in the warmth of his hand entwined in hers.

"Public performances?" she asked, trying to distract herself from wondering what kind of teeth the howling animal might have, and how close it might be. "Isn't that part of the charm of Lookout Point? Bare asses flashing in the moonlit back window of dad's borrowed car?"

Dante snorted. "Exactly. Why would I share my bare ass with everyone?"

Isabel realized then that Dante's reputation, legendary as it was, might have been rough for him. Sure, he'd obviously earned at least some of it. He'd said himself, he'd been wild. But that probably came with consequences.

She could imagine the crowd outside his car window, a stopwatch in one hand as they counted how many times his ass flashed in the window. Scorecards, game rosters to track who he was with. Full commentary at lunch the following day.

She shuddered. Intimidating.

"So you found your own spot, hmm?"

He shrugged as they broke through the woods. There, in all its moonlit glory, was the lake. It looked like a glittering expanse of black glass. Smooth, shiny and deep.

"Oh," she breathed, "it's beautiful."

"Yeah." He stood there, his hand in hers, and took in the view. A smile—she'd almost call it sweet if it wasn't for the wicked quirk of his brow—flashed. "It hasn't changed. I'd wondered if it would."

"With a view like this, I'm surprised you didn't end up with the crowds here, too."

Dante shrugged and headed toward the lake, pulling Isabel along. The air was chillier here. Another howl filled the air, sending a shiver down her spine. She'd finally made it to Lookout Point; it'd suck to end up eaten by a wild animal.

"Like I said, not too many people knew about this spot. It's not easy to get to, and you have to walk to see the lake. For most people, it was a lot easier to hang out in a warm car."

"Good point. And most cars come equipped with backseats." She frowned, stumbling through the thick undergrowth as she tried to keep up with him. Despite his hand wrapped in hers, it wasn't an easy trek. "Didn't you always ride a motorcycle?" He nodded. "Then where did you…"

He glanced at her and laughed. The rich sound echoed wickedly in the night air.

"Backseats are cliché. There's plenty of space here." He made a wide, sweeping gesture to indicate the space.

Isabel looked around and swallowed. Do it outdoors? That definitely wasn't on her fantasy list.

At Dante's urging, they settled on a large, flat rock, his arms curving around her waist. Isabel, oddly disappointed in the sweet, yet almost friendly gesture, held herself rigid for a few seconds. But he wasn't having any of that. He tugged her close until she leaned back against him. Stiff at first, she stared out over the smooth water. Soon, his heat, the soothing view and the magic of the evening seeped in, relaxing her.

Isabel sighed. She was usually so focused on her goals, on setting them and on achieving them, that she rarely took time out to just sit and relax. It was nice.

It lasted a whole minute and a half before her mind was racing. What were they doing? Were they going to just sit here all night? It was all she could do not to squirm on the cold, hard stone seat. Was Dante only here for some nostalgic relaxation and her presence was immaterial?

Maybe he was here for some nostalgic nookie?

She wasn't sure which bothered her more.

Isabel frowned at the water as it lapped gently on the rocky shore. Why would nostalgic nookie bother her, though? Her Man Plan was based on a decade-old crush, wasn't it?

Isabel considered. That was definitely how it'd started. But now? She wasn't so sure.

She thought of his easy laugh and the way his eyes crinkled when he grinned. With a sigh, she remembered his faith in her ability to choose what she wanted, unlike the way Lance used to insist he knew what was best for her.

Cuddling closer to his warm chest, she recalled his easy enjoyment of her friends, despite his occasional discomfort. And his acceptance of her.

That was the biggest thing, she realized. He acted like he accepted her—completely. Her quirks and foibles, her obsessive planning and her sexual fantasies.

She wasn't chasing him based on his past persona. After all, that'd been the stuff of legends. No, it was the present man—with his stubborn streak and hard body, his skill with a hammer and his loyalty to old friends—that she wanted.

And, of course, there was his amazingly talented mouth and the way he'd taken such pleasure in her satisfaction.

Yeah, she wanted him. But in the here and now, despite their little visit to memory lane.

But what, exactly, did he want? Was he waiting for her

to decide? Should she make the first move? Could she? Isabel drew in a shaky breath, trying to orchestrate it all in her head.

Outdoor sex. Hard rock, cool air. Not exactly romantic or even remotely sexy. This was supposed to be a turn-on? She shifted in Dante's arms, noting the platonic way his hands linked together at her waist. Well, it wasn't like he was turned on, now, was it?

"Relax," he said, his voice a soft hush. "Enjoy the view."

Wasn't she supposed to be enjoying him? She'd thought that was why there were there. But Isabel gave a sigh and let herself lean into him fully, her head against his shoulder. She looked out at the water and had to admit, it was beautiful.

"You must miss this," she said.

He was silent for a few seconds, then gave a surprised humph. "If you'd asked me, I'd have bet there wasn't anything I missed about Santa Vera. But…yeah, I do miss this."

She twisted her head to shoot him a naughty look. "By this, I mean the serenity of the lake and the gorgeous view. Not taking a willing girl to Lookout Point."

He laughed. "I didn't always come here with a girl. I'll bet at least half my trips were alone. Just to sit here like this. Relax, think. The water, watching it…it helped."

She lay her hand over his where he'd wrapped them around her waist. "Was it rough?"

His shrug tousled her hair. "My life?"

She nodded.

"I wouldn't call it rough. I didn't fit here. The harder people tried to force me to, the harder I'd resist."

Isabel frowned. She'd never quite fit, either. But her

answer was to try harder. Find a way. Volunteer, much to Audra's disgust.

"What happened? They pushed so hard, you finally left?"

"Something like that," he said quietly. "My dad and I had problems for years. I didn't fit, didn't live up to his expectations. Just before I graduated, things got ugly. He picked his side, and I wasn't on it. It was easier to leave than fight."

Isabel's heart shifted at the disappointment in his voice. It was a subtle thing, like the gentle way the moon highlighted the tree branches. Barely noticeable, unless you paid careful attention.

Did he even realize it was there?

"I can see how this would be a nice refuge. I've never been up here before," she admitted instead.

Dante gave a baffled laugh. "How the hell did you stay so innocent hanging out with Audra?"

Again, with the not-quite-fitting thing. Isabel sighed. She turned in his arms so she could see his face as she responded.

"Part of it was, you know, the whole not-wanting-to-disappoint-my-parents thing. But mostly it was a combination of my going to private school and Audra moving away. We stayed in touch, but didn't see much of each other until after high school."

His eyes narrowed. Realizing he was probably trying to do the math, she made it easy for him. "We were sixteen."

"A lot of chicks hit lookout early enough to eliminate the sweet sixteen myth," he said.

"Including Audra. Me? I was a late bloomer."

He quirked a brow, then lifted her hand to his lips. He pressed a kiss against her palm, his breath hot, moist—delicious against her flesh.

"Some of the best things in life bloom late," he assured her. "Time ripens them, lets them come into their own. They're the ones that are the most worth waiting for. Having tasted you, I'll attest to your delicious sweetness."

Isabel was grateful the dark night hid her blush.

"You might have bloomed late, but you've got a firm handle on your sexual fantasies," he pointed out. "I've never seen a list as hot—or as organized—as yours."

"You sound surprised."

"Well...I'll admit I'm not the most organized guy around, but I've never imagined listing sexual encounters by priority."

"It really makes sense, if you think about it," she assured him. "Let's say I started with the food sex. That requires actual nudity, light and a certain degree of trust if we're involving hot fudge. And I'd definitely want to involve hot fudge. So, really, it's smarter to work up to something like that."

"You have a fantasy hierarchy?" he summed up.

Isabel grinned. "Yes, exactly."

"Why not start with your hottest fantasy and dive in?"

"That's why you're wild," she explained, fighting off a shiver at the idea of actually *doing* her wildest fantasy. Nope, she wasn't ready for that. "Me, I need to take it slow. Toes in the water, so to speak."

"But you want it?"

"Well..." she considered. "I think I want it. But it kind of scares me a little."

"That adds an edge," he assured her. "A little extra punch to the experience."

"I don't know that I'm ready for punched-up sex."

"You're ready," he claimed.

The complete assurance in his voice made her feel

ready. Then she thought of her ultimate fantasy. The last one on the list—total submission. Her, Dante, silk scarves and hot, throbbing music pounding through the walls. Completely at his mercy, there to serve as his sex slave in any way he wanted.

Just the tied-to-the-bed part was enough to make her equally wet with desire and terrified of giving up control.

"No," she said, pissed that her voice was shaking. She drew in a breath, regained control and gave a little shake of her head in denial.

"No," she repeated calmly. "It's my list, my fantasies and I want to work down the list in order, so to speak. It's better for me that way."

"Scripted sex?"

"Oh, no," she assured him. One part of her was amazed to be having this matter-of-fact conversation about sex with the hottest man she'd ever known. The other part was simply turned on. Wet panties, quickened breath, pounding-heart excited.

"So it doesn't have to be followed in order? For instance, the *hot and wild against a wall* was okay for you, even though on your list it's like the *third* thing?"

"You know, you could give that back to me," she said, feeling a little naked. "I doubt you need the list for sexual ideas."

"Nope, it's mine now," he said with a wicked grin. "I doubt I'll follow it in order, but I'm damned sure we'll hit each and every fantasy."

Isabel swallowed hard. The order was what made the list okay. That was her safety net. The idea of giving it up was enough to make her scream.

Despite the icy cold air, sweat pooled in the small of her back. Maybe this whole fantasy idea was crazy?

Before her anxiety was able to get the better of her, he squeezed her waist and smiled. The look, and his touch, was pure assurance.

"For a woman with such a strong control issue, this list is a surprise. You're hot, you're gorgeous. Getting lucky obviously wouldn't be an issue for you. So, why the list?"

Isabel tried to rein in her panic. It wasn't like Dante was going to push her into anything. She was a big girl, she knew how to say no if she wasn't comfortable.

Holding tight to that theory, she gathered her thoughts.

"The list. Um, do you remember when I mentioned my birthday wish?"

"Sure. I got to kiss you." Satisfaction rang clear in his tone. She giggled, glad it was a good memory for him.

"I wrote that list, or I should say dictated it to Audra, on my birthday. I was tired of letting the good things go by, of being the good girl who settled for the big plan and not the pleasure plan."

"So you figured since the plan thing worked for business, you'd apply it to your sex life?"

"Right." She thought about it. "And look how well it's working."

Dante laughed so hard, something in the bushes rustled as it ran in startled shock.

Amused, tired of talking, and not able to ignore the ever-tightening tension coiled in her belly any longer, Isabel turned in Dante's arms.

The look in his eyes made it clear he'd been waiting. As usual, giving her the power of control. She shivered. She'd had no idea that control—and a man who was strong enough to let her have it—would end up being the biggest turn on she'd ever encountered.

"I want you," she murmured.

"Then take me," he advised.

To him, it was as simple as that. To Isabel, control was everything.

She leaned forward, brushing her lips over his. The gentle beauty of the evening seemed to call for sweetness, even though the desire snarling in her belly wanted sex— fast, hard and intense.

"You're holding back," he murmured against her lips.

"I was thinking this rock is going to be pretty uncomfortable," she admitted.

He laughed. "See, sensual."

In an easy move, Dante got to his feet. He grabbed her hand, wrapping it in his, and pulled her up, too. He led her along the path. Not back the way they'd came, but deeper into the wooded darkness.

After a minute of walking while Isabel tried not to be obvious about peering into the bushes for wildlife, they came to a clearing.

Dante led her over to a tree. It was huge, with a hollowed-out section that would easily fit two bodies. Just like a bed, albeit a very hard one.

Isabel cast a glance over the enclosure, then at Dante.

"That doesn't look much softer than the rock," she said.

"That's why you're going to be on top."

10

DANTE WATCHED THE EMOTIONS flash across Isabel's moonlit face. The soft moonlight lent an ethereal glow to her porcelain complexion, but didn't hide the flush burning her cheeks.

Damn, she was sweet. What was he doing? He'd never been into the seduction of innocents.

"I like that," she said, flashing him a look that could only be termed nervous naughtiness. "If I'm on top, I get to be in control, right?"

Dante snorted. "Interesting concept, but not quite accurate. Nobody makes me lose control."

"Nobody? Ever?" Her eyes went wide. He watched her throat move, her hands clench at her sides. The she took a deep breath and gave him a tremulous smile. "You say that like it's a challenge or something."

He grinned. "I'll make it a dare, if you want."

He watched her throat work. Was she the kind of gal to take a dare?

"I've only taken one dare before," she admitted.

Dante ignored the whisper of disappointment that curled through him. It wasn't like she had to be into the same things he was. The sex thing was enough.

"But…" She shrugged and gave him a look so hot, so willing and curious, his body shifted into overdrive. "You make me want to take dares. To push my comfort zone. So…now what? I try and make you lose control?"

He ignored the heat flaring in his heart. Hell, his entire body was on fire. Just because he felt like her words had shoved him over an emotional cliff didn't mean anything.

"Have at it," he challenged. "You've got the rest of the night."

"I'll do my best," she vowed, shrugging out of her coat. "I expect the same from you, of course."

Dante snorted. So much for innocent. She might blush and hesitate, but damned if the woman wasn't the sexiest thing he'd ever met. And quite possibly the only one who could actually meet his own appetites. It'd be interesting to find out.

"Why don't we?" he said, reaching out to slide loose one of the few buttons left on her denim shirt. "You're going to be cold," he warned.

"I'm counting on you to make me hot," she murmured.

Dante fumbled a button as desire blurred his vision. Riding the wave, he let go of her shirt and grabbed her shoulders to haul her up to his mouth.

Tongue, teeth, lips, they all melded together as Dante took her mouth, giving over to the ripping need clawing through his system. He'd tasted her tonight, slid his tongue into the slick, feminine heat of her folds. Now he wanted more. He wanted it all.

Delving deep, he slid his tongue along hers. He set a fast-paced, almost stabbing rhythm. Just like he wanted to set with their bodies. He wanted the quick, intense flash of heat as he pumped into her willing warmth. He wanted the rapid, insane rush of excitement as she welcomed him, wrapped around him, cried out his name.

He wanted it now.

"Strip," he demanded against her mouth.

"You first."

Dante gave a strangled laugh. He released her shoulders to unzip his leather jacket. With a shrug, it slid off. Visualizing exactly how he planned to take her, he draped it over a waist-high branch for cushioning.

Isabel spread her hands over his chest. Smoothing her hand down his shirt, she tugged the fabric free of his waistband. Dante's body tensed as cool air rushed over his belly, swiftly followed by the silky caress of her long, seeking fingers.

Mindful of the cold, Dante let her shirt hang open and reached under her tank top. His hands skimmed up the smooth flesh, reveling in how warm she was, how welcoming. With a snap, he released the front catch of her bra, filling both hands with the lush bounty of her breasts.

Isabel's fingers clenched on his chest, her nails skimming lightly. Dante vowed to feel those nails dig into him when she screamed out his name.

Rubbing his thumbs over her nipples, he leaned down and sucked one hard peak through the ribbed cotton of her tank top. She gasped. He pinched the other nipple, rolling it gently between his fingers through the soft barrier of fabric.

She strained toward him, but Dante didn't give in to her unspoken need to press their bodies together. Instead, he shoved the neckline of her top down, feasting on her breasts, their creamy softness making him groan. He pressed them tight together, his thumbs working her nipples as he kissed his way up her chest and throat in softly demanding bites.

When he reached the delicious warmth at the crux of her neck, he buried his face there, breathing deep her intoxicating scent. Isabel took advantage of the position, moving swiftly to press herself against him. She wrapped one foot around his leg, her heated center burning through their jeans. With gentle undulations, she made her need clear. She wanted him.

Good, he wanted her, too. But not until she was mindless and screaming with need.

Sure it would be a quick, wild ride to his goal, Dante leaned back to take her mouth.

But Isabel apparently had other ideas. She unwrapped her leg from his and cupped her hand over his dick as she pressed her mouth to his. Before he could react, she'd unsnapped his jeans. Grabbing her own jacket as a cushion, she dropped to her knees with a naughty smile that sent the blood rushing to his dick.

He had to give her credit for working the metal teeth loose, since he was pressed, rock hard, against the zipper. He watched her run her index finger over the soft cotton of his boxers, tracing the length of him. Tit for tat, she then pressed her mouth, lips open and moist, against his shorts.

Dante's breath caught at the wet heat, his hands tunneling into the silky tangle of her curls. She reached up, one small hand on either side of his waist, and grabbed his jeans and underwear. One tug and they were at his ankles.

His fingers still wrapped in her hair, he watched her lean back on her heels and take in the sight. As impossible as he'd have thought, he grew even harder. Obviously his dick appreciated the admiration on her face.

"Like the view?" he asked.

"I've wondered how you'd taste since you had me on the pool table," she told him as she leaned forward.

Hands gripping his thighs, she wrapped her lips around his head. Dante shuddered. Quick, wet friction pushed him from hot to wild in ten seconds flat.

He could barely control his body, already screaming in protest at not having been satisfied after feasting on Isabel earlier. He wanted satisfaction, and her mouth was offering pure heaven.

But Dante was stronger than that. Maybe if he told himself that often enough, his body would pay attention. Firmly holding to the image of Isabel's body spread beneath him, open and welcoming as he drove himself into her, Dante pulled away. He wasn't settling for less than that image.

"More," she murmured, glancing up. Slumberous gray eyes, hooded and filled with desire, stared up at him. Her mouth, lips swollen, glistened wetly in the moonlight. At the sight, Dante almost gave in and let her suck him back into her mouth.

Instead, he gripped her head and, with a lift of his chin, indicated she should stand. In a smooth, fluid move, she got to her feet.

As soon as she stood, Dante gave into the wild urge and grabbed her around the waist. He swung her around, settling her on the wide bed of the tree.

Grinding his teeth, he debated. He wanted his jeans off, but would have to stop to take off his work boots. And the ground was not only cold, but likely covered in sharp sticks and pinecones. To say nothing of wildlife. Distractions at the least, painful at best. And while he wasn't opposed to a little edgy pain with his pleasure, that wasn't his idea of a good time.

Opting for safe, but tacky, he focused on what *was* his idea of a good time. Isabel, naked and at his mercy.

His hands automatically went to her breasts again, his new favorite position. Dante used his mouth to push her tank top up, exposing her belly to his tongue. Tracing the line from her navel to the edge of her jeans, he reluctantly stopped rubbing the deliciously pebbled nipples to release her snap and zipper. A quick shove of her jeans and two seconds later, heaven was right there, glisteningly sweet, before his eyes.

Needing full access, Dante reached down to slide her shoes from her feet, letting her jeans and silky little scrap of panties fall into a pile on the ground. He gripped both legs, his fingers gliding along her smooth flesh, then grasped her slender ankles.

In slow, wet bites, he nibbled his way up her leg. Dante gently bit the soft flesh of her thigh, her gasp sending a shot of excitement through him.

Releasing her legs, he curved his hands over her breasts at the same time he feasted on the sweet bounty of her feminine folds. Slick, hot and delicious. He gave over to the wild pace, needing to hear her scream.

Isabel panted, trying to find some semblance of control. He was driving her insane. Between him and the feeling of being completely out of her element, she was lost in the dreamlike sensations.

Black night shimmered through the lacy canopy of bare branches. The soft moonlight cast a luminous glow over Dante's shoulders. She barely noticed the chilly air thanks to the warmth of his hands and the fiery heat of his mouth.

Desire, wild and wicked, flashed through her system as his fingers played her breasts like a fine instrument and his mouth…

Oh, God, his mouth.

She shuddered as his tongue shifted from soothing long strokes to hot, thrusting jabs. The wicked contrast of the smooth heat of his tongue and the scratchy stubble of his whiskers against the sensitive skin of her inner thighs made Isabel crazy. Struggling to catch a breath, she panted, rising faster and faster. His mouth mastered her body, sending it flying higher and higher. Need tightened, then snapped.

Isabel let out a cry, her fingers digging into Dante's shoulders, afraid to let go. He was her only anchor, the only thing keeping her from flying to pieces. Then, one last thrust of his tongue, and her body—her entire being—exploded in pleasure.

She was distantly aware of him shifting, his body still warming hers, but his movements slower now. Not soothing by any means. No, he was keeping her on the edge, skimming the border of wild ecstasy—not letting her cross over again, but not letting her come down either.

"Did you like that?" he asked, his voice husky and rough.

Isabel gave a faint nod.

"Uh-uh, babe. I want to hear the words. Tell me how it was for you."

Isabel's eyes fluttered open and focused on his face, the harsh planes a study of shadow and light. She swallowed, trying to find her voice.

"It was good," she whispered. "Like a dream, only sharp and wild."

"Want more?"

Only as much as she wanted her next breath. Isabel rose to her elbows and licked her lips. She eyed him, half-naked and sexy in the moonlight. Her hand trembled with the need to touch, to feel him beneath her fingers.

"What do *you* want?" she asked, not willing to be the only one wild with desire. Somewhere between the ride to the bar and this wild orgasm, things had shifted. It was all about the sex, yes. But it wasn't all about the fantasy anymore. Now she wanted more. She wanted *Dante, the man.* She wanted him crazy for her. Just like she was for him. "What's going to drive you crazy? Send you over that edge? What's it take to make you lose control?"

His eyes, so dark they looked black in the night, narrowed. Isabel bit her lip. What was she thinking, taking on a guy like this? Dante was in complete control, obviously. Her cocky declaration replayed in her head, mocking her.

Then she caught sight of his heartbeat, pounding a staccato beat in his throat. She looked closer. His knuckles were white on either side of her knees, his breath unsteady.

He was already hot for her. Could she make him go from hot to wild, crazy, insane with need? Isabel ran her tongue over her lip, watching his gaze follow the movement.

She gave him her slowest, most seductive smile and breathed deep. His gaze dropped to her breasts, his throat working.

Yes.

"Do you like it slow?" she asked softly. For the first time, she felt like she was meeting him on the same playing field. Woman to man, instead of dreamer to fantasy. "Measured and smooth? Or do you want it hot, wild and fast?"

"Music," he murmured.

Huh?

"Come again?"

"You asked what I liked. I like to do it to the beat of hard rock. Music."

Isabel looked around the wooded clearing and gave a helpless shrug. "You gonna sing?"

He laughed, then moved away for a second to grab something from his jacket pocket. Moonlight glanced off the small metal device, and the condom he'd obviously gotten from the bar's restroom. Isabel gave a little laugh. "You brought sex tunes?"

"Not deliberately," he said, his tone defensive. Poor guy, he clearly didn't want her to think he'd hauled her to Lookout Point for premeditated sex. As if she didn't know who'd clearly seduced who.

She reached out to take the small, flat rectangle from him. Larger than her MP3 player, she realized his was in a docking station with tiny speakers. Looked like they'd both get to enjoy the tunes.

She scrolled through his playlists, smiling when she found some of her favorite songs. Considering, she chose the one she wanted to start with, and set the piece of equipment on the branch.

She sat upright, scooting to the edge of the surface and pressed her thighs on either side of Dante's waist. Curling her hands behind his neck, she let her fingers slide through the deliciously silky texture of his hair.

"I chose the beat," she told him, leaning up to brush her lips over his. Her tongue flicked out, testing, tasting. "Let's dance."

Dante laughed, then his smile faded and he tunneled his fingers through her hair. Holding her head tilted back, he stared at her with such intensity, her own smile fell away.

Isabel struggled to catch a breath; his face was so serious. Her heart beat so loud, it drowned out the night noises.

"Do you know how powerful you are? How in-credible?" he asked in a tone so low she had to strain to hear his words. "I don't think I've ever been so turned on. You are simply the most fascinating woman I've ever met. You want something, you make it happen." He slid one hand from her hair to cup her cheek in a gesture so sweet it made her knees shake. "Now let's see you do that dare, hmm? Go ahead. Make me crazy. I know you can."

The man had so much faith in her, it blew her mind. Never before had anyone shown such complete accep-tance of her. Or such a complete belief that she could do anything, or in this case, everything.

It was more than she could resist. She'd have to find a way to deal with breaking rule three.

Before Isabel could lament the loss of her heart, Dante's mouth swooped down and took hers in a wild, erotic dance. A single tear trickled down her cheek for the heartbreak she knew would come, but she ignored it. Instead she gave herself over to the power of their love-making, the incredible taste that was Dante.

When he grabbed her around the waist, she locked her legs around his hips. She groaned at the feel of him against her center, but then he swung her down from the branch.

In a move so fast it made her dizzy, Dante turned her around so her back was to him. The long, hard length of him throbbed against her butt as he used the pressure of his body to anchor her, belly down, on the wide tree branch.

Isabel twisted around, giving in to the need to see his face. He stared through slitted eyes, making Isabel nervous as she realized his view consisted of the rounded curves of her butt, the lush spread of her hips and the long lines of her back. She hoped like hell he was focusing on her back.

Then he squinted, brow furrowed and leaned closer. She held her breath, waiting for his reaction. When he roared with laughter, her breath puffed out in a relieved giggle.

"Is that a poodle?" he asked, sounding baffled. "You have a pink poodle tattooed to your butt?"

"Oh, so you can have one but I can't?" she said, shooting him a sassy glance. That look, exasperation mixed with desire and a good dose of humor, seemed to make Dante laugh even harder.

Isabel grinned. Laughter *and* the best sex of her life? It was an addicting combination. One she wanted more of. Determined to feel him inside her, to see how good the best sex in the world felt, she wiggled her butt. The sight effectively ended Dante's amusement.

"Babe," he told her, "you can have anything you want."

"You. Now."

"Tell me how," he insisted.

Ready to scream, Isabel wiggled her butt against him again. His dick, rock hard, pressed against her, guaranteeing his interest. She wanted control, yes, but verbally? He was pushing her, forcing her out of her comfort zone even as he gave her the power to direct their passion. Pseudo-control, she realized. He still held the reins.

She pulled in a deep, shuddering breath. Determination mixed with desire. She'd send him over the edge. Somehow, she had to make Dante lose his rock-hard grip. On his body and, she realized with a hint of terror, on his emotions.

She stretched out her arm, using the tip of her fingernail to push the play button on his MP3 player. A hard-rock beat throbbed in the night air.

"Do me," she commanded in a husky tone. "I want to

feel you inside me—hard, wild, hot. You're going to go crazy. It'll feel so good."

He grinned, pressing against her, promising delight but not yet delivering.

"By the way," she tossed over her shoulder as he sheathed himself in the condom, determined not to wiggle and squirm like she knew he wanted. "You'll come first."

That's all it took. That challenge, a dare thrown down, and he was through teasing.

With a growl, he slid into her in one swift, intensely delicious thrust. Isabel had to bite her lip to hold back her scream of pleasure. Oh yeah, baby, he was good.

Dante moved in rhythm with the pounding beat of the music. Hard, fast thrusts mimicked a primitively sexual dance. Isabel lost herself in the movements, in the wild beat and the building power of his hard body inside of her.

She gripped the tree branch, the bark rough and cold beneath her fingers, even as her body slid in erotic pleasure over the smooth leather of his jacket.

Desire curled in a tight coil deep in her belly, screaming to break free in climax. But she was determined to win the dare. To send Dante over first.

Isabel struggled to find control, to think straight. She needed something, fast, because she wasn't going to hold out much longer. The sharp edge of pleasure was beckoning, pulling her closer and closer with each thrust.

The song changed, but the tempo remained the same. Need spiraled tighter. She clenched her thighs, trying to hold Dante, to slow the rhythm, to gain even a tiny bit of control.

He didn't let her have it.

Her vision blurred, her body teetering on the edge of an orgasm so intense she could barely breathe.

"Harder," she demanded on a gasp. "I want it harder."

His rhythm hitched and she felt rather than heard his groan.

Power surged through Isabel. "I love how you feel inside me," she moaned. "I want to feel you deeper. Faster. I want to feel you lose control. I need you to come. I need to feel you explode inside me."

Dante's hands clenched on her hips. He thrust, hesitated then plunged one more time, his guttural shout announcing his climax at the same time Isabel felt his body surge. A keening scream ripped from her throat as the his power sent her flying over the cliff of her own wild orgasm.

Isabel didn't know how long she spaced out, but the next thing she knew, Dante was rubbing her back. The sound of his murmured sweet nothings were barely noticeable over the music. She pulled in a deep breath and, using his jacket as a shield, slid from the branch. Dante wrapped the leather around her before bending down to gather her clothes.

They dressed in silence. She watched his face, frowning as his look of mellow pleasure was replaced by a tight, blank mask. As he slid the last of her shirt buttons closed, she cleared her throat.

His eyes met hers, the dark green cloudy.

"I won," she pointed out.

His eyes grew huge, the clouds clearing away as a laugh ripped from his throat.

"Ya think?"

"I *know*."

He shook his head, his smile making her heart melt.

"You probably want to keep this quiet," he advised, his

voice hushed in the night air. "After all, Santa Vera is a hotbed of gossip."

How big a deal was gossip? It couldn't be worse than knowing she'd done the unthinkable. She'd broken the most important rule. And lost her heart.

Even as the comfortable glow of satisfaction turned chilly around her, she had to wonder...

Just whose reputation was he worried about? Hers for being with a bad boy like him?

Or his, for being with such a good girl like her?

11

"THAT DANTE LUCIANO IS such a good boy."

Isabel smirked into her to-go cup of coffee, but didn't comment. She didn't figure Mrs. Brown would have the same take on just how good Dante was as she did.

"How can you say that?" someone asked. The male voice was so angry, Isabel couldn't tell who it was. "He's bad news, always has been."

Curious, she stepped around the diner's wall to peek into the seating area. Two tables had been shoved together, the surface covered with desserts. Ahh, that's right. The festival meeting to choose which sweets to offer in their booth. Isabel sniffed. She counted twelve people, including Lance. Only four were council members. She needed to find a way to be included in these events. Or, was it a matter of just stepping up and grabbing the opportunity? Along with the incredible physical pleasure last night, Dante had also made her realize sometimes all it took was asking to get what she wanted.

"Hey, everyone," she said as she stepped forward.

Greetings engulfed her, then died away as one of the gentlemen pulled out a chair for her. Huh, what d'ya know? She *was* a part of things. Isabel grinned into her coffee cup.

"Isabel can tell you," Lance suggested. She shot him a questioning look. "Dante Luciano is trouble. Remember all the stunts he pulled? The trouble he caused?"

She caught her breath. That nasty meanness that'd caught her attention had been Lance?

She cast a glance around the table, seeing nods and grimaces.

"But that was years ago," she said without thinking. As soon as the words were out, Isabel wanted to slap her hand over her mouth to call them back. Not smart, she inwardly groaned. After wanting so badly to fit into the town, she then publicly disagreed with them?

"Little lady's right," one of the men said. She wanted to jump up, run around the table and kiss his wrinkled cheek. "I'm not denying Dante was a pain in the ass back in his day. But he's changed. Just two days ago, he stopped by and fixed my fence. Falling over into the neighbors' yard, it was. Wouldn't even take money. Did visit a bit though. He's grown up. Frank should be proud."

Was that rage that flared on Lance's face? Isabel gaped, but the look was gone too fast to tell.

"Dante's doing right by his parents," Lorna said. "I'm sure we've all done things we regret. He just shoved all his into his formative years."

"For all we know," Lance pointed out, "he hasn't changed. Fixing a fence doesn't make up for the fact that twelve years ago he drove his father's truck through the same yard. Even when Frank coached the high-school football team, Dante did everything he could to humiliate his father. He's trouble."

"I've spent quite a bit of time with him," Isabel

admitted slowly, carefully weighing each word before she let it slip from her mouth, "and I haven't seen anything to make me think he's either irresponsible or trouble. I'm confused, though. I thought he was leaving soon, so why is this even an issue?"

"He wants to make a donation to the festival," Lorna told her. The older woman's craggy face softened as she gave Isabel a long, considering look. "Someone put a bee in his ear about how important the event is. He suggested we get a few of the teens to help with the construction work his daddy had to turn away cause of his foot. Dante said he'd foot the bill to pay the kids. Keep them off the street, make them feel involved."

Isabel couldn't help it, her smile was big enough to crack her face. The man was amazing. Orgasmically sexy, incredibly talented with both his hands and...well, his hands. And now this? Warmth wrapped around her heart, making her want to sigh.

Discussion flowed around her, but she was too caught up in her feelings and thoughts to notice it until Lance leaned over and put his hand on her knee.

Eyes huge, she stared. First at it, then at him. He'd never even held her hand in public when they were dating and now he made a move?

"What?" she hissed, shifting her leg so his hand fell away.

His frown was brief and hurt, making her feel bad. Friends. They were supposed to be friendly, now, weren't they? Guilt made her smile brighter, sparking an answering one from him. And, unfortunately, the return of his hand. Isabel grimaced and, with a quick pat, moved it off her knee.

"Eileen suggested I bring you the rest of the zoning

paperwork," Lance informed her in a quiet tone, curving his arm around the back of her chair. "She also asked me to invite you to join the board for their dinner meeting this Wednesday. I can pick you up."

Wednesday? She frowned. She and Dante didn't have any plans, but she'd like to keep as much time open as possible just in case he wanted to check off a few more items from her fantasy list. But she couldn't turn away her future, either.

"I've got a lot going on at the store." She hedged. "How about I just meet you there?"

Before Lance could respond, she glanced at her watch. "I've got to go," she told him, raising her voice to include the group. "I'm due in Sacramento to see the printer about brochures."

And a quick stop at Audra's shop. If she and Dante were going to keep having outdoor sex, she was going to need warmer lingerie.

"WHAT THE HELL DO YOU MEAN, Sweet Scentsations failed inspection?" Dante demanded. His fist wrapped so tight around the cell phone, he was surprised it didn't crumble. "We weren't even scheduled till next Tuesday."

Straddling his bike on the side of the road, Dante glared at the passing traffic. When Isabel had called, he hadn't wanted to sort through his own confused emotions let alone hers, so he'd let it go to voicemail.

His ego had shriveled pitifully when he'd heard her message about a problem with the building inspector. He'd immediately called the inspectors' office, only to get this runaround.

"It seems your inspection was rescheduled," the clerk explained, her voice vaguely conciliatory. It was hard to tell through the sound of her eating lunch as she spoke. The problem obviously hadn't affected her appetite. "I don't see who moved it, and there aren't any notes to tell me why it failed. Perhaps if you contact the offices tomorrow, you can speak with the inspector and get the details yourself?"

"I can't work on the job until I find out why it failed," Dante explained, wondering when the hell he'd developed patience. "If I have to wait until tomorrow, I lose an entire day."

"I can page the inspector, leave him a message. He took today off, though."

"Maybe one of the other inspectors can help me?"

"He has a note here saying this job is a special assignment, so I don't think so."

Dante frowned. Special assignment? What the hell?

"Why special?"

Crunch crunch crunch.

"I'm sorry, but I don't have that information."

Dante shoved a hand through his hair and blew out a breath, turning the air to white smoke.

"I don't suppose a smart lady like you would know where to find that information, huh? I'd definitely appreciate any help you can give me."

"Well, I'm not supposed to give out things like that."

But Dante, hearing her hesitation, turned on the charm. A few minutes of flirting, a couple of sexy jokes, and she gave a sigh.

"You're so bad," she giggled. "Tell you what, hang on. I'll pull the files."

He zipped his jacket a little higher, switching his phone to the other ear so he could shove his hand in his pocket to defrost it. Oddly enough, even the cold wasn't making Northern California as unappealing as it usually did. Probably because he was still flaming hot after his incredible night with Isabel.

He was freezing his ass off, but his body reacted like one of Pavlov's dogs, getting hard and horny even as the cold seeped in.

Dante swallowed, his vision blurring as the image of Isabel flashed through his brain. The saucy smile she'd shot over her shoulder as he'd teased her about her tattoo.

God. The woman was incredible. Sexy, yet reserved. Wild, yet uptight. Obsessive, yet impetuous.

She seriously scared the hell out of him.

"Mr. Luciano?" the clerk said through the phone, hauling him out of his horn-dog roadside fantasy and back to business. "I've got the file but it's kinda weird. Usually when there's a special assignment like this, it's noted who made the request or why. You know, so we know what to watch for. But this says *private*."

Dante's brows shot up.

"The inspector's in tomorrow?" was all he asked though.

"He's due in at nine," she said. Obviously realizing she was sitting on a time bomb, she asked, "You know, I could lose my job for giving out confidential information."

"Don't worry, sweetheart. I'll stop by and have a talk with him. He'll be the one to give me the info."

With a brief thanks, Dante ended the call. He slid his phone into its case on his belt loop and snagged his helmet off the bike's handlebar.

Missing supplies. Bribed building inspectors. And although at first he'd chalked it up to careless mainte-nance on his father's part, now he realized there had been equipment sabotage as well.

Someone was clearly trying to blow this job. Whether it was him they were after, or Isabel, he was taking it personally.

Dante didn't like people screwing with him and he planned to find out who it was. After he beat the hell out of them, then he'd find out why.

Ten minutes later he stepped into Santa Vera's only convenience store, needing food and caffeine. He grabbed some lunch, selected a chocolate bar he remembered Isabel saying she liked, and tossed it all on the counter.

"Why aren't you working, boy? It's noon. Only bums are dragging ass into work this late in the day, and damned if anyone on my payroll is going to be a bum."

Tension, like a steel bar, slammed through Dante's shoulders. He clenched the paper bag and, with a smile of thanks to the convenience-store clerk, took his change.

Things had been going too well. He should have known, like the infamous raincloud, Frank Luciano would show up eventually.

"Dad," Dante said as he turned to face the man he'd spent his teen years alternately hating and idolizing. The last time he'd seen the old man, Dante had been on the wrong side of a jail cell's bars. If he remembered correctly, his father's last words had been to disown him.

The old man looked like hell.

"Should you be on your feet?" Dante asked neutrally, hiding his shock. "I thought you were supposed to rest for another week or so."

He had to work to keep his expression clear. The old man, invincible in Dante's mind, looked...well, old. Gray, barely hinted at the last time Dante had seen him, capped his father's head and wrinkles had settled into craggy lines on his face.

"Your mother's a worrywart. I'm fine."

"Doc Lawson?"

"He's a worrywart, too. What does he know? I've got a business to run. I can't be expected to lie around while it goes to hell, now can I?"

Which obviously meant Dante was in charge of the drive south.

"Mom's gonna be worried," was all Dante said though.

Frank frowned, his concern at hurting his wife clear in his gaze. For all the man had been a total hardass with his son, he worshiped his wife.

"She knows I'm out," the old man said gruffly. He gestured to another gray-haired guy busy filling coffee cups. "I'm on my way to the Legion hall for lunch. Ol' man Sinclair makes crappy coffee so we were buffering ourselves ahead of time."

Dante nodded.

"Your mother thinks you came back to help." Frank's tone made it clear he thought that was bullshit.

"But you don't?"

"Of course not. You never gave a damn about Luciano Construction before. Why would you now?"

"Just because I didn't kiss your ass didn't mean I didn't give a damn."

Frank's face flushed and his fists clenched tight on his aluminum crutches.

"Work ethics aren't ass kissing."

"No, but taking the blame for things I didn't do would have been."

"There were witnesses, boy. Eye witnesses who saw you break in and steal the supplies. That means your work ethics sucked."

"You never would tell me *who* those eye witnesses were," Dante pointed out. Or who the liars were, to be exact. To this day, he didn't know if he'd been deliberately set up or if the entire incident had been an exaggeration based on his reputation. People pointing fingers, gossip growing into fact. But while Dante had done many things in his day that were questionable, quite a few that were illegal, he'd never stolen.

Especially not from his own father.

"What difference does it make? You never denied it."

"I shouldn't have had to. If you believed I'd steal from you, nothing I said would have changed that." Old resentments flooded back, making Dante want to put his fist through the wall next to him. All he'd ever wanted was his father to take his side, no questions asked.

"Bullshit. You could have told me why. I gave you plenty of chances."

Dante took a deep breath and then shrugged. There wasn't any point in giving in to the fight. As wild as the thought was, he realized he'd finally matured. He didn't want to spout crap with the single goal of pissing off his father.

Besides, the old man had aged. Dante wanted to let it all go. The anger, the resentment, the past.

Watching the old guy try to maneuver on the crutches to get out of the way of incoming customers, Dante wondered if the nagging tension in his gut was regret.

Maybe it was time to make peace? If nothing else, for Sylvia.

"Your mother says you're doing good work on the Santos job," Frank said gruffly, his thoughts obviously aligned with Dante's. "I stopped in myself yesterday." The old man's fists clenched and unclenched on the grips of his crutches, then his eyes met Dante's. "It looks good."

Dante smiled. How long had it been since his father had complimented anything he'd done? Grade school?

"I noticed you've learned a few things over the years," Frank continued. "I'd have thought construction was construction. But you have a few time-savers in there that I hadn't seen before. Sturdy, inspector approved. Where'd you learn it?"

Part of him reveled at the question. Part of him wanted to find his father a chair, sit him down and spill every detail of his last ten years. Job included. But that'd include discussing Tremaine. And while Luciano Construction might be a small-town venture, Frank Luciano wasn't a stupid man. Chances were, he'd heard of Tremaine's company. Even if he hadn't, he'd put two and two together with no trouble once Tremaine's recent purchase was made public.

Not that Dante'd deny it if directly asked. But his father was looking at him with respect. He didn't want to be the one to hand over the info that'd change that.

"Are you asking what I've been since I left home?" Dante hedged. "I didn't do construction work in jail, if that's what you're thinking."

"It's that kind of smart-ass remark that always got you in trouble," Frank pointed out. "Your mouth was always too fast for your own good. Embarrassing, to say the least."

"Good thing I'm not a kid anymore, then, isn't it? And lucky for you, what I do or say isn't your problem now."

"You haven't changed, have you?" The old man looked like he wanted to swing his crutch out and whack Dante upside the head.

"Have you?" Dante asked quietly.

Forget peace and screw regrets. He'd done fine all

this time without his father's support, he didn't need it now. And if his heart wanted it? Well, he was used to ignoring things like that.

"Gotta go," he said, lifting his bag. "Lunch break is over."

"It ain't a break if you haven't started work yet," Frank growled.

"Good thing I don't work for you then, huh?"

Without another word, or even looking at his father, Dante skirted around the old man and left the store. He carefully stored the sack in his saddlebag, zipped up his jacket and unhooked his helmet.

He swung his leg over the bike and was just about to put on the helmet when his phone rang.

His first inclination was to ignore it, but that'd hit too close to his father's assessment of him as an irresponsible asshole.

Already edgy and irritated, Dante flipped open his cell phone.

"Luciano," he barked.

"Dante?"

His anger fled at the fear in Isabel's voice.

"What's wrong, babe?"

"Someone vandalized the store." Her voice shook, then he heard her take a deep breath. When she spoke again, she was her normal, assured self. "There's paint everywhere and they broke the front window."

"I'll be there in five," he promised, ignoring the worry strumming through his system.

Firing up the Harley, Dante decided he didn't give a damn about the why. Whoever had done this had hurt Isabel. He'd settle for beating the shit out of them and screw the reasons why.

12

ISABEL SURVEYED THE MESS that had been her store and tried not to cry. Why would someone do this?

She wasn't the only one who wanted to know. Half a dozen townspeople milled through the vandalized store. Everyone had the same look of horrified anger on their faces.

"Who'd do something like this? Any ideas?" Lorna from the diner asked. She'd obviously seen the mess from her large window and brought the universal cure all. A three-layer chocolate cake with fudge frosting. And sprinkles. Isabel figured it was the sprinkles that would get her through this incident.

"I guess it could be kids. I don't understand why, though." Isabel rubbed at the white paint strewn over her once-beautiful rag-rolled peach walls. It didn't wipe off. Apparently whoever had thrown the tantrum had done it as soon as she'd left for Sacramento that morning.

"Not kids around here," Mr. Whittaker said. "We've never had hoodlums in this town."

Isabel gave a rueful laugh. "That's not the way I hear it," she said.

"Horse hockey." Lorna exclaimed. "Santa Vera's had her share of troubles, but never hoodlums."

"Not even Dante Luciano?" Isabel couldn't resist

asking. From Lance's description, Dante had been a complete juvenile delinquent.

"Even at his wildest, Dante wouldn't have done something like this," protested Therese Rankin, the owner of the dress shop across the way. "He was bad, sure, but he was never a destructive boy."

"You really shouldn't listen to gossip, dear." Lorna patted her arm and made a tut-tutting noise. "No matter what people say, I think you're the best thing to happen to the Luciano family in years."

"Huh?"

"Well, thanks to you, Dante's home."

"Me? Dante's home because his father broke his foot and his mother conned him into helping out."

"Word is he's smitten with you. His momma's hoping that translates into more time in town. Oh, sure," Lorna said, now confiding in Therese, "the chances of him actually moving back are slim. But Sylvia'd be thrilled with regular visits."

What happened to not listening to gossip? Isabel couldn't hear the rest of Lorna's words through the blood rushing to her head. Dante and her, long-term? The idea of him sticking around terrified her. She couldn't hide her feelings that long.

A loud roar thundered, then halted outside. She and everyone else in the room turned to watch Dante swing off his Harley, toss aside his helmet and stride to the door. His anger was a palpable thing, almost scary to see.

Everyone except Isabel stepped back toward the storeroom when he shoved open the door. Apparently he wasn't so scary they'd leave, though. Gossip notwithstanding, the crowd was obviously anticipating a good show.

"What the hell?" Dante growled. His swift glance took in the mess, the audience, then ignoring both he strode over to Isabel. "Were you here? Are you okay?"

His hair, the silky texture she'd gripped while he pleasured her with his mouth, was pushed back off his face like he'd been shoving his hand through it. She stared up into his gorgeous face, emotions flying through her at the speed of light. Relief mingled with desire, joy with embarrassment.

He obviously caught the last one, probably because her cheeks went cherry-red.

"What?"

"Nothing," she whispered, mortified at both his perception and the fact that she was acting like a silly schoolgirl. A woman didn't write a wild, sexual Man Plan, implement it by winning a hot, sexy dare and then blush about it in the daylight. That was just silly.

"I'm okay," she said quickly, hoping to distract him. "I'd gone into Sac to see the printer. I got home right before I called you. The paint was already dry."

As he stared down into her eyes Isabel licked her lips. His concern was a physical thing, but so was the sexual awareness. As if he were stripping her bare, with all her inhibitions tossed aside, so he could look into her soul and make sure she was really okay.

"Good."

She blinked as he turned away. Or maybe she'd imagined that intensity. Only her pride kept her from grabbing his arm and pulling him back so she could ask him if he'd spent the night reliving their sexual encounters. Well, pride and the gawking crowd.

"Did anyone see anything?"

Isabel started to answer, then realized he was talking

to the others. As if his question opened a door, they all poured forward, talking and gesturing at the same time.

Isabel watched in fascination as he interacted with the townspeople, all who had obviously known him most of his life. This was the first time she'd seen Dante with anyone local. Well, anyone other than Lance and Eileen, and they apparently weren't an accurate gauge.

He was both distant and respectful to everyone. They, however didn't have the same reserve. They poked, prodded, instructed and interrogated. Dante took it all in stride. Isabel didn't know that she'd have stood up to their onslaught, but he just grinned, rolled his eyes and answered politely.

"What d'ya make of it?" Lorna asked. She cast an indulgent look at Isabel, then leaned toward Dante to whisper loudly, "Someone thought it was kids. Have you ever heard such a thing?"

Dante shrugged but didn't comment.

"Nobody saw anything?" he asked again. They all shook their heads. He wiped at the wall, then frowned and leaned close to scratch the paint splattered over it. "This isn't paint, it's primer."

"Does that matter?" Mr. Whittaker asked.

Dante shrugged again. His gaze met Isabel's, a frown furrowing his brow. "It might," was all he said.

"What can we do?" Leigh asked.

Isabel was about to thank them for their time, since there was obviously nothing anyone could do except the cleaning and repairs. The sooner they left, the sooner she could get started. She fought back tears at the attack and at what it did to her timeline. She was so far behind, at this point it'd take a miracle for Sweet Scentsations to open on time.

"Help clean it up," Dante said immediately.

Isabel made a sound of protest at the presumptuous command. It was drowned out by the sound of people hurrying to do as he'd asked.

Twenty minutes later, two people scrubbed at the floor while another three manned rollers, spreading the under-coat of apricot paint over the primer splatters. Isabel was trying to sort through the hurricane-styled mess that had once been her files when Dante asked her for a phone book.

"What number d'ya need?" Lorna asked. "Between us, I'm sure we know every one of them here in Santa Vera."

"I want to find a lumber store in one of the next towns over," Dante said.

"What?" Therese protested. "Why would you go outside town for supplies? Oliver Herndell's hardware isn't good enough for you? Your girlfriend's a member of this community, why wouldn't you use locals to fix her place?"

"Girlfriend?" Dante's sneer was clear, even though Isabel was staring at the back of his head. "Don't you people have anything better to do than make up crazy gossip?"

Even though Isabel had denied it herself when Lorna had made the same suggestion, Dante's words hit her in the gut. Tears flooded her eyes before she could stop them. Why, she had no idea. She knew he wasn't into her like that. She didn't want him to be. Sex. A Man Plan, fantasy fulfillment. That's all he was.

At Lorna's tut-tutting, Dante turned. Seeing the look in Isabel's face, he reached out.

"I need to be alone," she muttered as she waved him off. With a quick apology to everyone, she slapped at the tears on her cheeks and raced to her office.

Head in hands, she tried to sort through the tumultu-ous emotions ricocheting through her. Thoughts of Dante and the break-in warred in her head. She focused on the break-in, since it was safest. On her anger at the vandalism. On her fear, if she were honest, at the idea that someone could break into her shop so easily and create such a mess. And that they'd want to.

Why? She had no idea.

Which left her to focus on Dante Luciano. Baddest bad boy she'd ever met. The shining star of her Man Plan and her ultimate fantasy.

She'd had the best sex of her life with him last night. Mind blowing, so far out of her comfort zone she still blushed thinking of it, wildly fabulous sex.

Like, once in a lifetime sex.

Isabel wanted to cry.

Instead, she did the next best thing and grabbed the phone.

"Hey," Audra said when she picked up.

"Hey."

"Uh-oh." There was a pause on the other end, some rustling and the sound of a door shutting. "Fess up, he sucked in bed, right?"

Isabel snorted before she could stop herself.

"See, that's my deepest fear," Audra said with a sigh. "That the hottest guys that we spend so many years fantasizing over are either gay or simply suck in bed."

"Aren't your fantasizing days through now that you have Jesse?"

"Uh huh, you go ahead and tell yourself that," Audra said with a laugh. "Granted, my fantasies are pretty much all about him now. But every once in a while there's this threesome thing I wouldn't mind living out."

"Johnny Depp again?"

"That guy is pure sexual eye-candy."

"You're bad."

"Right. And that's not why you called, sounding freaked out and stressed, in the middle of a workday." The teasing left Audra's tone. "What happened?"

Isabel started to use the vandalism as an excuse, then stopped. That wasn't why she'd called Audra.

"He didn't suck," she admitted.

"That scares you?"

"Maybe? I don't know. I like sex, so having incredible sex was, well, awesome. Why would it scare me?"

"Did he respect your boundaries?"

Isabel thought about it. He'd pushed her, definitely. But not in any way she was uncomfortable with. At least not in the physical sense.

"We didn't go anywhere I was uncomfortable with."

"Did you regret what you'd done after you woke up this morning?"

Since she'd relived their encounter all night long, she didn't think she'd actually gotten any sleep. But that probably wasn't what Audra meant.

"No regrets. And I still respected him in the morning."

Audra snickered.

"I don't know what it is," Isabel said, pushing her hair back off her face. "I'm all wigged out."

"Best sex of your life, hottest guy you've ever known, a scenario you've fantasized about for years?"

Isabel pursed her lips. "Yeah, that's about right."

"You're not thinking crazy, are you?"

"Define crazy."

"Rule number three, remember? That no-falling-in-love thing. Are you thinking this is more than sex? Trying to pretty up hot, raunchy orgasms into a neat emotional package?"

"Can't hot, raunchy orgasms come with emotions?"

"Sure. I have them all the time," Audra assured her. "But that's not what this was all about, was it? You were pretty adamant with those rules."

"Sometimes emotions are a bonus."

"Or a curse."

"Or a curse," Isabel agreed slowly.

And *that* was why she'd called Audra. Because she was cursed.

"I blew it," she whispered.

"Not yet," Audra said, her voice way too cheerful for Isabel's morose mood. "You didn't make any silly declarations or beg Dante to move to town and be your love-slave, did you?"

"Of course not." Isabel considered. "Although the love slave angle has potential."

"Down girl."

Isabel leaned back in her chair, letting her head rest on the cushioning leather. She'd realized she was falling for him last night sitting on that rock. As much as she'd like to write it off to good—no, spectacular—sex, she knew it wasn't that.

Dante got her. He understood her drive for control, her need to call her own shots. And he wasn't intimidated by that. Even better, he totally believed in her ability to be just as strong as she wanted.

"A little emotion never hurt," she suggested.

"No, sex is always better with emotion," Audra conceded. "But heartbreak sucks."

"What about heart bruising?"

Audra's sigh was so strong, Isabel almost expected it to ruffle her hair through the phone.

"Is it worth the risk?" Audra asked.

A knock on the door prevented her reply. Just as well since she didn't know the answer.

Before she could call out that the door was unlocked, it swung open.

Dante took one step in, and seeing she was on the phone, he leaned one shoulder against the white wood doorframe.

As it usually was when he worked, his hair was held off his face with a black bandana. His black T-shirt molded to muscles that had strained and bunched under Isabel's hands, and his jeans outlined thighs strong enough to hold her weight as he drove himself into her.

She met his gaze, the unfazed calm of the green depths giving her the answer.

"Yeah," she told Audra. "Whatever the risk, for however long. It's worth it."

WHILE ISABEL ENDED her phone call, Dante let his gaze wander over her. A hunger like he'd never known grew in his belly. She was like an addictive puzzle. He couldn't figure her out, yet he couldn't get enough of her.

"Sorry I ran out like that," she said as soon as she tossed the phone on the desk. "I should have come out and apologized."

"No biggie. Lorna said you were probably over-whelmed by the mess." He'd been relieved, since he'd worried it'd been his words that'd sent her running.

"I shouldn't have gone off and left you to deal with both the mess and the crowd," was all she said.

Dante shrugged, more concerned with the stress evi-denced on Isabel's face than a bunch of busybodies and a trashed store.

"They cleaned up most of the mess, so they served a purpose." He stepped into the room, close enough to get a better view of Isabel's face but not near enough to touch her.

"I still feel bad."

"Your choice." He shrugged, then not able to help himself, took another step closer so he could lean his hip on her desk. Now he could smell her perfume. The same scent he'd smelled on his body all night long. Damned if he'd considered not showering because he didn't want to lose that trace of her. What a wuss. Dante couldn't remember ever being this insane over a woman.

It had to be Santa Vera.

"Want to take a ride?" he offered before he even realized what he was thinking.

"What?"

Dante considered. He'd woke up that morning figuring he'd be smart to back off and keep things loose and distant with Isabel. After all, she'd pushed too many buttons, made him think about her way too much.

So asking her to go for a ride was about the stupidest move he could imagine making.

"Let's take a ride. C'mon, it'll do you good to get away from here."

"I need to deal with—" she waved her hand toward the store. He wondered if she knew her face paled when she glanced that way. She definitely needed a break. "You know, all that. Clean up, inventory. Call the insurance company."

"The first two are done. The destruction was all cosmetic and that's repaired. No supplies are missing. It was a temper tantrum, that's all."

Her sigh was his undoing. Dante reached out and brushed his hand over her cheek, a gesture sweet enough to shock him as much as it apparently did Isabel.

"Call the insurance company later," he insisted.

Reaching down, he took both of her hands in his and gave a gentle tug. She came easily to her feet, standing in front of him, but not in his arms. She was obviously waiting, watching him with those huge gray eyes to gauge his next move.

Damned if he knew what it'd be.

"You need to take a break," he suggested again.

"I'm not dressed for a ride."

He glanced over her silky dress, the deep purple color reminding him of a cold night sky in winter. The way it draped over her curves, highlighting but not hugging, made his mouth water.

"Fine, no ride. Want to get food?"

"Did Lorna leave the cake?"

"Yeah, a huge slab of chocolate."

"I want that," she decided.

Dante laughed. He'd never get women. They could be dragging-ass miserable, then you mention chocolate and they perked up like they'd been promised the greatest sex in the world.

Dante considered. Maybe there was something to that idea? Sex and chocolate? Like his-and-hers favorites.

The idea turning in his head, he nodded toward the now-empty store.

"C'mon, we'll get your cake. Want to take it somewhere private and share?" As soon as the words were out, he knew he should recall them. But damn, he didn't want to.

She stood there in front of him, close enough to wrap him in the delicious warmth of her scent but not close enough for him to glory in the feel of her body. Dante wanted that body again. To see her spread out beneath him. Or better yet, this time, rising above him.

He drew in a long breath, telling own his body to power down. The way he reacted to the image boded ill for his chances at winning a rematch on the who-will-come-first dare.

And despite his misgivings, his body demanded that rematch. Dante rarely refused his body anything that he knew would feel incredible, even if the cost was high. Emotional paybacks, reputations, even worries about Isabel getting the wrong idea, none of that held up to the wild need clawing through him.

"How private?" she asked, drawing him back to his proposition. "And, more importantly, who's in charge of the cake? You know how I feel about sharing chocolate."

Dante shook his head. Damn, the woman was something else. He gave in to the need and pulled her to him, not able to hold back his affectionate hug.

"Take turns?" he suggested.

"I'm first."

"Always." Later, he'd worry about why that concept scared the hell out of him. Right now he was hungry.

He took her mouth like a starving man, desperate to fill himself with her taste, her texture. Releasing her shoulders, Dante tunneled his fingers into her hair to tilt her head back, controlling the pressure, the angle, the intensity of their kiss.

She pressed her hands to his chest, fingers gently clawing down to his belt. With a simple slide of her hand, she cupped his dick and, just like that, claimed complete control.

"What about the cake?" he murmured as he nibbled his way over her jawline and down the sweet curve of her throat.

"We'll take it upstairs," she said in a breathy voice. "I'm thinking it'd taste absolutely delicious eaten in bed."

"I'm thinking it'd taste even better eaten off each other," he returned.

Isabel pulled back, her gaze smoke-and-flame. "You realize this is going to make a total mess, right?"

"Yeah." He knew she was talking about a lot more than chocolate smeared over her sheets. "Does it matter?"

She took a deep breath, staring into his eyes. Whatever she saw there must have reassured her, because she gave a little shake of her head.

"Nope. The only thing that matters right now is how you taste in cake."

13

"I THINK THIS IS A MISTAKE," Dante warned as he slid into the banquette seat next to Isabel.

"Quit being so paranoid."

"Dinner in the only upscale restaurant Santa Vera calls its own? With me, in an obvious non-working situation? I don't call that paranoid. I call that asking for attention."

She rolled her eyes and spread the linen napkin over her lap. With a pleased glance, Isabel took in the chichi atmosphere of the restaurant. So she'd manipulated her list a little to convince Dante that a romantic dinner out was the prelude to one of her turn-ons.

He was leaving soon and she desperately wanted the memory of a real-date experience.

"I've never been here before," she told Dante, gesturing around the dimly lit restaurant. The quiet buzz of conversation was a soft backdrop to the live piano music. "I'll have to come back sometime and talk to the manager. No amount of candlelight is going to hide those ugly plastic flowers. Do you think they'd consider live seasonal blooms? I'd give them a really good deal."

As she'd intended, Dante laughed and visibly relaxed. As she watched the tension ease from his shoulders, Isabel realized she'd been just as uptight. Maybe there was more at stake with this date than she'd realized.

Even Dante looked different. As usual, he wore a T-shirt, this one dark purple. But the sport jacket over it made him look hot. Sexy. He hadn't cut his hair or anything; it still waved back off his forehead, but instead of its normal sexy tousle, it was smooth, like he'd taken time to gel it or something. At seven in the evening, his cheeks were baby-butt smooth. He'd shaved before picking her up.

Like a real date. One of those romantic, more than just sex, getting to know you and we might connect in a big way dates. Like it was important to him, too.

Pressing a hand to her stomach to calm the fluttering nerves, she was grateful when the sommelier arrived with his wine selection.

Dante proceeded to order, showing a proficiency and knowledge of wine that buried her nerves in shock.

"You do that very well," she commented when the sommelier left.

Her surprise must have been clear, since he laughed. Stretching one arm along the banquette seat behind her, Dante turned his body so he could lean into her.

Isabel had eaten cake off the man's naked belly, for crying out loud. But the sight of him—his attention totally fixed on her, flirtation clear in his laugh—it was enough to make a girl squirm.

When Dante traced his finger along her jaw, smoothing it down her throat before fingering the lace of her blouse, Isabel did squirm.

"I do quite a few things well," he told her in a husky tone. "You've only seen the tip of the iceberg." He wiggled his brows in a way that made her giggle. "So to speak."

"And quite an impressive iceberg it was, too."

"Like I said, that's just the beginning."

Isabel's breath hitched as she tried to imagine what else he had in store for her. No, she reined back her thoughts in panic. Not what he had in store for her. This was *her* plan. *She* was in control. She needed to focus on what she had on the list for him to do next.

Sucking in a breath, she tried to toss off the sexual haze and to focus.

"Tell me about your job," she asked, desperately needing a distraction while she regrouped.

"About the job I'm doing for you?"

"No. Your real job. What you do when you're not saving your dad's business."

Dante snorted. "I don't think he'd see it that way."

"Whether he would or not, it's the truth, isn't it? He'd have lost business if you hadn't come to his rescue."

He shrugged. She couldn't tell if he was uncomfortable or pleased with her comments. Either way, it was obvious he wanted the subject changed because he started talking about his job.

"So now I'm basically a troubleshooter," he wound up. "I don't do the hands-on construction much anymore, go from job to job, site to site."

"Don't you get homesick? Oh, not for Santa Vera," she said with a laugh when he pulled a face, "but for one place. One job. You know, settling in and being a part of the regular day-to-day rut."

"As fun as ruts sound, I hadn't missed that aspect before." His frown and the way his words trailed off made her wonder if he might be changing his mind. "There's not much to keep me in one place."

"Home?"

"Half-furnished apartment." He shot her a naughty look and added, "With a killer sound system."

Images of his body poised over hers, moving in time with the beat of some rock tune, flashed through Isabel's mind. She blew out a breath and took a sip of her ice water.

"Friends?" she asked, trying to keep focused.

"What kind?" he hedged.

She laughed at his discomfort. "You tell me."

"I have friends. We get together when I'm in town, but it's not like they are hanging on hold until I arrive. I don't do relationships, if that's what you're asking."

Isabel propped her arm on the table and leaned into him. With a wicked smile she traced her finger over the collar of his jacket.

"I hadn't been. But you opened the door, so let's check it out." He rolled his eyes but didn't protest, so she asked, "How do you define relationships? And why don't you do them?"

"Anything that means obligation, and I don't do them because I'm a bad bet."

Tapping her fingers on his chest, Isabel considered his answer.

Before she could decide how she felt about it, the waiter arrived to take their order, followed by the sommelier with their wine.

"So why aren't you doing the big city?" Dante asked when they were alone again. "With your brains and talent for planning and organizing, you could be getting rich at some high-paying corporate job."

She debated steering the subject back to his being a self-professed bad bet, then decided his explanation would probably just make her miserable. So she shrugged instead.

"I'd rather work for myself. I prefer to be in complete control."

"That covers the corporate-job angle. What about the small town? Even as a florist, you'd stand to make a lot more money in a big city."

"I want the small-town feeling. That closeness and sense of belonging. A sense of belonging and support I wouldn't be able to get in a big city." She pursed her lips, aware that he could debate whether she'd managed to get that in Santa Vera, but Dante just quirked a brow for her to continue. "There's something about growing up an only child that is a little…"

"Stifling?" he suggested at her hesitation.

"Okay, yeah. I guess you'd know, too. It's all that parental attention and focus and, well, expectations. Mine expected me to be a good girl, to meet their standards and, because they were so much older, to not be any trouble."

Dante nodded. "Mine expected similar. Except the trouble part, of course. My mom used to say they knew from the moment I started walking I'd be a pain in the ass."

Isabel laughed. She'd give anything to see Dante's baby pictures. He must've been absolutely adorable. Her gaze traced his features and she sighed. Yeah. Adorable.

"So we both obviously met our parents' expectations?" she commented.

"I guess so. That doesn't explain the small-town thing, though."

"Only child to elderly parents," she summed up. "And I want to be a part of things. After all, it's easier to control variables in a smaller venue." She gave a one-shouldered shrug. "I don't want to get lost in the crowd, you know? In Santa Vera I can be a part of the community, make a difference. Or I'd hoped I could."

Dante pulled a face, then took her hand. "Look, you want to be an integral part of this town, you will be. They'd be idiots not to appreciate you."

"I thought you considered them all idiots anyway."

He traced her fingers with his, considering.

"Maybe not so much. Some of them, yeah. Like Anderson."

Isabel rolled her eyes. "One day you should share just exactly what the issue is between the two of you."

Dante considered. The look in his eyes, sad and a little hopeless, made her heart ache.

"Anderson's always wanted to be the golden boy, and he tended to twist situations to make sure he looked good. My dad was the football coach, Anderson a second-string quarterback. I never knew what Anderson's issue was, since I didn't play. But he took a shine to the attention from my dad and seemed to resent anyone else getting any."

"He caused problems?" Isabel was surprised. Lance was such a cheerleader, she couldn't imagine him trying to tear someone else down. Then again, he did seem to have an odd animosity toward Dante.

"Subtly. It'd be little things, nothing I could ever point out without looking like an ass." Dante shrugged. "Especially since the general opinion was jealousy."

"He was jealous of you?" She considered and nodded. "That makes sense. I'd think most guys would been. Even one with as drastically different focuses like Lance."

Dante laughed. The sound was so bitter, Isabel was surprised it didn't turn the wine bad.

"Hardly. The way the rumor went, I was jealous of him."

Isabel snorted. She slapped a hand over her mouth,

horrified to have made such a rude sound, but she couldn't help it.

"You? Jealous of him? How on earth could anyone think that?"

Dante grinned, lifting her hand to his mouth and pressing a kiss to her palm. "You're a sweetheart. I don't know where the jealousy gossip started, just that it was there. And my dad did a lot of comparisons. The whole 'Why don't you get grades like Anderson, here?' and 'Wouldn't hurt you to be more community oriented. Why don't you ask Anderson to help you out?'" Dante shrugged. "You know, that kind of crap. So when I was arrested, I was already looking pretty bad."

"You were arrested?" Lance had hinted at it. She wondered if Dante expected her to be horrified, too. "What for?"

"Burglary."

Dante released her hand. She wondered if he let it go that fast so she couldn't do it first. Isabel frowned and held back her comments as the waiter served their salads.

Once he'd gone, she tasted the field greens and gave a hum of appreciation at the tangy spice of the dressing. Then she set down her fork. Turning again to face Dante, she raised a brow.

"Did they ever clear it up? Find the truth?"

"You're assuming I didn't do it?"

"You're many things, but a thief isn't one of them. I could assume you've changed tremendously over the last ten years, except that I know Drew. And he wouldn't have been your friend back then if you were the type to steal."

"That simple?"

"Shouldn't it be?" Isabel frowned, then taking a huge risk, reached out to take his hand. She realized she'd never emotionally reached out to anyone before. Other than her parents, Audra was probably the only person she'd ever let get close enough to her to risk rejection.

Until Dante.

When his fingers closed over hers, she let out a sigh.

DANTE TRIED TO HIDE his stunned expression. Nobody had ever had such unquestionable faith in him before. He'd never tried to be anything other than himself, never tempered his wild ways. But to have someone accept him, bad-boy image and all, and still believe he was innocent?

Damned if she hadn't ruined him. One sweet gesture and she'd pushed him over the steely emotional fence he was so careful with. Now what?

What else? Hang on and enjoy the ride. And if he recalled Isabel's incredible fantasy list, there were a few rides he was definitely looking forward to enjoying.

"Let's talk about your list," he suggested, more than ready to change the subject.

He grinned as her cheeks turned the sweetest shade of pink. For a woman who could bring him to his knees with pleasure, she was pretty damned reserved.

"What's to talk about? You've already either done, or revised, at least half of it," she returned with a laugh.

"What prompted you to make a fantasy list in the first place?"

"Ooh, that." She puffed out a breath and lifted one hand. "It was just one of those things. Audra and I got to talking about sex and fantasies, and the idea of the list was born. Audra, in her infinite wisdom, told me to think of my ultimate fantasy guy and—"

She turned bright red this time, her gray eyes huge.

When the waiter arrived with their entrées, she looked like she was going to jump out of the booth and kiss the guy in gratitude.

Interesting. He knew from both the little bit she'd said and the town gossip that she'd dated Anderson for a while. That'd be enough to inspire any woman to fantasize about other guys, for sure. But why the secretive attitude? Dante puzzled over the tight ball of anger in his belly until he finally recognized it.

Jealousy. He was jealous that Isabel had written that hot, wild list of sexual wishes based on someone else.

Damn. So this was how it felt when the mighty fell. Lousy.

"So tell me more about this fantasy guy," he teased after they'd had a few bites of their meal.

"Why? Are you interested in a threesome?"

Dante choked on his bite of steak, his eyes filling as he tried to swallow and laugh at the same time.

"No," he replied when he finally found his voice again. "I'm not big on sharing. If I'm in bed—or anywhere else—with a lady, it's just about the two of us."

Isabel patted her napkin to her mouth, the white linen a marked contrast to the lush red invitation of her lips. Her gaze holding his, she leaned close. Dante almost groaned at the delicious pressure of her breast against his forearm.

"Do you know what I think would be the perfect end to this evening?"

His smile was a slow, wicked thing. He couldn't wait to hear her idea of perfection.

"A ride, maybe to Tahoe. A moonlit walk by the lake."

Before he could counter her suggestion with one of his own, someone stopped in front of their table.

Dante tore his gaze from Isabel's to glance over.

"Dad?" he asked, shock clear in his raised voice.

"Dante. I'm surprised to see you here." Since Frank Luciano's face was a study of fury, Dante figured it wasn't a pleasant surprise.

"Not as surprised as I am to see you." Dante leaned back in a show of casual relaxation and he slid his arm along the back of the booth. From the look Isabel shot him, he hadn't hid the tension from her, but as long as his father was clueless, he didn't care. Another thing to worry about later, that he was willing to expose his true emotions to Isabel.

Then he saw who sidled up to his dad's side and figured it'd be much later.

"Lance? What are you doing here?" Isabel exclaimed. Dante didn't look away from the two men, but he felt her tension ratchet up to match his. Nice.

"We're here with a few others in an emergency council session," Anderson said, his face tight and pinched looking. Why did Dante get the feeling that uptight expression was somehow directed at him. Or, from the glare in the guy's eyes as he focused on Isabel, the two of them?

"Pretty upscale for the town council," Dante pointed out.

"We each pay our own way," Lance snapped.

"Didn't suggest otherwise."

"Your tone certainly did. I'm just as surprised to see you here. What? Isabel's paying for dinner?"

Dante didn't even bother to roll his eyes. What an ass! "That's the best you can come up with?"

"Enough," Frank growled.

At the same time Isabel leaned forward to protest, "Hey, don't put me in the middle of your pissing match."

Lance's jaw dropped at her words, but Dante almost grinned when he saw that his dad had to hold back a laugh. Their eyes met and for the first time in a decade shared a look of humor. Then Frank seemed to remember his son was the enemy, because his gaze turned to stone again.

"We've got a problem," Frank said before anyone could make another smart-ass comment.

"One of the job sites?" Dante asked, figuring that was the only reason to bring him into a discussion.

"Definitely one of yours," Lance said.

Dante frowned. What was with the innuendo?

"Dad?"

"I'm surprised at your timing. I'd have thought you'd wait till you left town before springing this on us," Lance continued.

Dante shot him a killing look. "Enough from you. I want to hear your opinion, I'll ask. Until then, the only person I'm talking to is *my* father."

Innuendo went both ways, and surprise surprise, Anderson was smart enough to get it. He pressed his lips together and glared, but didn't open his mouth again.

"That property on Main Street sold," Frank said, his gruff voice quiet. "The one across from your place," he told Isabel. Dante felt her nod.

"Apparently the buyer had an inside track." He gave Dante his patented glower. "He used it, and apparent connections, to bypass our zoning committee's contract for downtown properties. He found a loophole that will exclude him from the structural integrity we've worked so hard to build downtown."

Son of a bitch. Dante's stomach pitched. He'd figured the purchase would be sidelined when he had refused to help Tremaine. Without those loopholes, there was no point in buying property in Santa Vera. After all, Tremaine Industries didn't conform.

How had Tremaine gotten around the zoning commit-tee? That'd been the one thing Dante had counted on to keep him from pulling off his deal.

Knowing Santa Vera's obsession with the downtown project, someone was going to fry. The question was, how had they tied Dante to Tremaine? The anger on his father's face made it clear the connection was made.

Dante glanced at Lance. Noting the triumph glowing in the guy's pale blue eyes, he had his answer. Oh, not how Anderson had figured the connection, but he'd def-initely been the one to point the finger at Dante. Again.

"I don't understand," Isabel said. "I didn't even know the purchase had gone through. Isn't that information supposed to come to me since I'm head of the zoning committee?"

Dante's stomach, already clenched, took a dive right to his toes. No. *Not Isabel.* Not even Anderson would frame the situation in a way that would take her down. And down she'd go, if she was in charge of zoning. Innocent or not, Santa Vera didn't care.

"Records show they dealt with you, Ms. Santos," Frank said. His words, while cold, had an underlying regret.

"Nobody dealt with me," she protested.

"This is bullshit," Dante said quietly. "Someone's playing a game, trying to cause trouble."

"You used that argument once before, son. Didn't hold then, won't hold now. Nobody has any reason to set this up."

"Once again, you don't give a damn about the truth. Just a quick, circumstantial glance at the supposed facts and you cast judgment."

"Truth?" Frank said with a tired sigh. He looked old. Old, worn out and beaten.

"The truth," Lance said, putting a calming hand on Frank's arm. Dante almost growled watching his father chill out at the asshole's gesture, "is actually quite clear in this situation."

"To you? I'm sure it is." Dante sneered.

"To me and anyone else who cares to read," Lance returned. He pulled a thin stack of papers from the leather portfolio he'd been carting around and tossed it on the table.

Dante picked it up. He only had to glance at the letterhead to know he was screwed. A flip of the first page showed his initial report on the Main Street property, complete with signature. Shit. He glanced at the last page, the clerk's document. The signature was forged, sure, but it wouldn't do him any good to deny it given the evidence of the first two papers. With a growl, he crumpled the pages in his fist. Damn Tremaine.

"There's more, of course. It'll all be discussed during the emergency town-council meeting." Lance gave Frank a long, pensive look, like he was asking the older man for advice. "We'll need to start damage control right away, don't you think? I'm mapping out a plan already."

Frank gave a bad-tempered shrug. Dante smirked. Didn't Lance know better yet? Giving the old man cleanup options before he'd finished being pissed just irritated him more.

"This is all going to blow tomorrow. Save your mother some embarrassment and get the hell out of town." With that and an angry growl that Dante remembered so well, Frank stormed off as fast as his walking cast would allow.

Lance, the asshole, stood there until Frank was out of earshot, then smirked.

"I'd like to point out, Isabel, that I did warn you about Luciano." He gave Dante a look that made it clear he felt he was the superior being, then gave Isabel a look of pity. "But you didn't pay attention. And now you're paying, not only with your reputation, but possibly with your business. It's a shame, of course. One of those things listening to wise advice would have prevented."

"This doesn't make sense," Isabel said quietly. "Zoning is supposed to come through me. That's my committee. I've taken care of all of the paperwork, sent out all of the proper forms. This guy didn't apply for zoning through the clerk's office, or I would have handled it."

Lance tut-tutted and shook his head. "Apparently he knew how to circumvent our system. From what I understand, that's what Luciano's job is, isn't it? Help Tremaine buy up properties in small towns, turn them into nightclubs or bars in order to run other business out. Then buy up the rest of the property cheap. I checked. What'd you turn that last one into? A warehouse store? Before it was sold to Wal-Mart?"

All of which would ruin downtown. Dante slanted a look at Isabel's stunned face. Since it was only by circumventing zoning that Tremaine could pull it off, Santa Vera would blame Isabel. After all, that was her committee.

Lance gave Dante a look, his gaze filled with triumphant glee. Dante had to wonder how long the guy had been planning this moment.

"Why don't you fill Isabel in on the details, hmm? Or better yet, give her those papers. It's only fair that she realize why her association with you is about to make her persona non grata in Santa Vera."

With another smirk, Lance turned and left.

The incriminating documents balled in his fist, Dante waited for the fury to come. But all he got was a cold emptiness. Once again, his father had told him to get his ass out of town. And once again, Anderson was by his side, smirking. It'd be worth kicking the guy's ass on principle.

Except Dante was numb.

Because this time, instead of his reputation that was destroyed, it was Isabel's.

"Let's go," he said quietly, tossing cash on the table to cover their bill. "I need to ride."

Without a word, her face still as white as the linen napkin she tossed aside, Isabel slid from the booth and shrugged into her coat.

"One question?" she asked.

He looked at her.

"That Victorian, you told me you were looking at it. Were you inspecting it for this company? Do you work for this Tremaine guy? Is that what the letter says?"

For the first time in his life, Dante wished he were a liar. But he wasn't, so all he could do was nod.

And just like that, she shut down. She gave him a look so cold, he swore he could feel the ice forming on his face.

So much for faith. When it came down to it, Isabel was no different than any of the rest of them. Not only ready to believe the worst of him, but just like his father, she'd already convicted him of the crime.

14

ANGER COURSED THROUGH Isabel in a wave so strong it scared her. Her fist clenched tight to Dante's leather jacket as he sped down the highway.

What an idiot she'd been. She'd been so busy focusing on her goals, her lists. So excited to be actually living her dream fantasy, that she hadn't once questioned her judgment. Leave it to her to have lousy taste in men. She thought back to her conversation with Dante about the house across the street and ground her teeth. Once again, she hadn't paid attention. Just like with the married jerk, the signs were there. But she'd been too busy with her head in the clouds to notice them.

She'd waited until they'd got outside the restaurant so she'd have time to gather her thoughts, to try to process the train wreck that had been their romantic dinner. But when she'd asked Dante questions, like what the hell was going on, he'd just stared at her and shrugged. Mr. Big Bad and Silent, he'd handed her the helmet and swung onto the Harley. All he'd said was he needed to ride. They were riding.

What had those documents said? It must have been bad for both Lance and Mr. Luciano to convict Dante so readily.

Questions rushed through her mind as fast as the wind rushing over her body. Was it something she could have prevented? She'd thought she had a firm handle on the committee position, on her job description. All she had to do was make sure any new property owner signed the zoning contract before they settled the sale. The only way the sales were supposed to run through the downtown area were with zoning approval. Which was her committee now. That was the way it was set up. Wasn't it?

If she hadn't needed to use both hands to keep from falling off the bike, she'd have pressed one to her aching forehead.

Dante? Lance's accusations ran through her head. Isabel gave it a shake to knock them out. She might be blind to some things, like Dante's connection to Tremaine Industries and the purchase of that property. But she wasn't blind to who he was.

No matter what Lance or Mr. Luciano might think— hell, what the whole town might think after Lance was through—Dante hadn't done anything wrong.

She just had to find a way to prove it.

When the bike throttled down, she lifted her head and looked around.

"You have to be kidding," she yelled, even though he couldn't hear her over the roar of the engine.

Lookout Point?

He killed the engine and, as if she wasn't plastered to his back, he swung free of the bike. His moves controlled and tight, he unhooked his helmet and pulled it off. Then he threw it aside with such force it broke one of the winter-brittle tree branches.

Whoa. Heart racing, she took in the anger clear on his face, an anger that looked ten times hotter than her own. What kind of deviant was she that the sight turned her on?

"Look," she said, when she'd taken her own helmet off and hooked it to its peg, "this has to be fixable."

At his hard, blank stare, she was tempted to grab the helmet back and follow his example. Except it'd be his head she aimed for.

"Can I see the papers?" she asked quietly. She needed details. Information. She needed to fill in some of the blanks in order to fix this mess. She wanted to know what had made his father turn his back, positive Dante had sold them out. She had to know.

"What difference will it make?"

"It'll help me make a plan—" she started to say. Her words were cut off by his growl.

"Some things don't fit into a tidy list," Dante said, the deep timber of his voice carrying low over the lake sounds. Unlike their last visit, there was no moon tonight. His face was a study of shadows. "Is there a column there for betrayal? How do you juggle things to cover that?"

Her breath hitched. She was about to lose everything she'd worked for, planned for. The town had built its reputation on the quaint old-fashioned air of Main Street. If Lance was to be believed and this guy was going to turn that Victorian into a nightclub, that image was about to be blown to bits.

At his refusal to let her try to fix the problem, her anger, still simmering right there at the surface, boiled over.

"At least I try to make a plan," she yelled. "At least I want to fix things, instead of sitting there in stubborn silence while my reputation is ruined."

"You're worried about your reputation?"

There was an edge to his voice she didn't understand, but it made her take a step back. Eyes huge, she gulped. Damned if she'd back down, though.

"Yes, dammit. I am worried about my reputation."

"Don't you remember the warnings, Isabel? Hell, everyone told you. I'm trouble. You get involved with me, you're gonna pay." He stalked toward her, looming tall in the dark night. Isabel tried to swallow but her mouth had dried up.

"I'm bad, remember?" He stopped inches from her body. ·

"Wild." He tunneled his fingers into her hair, tilting her head up to stare into the angry green depths of his eyes.

"Trouble." His mouth swooped down, taking hers in an angry rage that sent her system into overdrive. Tongue, teeth, lips. They all melded together in a frenzied dance of pleasure, with Dante leading. Each time she thought she'd found the rhythm, he changed it, shifting, pulling her along like a puppet.

Emotions surged, dark and wild, intense like she'd never felt before. Desire, always present around Dante anyway, flamed in hot, livid passion.

A part of her—the sane, rational part—took a mental step back to ask what on earth she thought she was doing. The biting need ripping through her system shoved that rational part aside. The only thing that mattered was Dante and the viciously wild desire wound tight in her belly.

He slid his hands out of her hair, skimming them down her arms and around her back. He grabbed her ass, his fingers curving into her cheeks and pulling her tight to the throbbing pleasure of his erection.

Losing control, Isabel ground herself to him. It wasn't enough. The angle, the pressure. She wrapped one leg around his thigh, trying to find relief for the spiraling need that ripped through her.

His hands squeezed her butt, lifting her to the right position at the same time he released her mouth to bury his face in her neck. The heat of his fingers, the pressure of his hard body, the feel of his mouth against her sensitive skin. The combination of it all sent Isabel into a tailspin.

With a keening moan, she pressed against him, undulating in pleasure as the first wave of her orgasm swept over her. Her body clenched as she tried to hold tight to the climax.

"You like?" he asked against her throat.

"More," she gasped.

Not willing to be the only one crazy here, she released Dante's shoulders to shove his jacket free. He had to release her butt to shake it loose. Before it hit the ground, he had one hand back on her ass and the other cupped over her breast. Tweaking fingers circled her straining nipple, making Isabel crazy with the need to be naked.

She raked her fingers down his chest to his belly. A quick tug pulled his T-shirt free of his jeans. She scraped her nails back up, reveling in the power as he shuddered in pleasure. When she reached his chest, she paid him back for the delicious torment by tweaking his nipples. He groaned his delight.

Pulling away from her, he unbelted her leather jacket, then pushed it off her shoulders. It fell with a thud to the cold ground by their feet.

Dante's hands gripped both sides of her blouse. For a second, she thought he'd rip it right off her. The idea of that, of him wanting her so bad he'd tear the clothes from her body, almost made her come again.

But he stopped, instead, and pushed her back. He pressed both hands to her shoulders to make her stand in front of him. Then, his eyes black in the night, he held her gaze as he slowly, deliberately slipped each button free.

This studied, intense break from the wicked biting passion was all the more seductive because Isabel knew it was only the eye of the storm.

Through with her buttons, but still holding her gaze, Dante unsnapped her bra. He didn't touch her.

The wait was killing her.

"Please," she whispered.

"I'm calling the shots this time," he told her.

As if she weighed nothing, Dante swung her up in his arms and carried her to the bike. Isabel licked her lips, her breath coming in quiet gasps in the still night air.

When he straddled the seat, she frowned. Then he swung her around to face him, her legs on either side of his thighs.

"What are you doing?" she gasped, the leather seat of the motorcycle cold against her bare thighs.

"We've done your fantasies," he said quietly. "Now we're doing one of mine."

What? Before Isabel could voice a protest, he leaned forward to bury his face between her breasts, his hands cupping, squeezing, driving her crazy.

He wouldn't let her touch him. Wouldn't let her do anything except follow the commands he made on her body.

She tried to think, to put a name to the sudden terror burning in her gut. But sensations ruled her body.

Dante nibbled, licked, tormented her nipples. One, then the other. Every time Isabel tried to touch him, he shrugged her off. It was all about control. She recognized it, even as she struggled against his power to take hers from her.

Determined to hold her own, Isabel ignored Dante's

unspoken command that she keep her hands to herself and slid them along the smooth denim of his thighs. Knowing he'd stop the delicious nipple action if she touched his dick, she kept her moves smooth, subtle. Long, soft strokes on his thighs. Up, to the crux of his legs, down, to his knee. Gentle, barely there strokes until she felt him return his entire attention to her breasts.

He sipped at her nipple, soft, gentle laps of his tongue. Isabel's head fell back as she lost herself to the pleasure of it. The sudden nip of his teeth sent a sharp, stabbing spike of pleasure to her belly. Isabel gasped, her body arching toward him. Unable to help herself, she reached for the staining flesh behind his zipper.

At her touch, Dante groaned and pressed himself to her. But when her fingers touched the snap of his jeans, he pulled back. With a frown, he shook his head.

"Hey," she protested.

"No words. Just feel."

With that, he pressed her back so she lay against the bike's gas tank. He bent to the side, grabbing her jacket and pillowed it under her head. Then he leaned back and gave a wicked grin.

Isabel's breath caught at the look on his face. He still looked angry. His jaw was clenched and the tension came off him in physical waves.

But beneath the rigid control, his eyes made no secret of the fact that he liked the view, his hands running up and down her legs where they lay across his.

She lay there, half naked in the dark night, and felt like an offering to some pagan sex god. When Dante slid his fingers beneath her skirt, she shuddered. The warmth of his hands was a vivid contrast to the cold night air as he pushed her skirt higher, higher until it reached her waist.

He finally released her eyes and let his gaze travel down her body. Determined to shake his control, to hold her own in this encounter, Isabel gathered her courage and every ounce of bravado she had and cupped her own breasts. Dante's gaze narrowed as he sucked in a breath.

Power surged through her. Isabel rubbed her fingers over her nipples and let a slow smile curve her lips as Dante groaned.

Try to control her, would he?

That was her last sane thought. Like a panther, Dante pounced. His mouth took hers, fast and wild. Between his plunging tongue and the riff of his fingers over her panties, she could barely breathe.

Then, in one swift rip, he tore her panties way, leaving her bare to the night and his taunting fingers. She gasped as he plunged his finger into her, matching the wicked dance of his tongue.

Isabel squirmed. She needed more. She had to have him. *Now.*

"Please," she gasped, pulling away from his mouth. "You're driving me crazy."

"I'm going to drive you even crazier," he promised as he slid his tongue down her body.

Isabel gave a little scream when he slipped his hands under her butt, lifting her so her legs wrapped over his shoulders. That wicked, all-male grin was back as he looked down her body. She braced her hands on the bike's seat and hoped like hell he had good balance.

His hands holding her up, he feasted on her like she was the most delicious chocolate dessert he'd ever tasted. Nibbling bites along her thighs gave way to deep sucking licks of her clit. Isabel let out a keening cry as her orgasm crashed over her.

And he kept going. Not satisfied with sending her up once, he did it again.

Even as she gave over to the pleasure, she cursed him for his command over her body.

She barely registered him releasing her to the bike seat again or the sound of his groan when he unzipped his pants. The ripping sound of the condom clued her in, though, that she was about to go for another ride.

Dante slid his hands down her calves, over the leather of her boots and grabbed her ankles again. He hooked her feet around his waist, then, his hands fisted on the bike's handlebars, he drove himself deep inside her in a single, wild thrust.

Isabel couldn't keep up with the sensations. She stopped trying to catalogue the wild rush of emotions filling her and just let go.

Her fingers gripping the leather seat so tight she was sure it'd leave marks, she met Dante's thrusts.

Harder, faster. More.

Her breath came in tiny pants now, stars flashing behind her closed eyes. Higher and higher she climbed, tighter and tighter the coiling need wound in her body.

Then Dante's thrusts increased. He lost the steady rhythm as he gave over to his own desire. Isabel tried to touch him, to hurry him along, but because of their position, she couldn't let go of the seat without chancing both of them falling over.

She felt his release, the power of it as he bellowed his satisfaction. It was the last push she needed to send her flying over the cliff of the wildest orgasm she'd ever had.

He dropped his head to her shoulder. She could feel his gasping breaths as he recovered from his own satisfaction.

Tiny waves of pleasure were still rippling through her body when the fear set in. Isabel tried to catch her breath. Tried to rein in her sense of control.

Control, hell, she'd lost it. Completely. And that, more than anything else that had happened this evening, terrified her. Panicky fingers clawed through her mind. Isabel tried to catch her breath, tried to push away the black edges of fear. Without control she was vulnerable. Powerless. Wide open to the whims of fate.

Like she had been here. Helpless while Dante called the shots.

He'd ripped from her the one thing she valued most. *Her control.* She had to get it back. Had to. Because without it, she had…what? Instincts? She'd been warned against Dante. Told he was trouble. But had she listened? No, she'd went with her instincts, trusting that inner voice that said he was misunderstood. That he was more than a bad boy with an eye only for himself. And now? Her instincts had led her here, bare-assed on a motorcycle with her feet in the air. Screwed over, in every sense of the word.

Isabel retaliated in the only way she knew.

Words. Words and retreat.

Dante's breath shuddered as he pulled away from Isabel. Damn. Maybe he'd have to see if she'd be willing to live out a few more of his fantasies. He'd had no idea, no freaking clue, that it would be such a rush to completely let go. Of course, he'd never been with anyone he trusted enough to let go like that before, either.

He looked down at the woman beneath him, pleasure settling deep in his heart. She was gorgeous. Pure beauty, inside and out.

He couldn't lose her.

Dante thought of the mess thrown at them at the restaurant. Who needed that kind of crap? Even if Santa Vera wasn't the hellhole he'd remembered, the games still pissed him off.

He wanted to take her with him. Take her away from Santa Vera and all the bullshit he knew was about to explode.

Before he could suggest it, she moved, her wild curls fading into the inky black of the leather that cushioned her head.

Isabel pushed the curls off her face and sighed. "I used to dream of this. Wild sex. You and me." Her voice had an edge to it he didn't understand. "And, of course, your motorcycle. I don't think you had a Harley back then, though."

"No, I didn't get the Harley until about five years ago," he answered automatically. Then Dante frowned. "Used to?"

She shrugged and shifted her legs so she could swing to the ground. A few shakes of the fabric and her skirt was once again a ladylike flow of fabric, those glorious legs covered.

He'd been accused of many things over the years, but stupidity wasn't one of them. Even with the last dregs of lust still fogging his brain, it didn't take Dante long to connect the dots. He yanked his pants in place, zipping and snapping with jerky moves.

"*I* was your fantasy guy?"

Isabel paused in buttoning her blouse and met his eyes. He saw the truth there.

"Once, back in high school, you kissed me." She gave him a self-deprecating smirk. "You were drunk, so I'm sure you don't remember it."

"I hit on you?" It wasn't a far-fetched concept. Isabel was hot now, he'd bet she'd been hot as a teen. But she had that good-girl air that he'd have run from a decade ago.

"I hit on you," she admitted. "It was a dare."

Son of a bitch. He'd thought she was different?

"So this wasn't about me? Just my… What? My reputation? Points scored for doing the bad boy?" He felt like he'd been kicked in the gut. He'd been so sure Isabel wasn't like the rest of them.

She flinched. Then her face tightened, anger clear in the gray depths of her eyes. "What difference does it make?"

What difference did it make that the first time he'd trusted enough to give his heart, it'd all been a game to her? A chance to do her fantasy list and win at the same time.

"Now? Not a freaking bit of a difference. But before, hell, if you'd told me it was all about that bad-boy fantasy we could have played it up a little. You know, hit the old school haunts. Played era tunes to rev up the fantasy factor. After all, you're looking for the label. Not the real guy. We're all interchangeable, right? Maybe you should have checked with that blonde chick—what was her name? Eileen? I'm sure she had some ideas you could have used, too."

She pressed her lips together, then shrugged. "Well at least your maturity level is in keeping with high school."

He ground his teeth, knowing he sounded like a complete asshole but not able to stop from spewing angry words to cover his hurt.

"Your list was definitely beyond high-school level, though. You probably studied up, spent a lot of time considering just what fantasies rocked you, got them in the perfect order. God forbid you try spontaneity."

"You're one to talk," she snapped. "Did you spontaneously decide to sell out the town when you got here? Or did you have that all planned out? Such an intriguing question, hmm? I mean, it's not like you could break your dad's foot and arrange to come back here."

"You really think I'd do that? That I'd come back to the town where my parents still live planning to screw them over?" Dante ignored the fact that he had arrived with those instructions. He'd never have followed through. He knew that now. "That I slept with you, all these times, all these ways, the whole time planning to betray the town you're trying to be a part of?"

She finished buttoning her blouse and pulled on her coat, her movements short and jerky. Then she gave him a glare worthy of queen about to have her minion beheaded.

"How should I know what to believe? You won't talk to me. Whatever your intentions, the results are what matters."

She lifted her chin and wiped a shaky hand over her cheek, making Dante aware for the first time that the glistening on her face wasn't a reflection off the lake. It was her tears. He flinched.

"And the results are what you have to deal with, right? So what are you going to do about them?" She pressed her lips together, then shook her head. The sadness in her eyes, like a gloomy winter day, broke Dante's heart. "If you follow your standard M.O., you'll simply walk away, won't you? Just like you did when you were arrested."

"What's the point of sticking around? People either believe you or they don't. You're just like my father. Believing I'd betray you, sell you out. Then and now."

It didn't take her long. "Then? When you were arrested?"

"Right. Back when good ol' dad believed I'd stolen

his supplies and sold them for cheap thrills. Of course, he had a lot more to go on than some incriminating letters. He had a witness. Secret one, though, since nobody would ever come forward and actually make the accusations to my face."

Fury surged through Dante as he shoved his arms into his jacket. Noticing the documents in his pocket, he yanked them out and tossed them to her.

"Hate to deprive you of fodder for your list. After all, I know how important those things are to you."

Her mouth worked but nothing came out. She didn't even bother to read them. Instead she shoved the wadded up mess into her pocket, her face a study of outraged fury. Finally she shook her head and threw her hands up in the air.

"You were actually arrested for stealing from your own father? And he didn't mean enough to you to fight? Obviously I'm crazy to think you'd do something to save this disaster. Why on earth would you?"

So now she believed he'd stole from his father. Apparently her loyalty shifted when the stakes were personal. Dante didn't know where the pain came from, but he settled for his tried and true method of dealing with emotions. Or as she called it, his standard M.O. He wrapped himself in anger and retreated.

Handing her the helmet, he gestured to the bike.

"Let's go. I have things to do."

She met his eyes, questions clear in her stormy gaze. Misery washed over him. For once, he'd thought he'd found someone who'd believe in him, no matter what. Ha.

"There isn't anything left to say, so why drag it out?" Besides, he needed this to be over. "We're obviously done."

She gave him a sad kind of smirk, as if she'd known that was exactly how he'd react and shrugged.

"It's too bad you can't grow up and deal with real life for a change. Instead, you just keep running away."

15

DANTE WAITED, HIS FINGERS tapping out an impatient beat on the motel-room dresser. Finally the tinny destruction of some classical piece ended and Tremaine picked up his line.

"Yes?" Dante's boss said.

"What the hell are you doing?"

"Considering it's eleven o'clock on a Saturday night, for the lady's sake I'd prefer not to offer details," Tremaine responded in even tones.

Dante smirked through his anger.

"I hope you're doing her as well as you did Santa Vera."

"Your little town? How do you think I screwed it over?" Tremaine asked, not bothering to pretend he didn't understand the insinuation. "I bought the property fair and square. But you knew that, I told you last week."

"Right, but you squirreled out of signing the zoning contracts. It's one thing to hide your identity, to sneak in under the wire and buy up properties you know people might hesitate to sell to you. But it's another to completely circumvent their system. Just because you can dance around the law doesn't make it right to thumb your nose at the traditions of a town trying to survive."

"You've never cared about traditions before,"

Tremaine mused. "Not for other towns, and certainly not for this one."

Guilt flashed. The truth sucked. How often had he given Tremaine the info he needed to do this same exact thing to other towns? To go in and buy prime real estate, tear it down and build his chrome-and-glass monstrosities? Too often for Dante's comfort.

"You can't level a perfectly good building and put up a new one that will ruin not only the uniformity of the downtown architecture, but will severely impact the town's economy."

"You don't think my revenues will boost the economy?"

"Not enough to make up for how damaging your building will be to the look and feel of the downtown project. You'd be ruining years of work these people have put into creating a look and feel for their town, their festival." Dante pinched the bridge of his nose and sighed. "Besides, we both know you'll flip the property in a couple years, after the damage is done. You are needlessly ruining lives."

"I had no idea you could be so melodramatic."

"Screw you."

"I was working on that when you interrupted." Rare laughter burst through the phone line.

Dante shook his head. Maybe the world had ended and nobody had seen fit to let him know? Tremaine making jokes, Dante forcing issues rather than walking away. It wasn't normal.

Figured. Nothing felt normal now. Not since he'd seen the tears on Isabel's face.

Her words still rang out in his mind. Before, he'd always felt walking away was the way to go. Why shove his innocence, or lack thereof, down anyone's throat? But the way she'd said it, he felt like a coward.

He'd never cared before what people thought of him. But he'd be damned if he would make himself look bad in Isabel's eyes. Or, damn it, let anyone else make him look bad.

"Did you sell me out?" he asked, having to swallow twice before getting the words out. Dante wasn't used to worrying about his reputation, so asking questions like this were beyond bizarre.

"You're joking, right?"

"Someone from Tremaine Enterprises sent a detailed letter to the town council outlining my job description and role in the company. They also sent a copy of the initial spec report I'd done, complete with my signature. It specifies I was the guy handling this project for you."

"Well, well." Dante could hear the clink of glass and ice. So, the conversation had finally gotten Tremaine's attention. "As you know, that's against policy. I'll take care of it, of course."

He didn't know why that made him feel better, but it did. Not enough to let the topic rest, though.

"You can't do this," Dante decided. "I can't support it."

"Care to elaborate?"

Dante only had to think about it for a second, then he shrugged.

"I'll quit."

"Threats?"

"No. I found a moral base I didn't realize I had. Honestly, I'm not sure I won't quit anyway." He hadn't even realized he was thinking about it until the words were out. "I'm tired of travel. Maybe it's this visit, maybe something else, but I'd like to chill on the constant moving around."

"What's her name?"

Dante gave a little laugh. Not much got past Tremaine.

"Doesn't matter," was all he said.

There was a few seconds of silence. It didn't bother Dante, since he knew his boss always carefully considered his words.

"As enlightening as this has been," Tremaine finally said, "I didn't circumvent the zoning restrictions in this situation."

"Sure you didn't."

"Dante, I'm many things, but I'm not a liar. If you'd like to get to the bottom of this puzzle, I suggest you start right there in Santa Vera."

Dante's stomach took a nosedive. The accusations couldn't be true. Isabel was too careful, too meticulous, to have let something like this slip up. Which meant she'd have had to deliberately made arrangements for Tremaine to bypass zoning. She'd have had to tell him which people to talk to, how to do it.

And let Dante take the blame? He recalled her anger, her apparent innocence. Dante relived the wild intensity of their lovemaking on the Harley. Her final words, challenging him to grow up.

Isabel didn't play games. If she'd wanted to screw the town over, she'd have found a way to do it right there in their faces. No subterfuge, no lies.

"It wasn't Isabel," he stated adamantly.

"Isabel? I haven't had the pleasure. Yet. I hope you'll correct that in the future."

Dante frowned. Future? Apparently his threat to quit wasn't a direct shot to the unemployment line.

"Sure. After I deal with this mess. You said look at the town itself?"

"Your councilman is amazingly resourceful," Tremaine offered.

Anderson?

"Son of a bitch."

"Exactly."

TWO HOURS LATER, DANTE stood on the one place he'd promised himself he'd never be again. Wiping a hand on his jeans, he lifted his fist and knocked.

"Dante?" Shock was clear in Sylvia Luciano's voice, but the pleasure underneath was just as loud. She fiddled with the pearls at her throat, a gesture Dante recognized as nerves. "Sweetie, come in."

"Ask him if it's okay first."

His mother rolled her eyes, the deep green so like his own flashing impatience, and grabbed his arm. She tugged him over the threshold and shook her head.

"You're as stubborn as he is, you know." One hand still gripping tight on Dante's wrist, she yelled down the hall, "Frank? C'mon down."

"You've got to be kidding," Dante said quietly. "He's still using the upstairs bedroom with that broken foot? Wouldn't it have been easier to move to the room down here?"

"Like I said. Stubborn."

That stubbornness was clear a minute later when Frank Luciano glared a hole through Dante.

Too damned bad.

"I didn't sell out," Dante said without preamble. "I work for Tremaine, yes. But other than looking over the property, doing an initial inspection, I told him to blow. I wouldn't help him bypass the city ordinances."

Frank's glare downgraded a few notches, but he didn't comment. Dante ground his teeth. Why bother? His old man didn't listen. Didn't care.

"Fine, whatever. You don't have to believe me. I don't want this falling on Isabel's head. It's one thing for you to roll over and let the uptight jerks in town railroad me out, but it's not okay for them to do that to her."

"Dante—"

"No. Let the boy talk, Sylvia."

"Nothing else to say." Dante turned to leave, then stopped. "You're on the council. People listen to you. Just make sure they don't railroad Isabel."

"And I have...what? Your word she didn't give this guy inside information? If you're telling the truth, you didn't do this. If it wasn't you, it could only be her. It's her job to handle zoning—*she* blew it."

"Bullshit. She couldn't handle what she wasn't given."

"You're saying someone deliberately set this up? And it wasn't you?"

He shrugged.

Sylvia said, "Dante, if you know who would do something like this, you need to tell us. Your father can't help the girl if he doesn't have the facts."

Dante ground his teeth. What difference would it make? Lance was Frank's buddy, his council-mate. It wasn't like his father was going to believe Dante over him. He never had before.

But it'd never mattered like this before. Because while Dante might be willing to toss his own rep aside, to walk away without a fight when it was his word on the line... This was about Isabel.

And he'd be damned if anyone screwed over the woman he loved.

"Tremaine's only talked with one person other than me in this entire deal. Someone with a special knowledge of real estate. Who knew enough to tell him how to work around the zoning laws, how to file to avoid red flags. Which clerks were amenable to a little gift."

Frank's gaze narrowed. "If it went through the clerks' office and bypassed the zoning contracts, it'd need an official signature. Or at least an unofficial verbal green light."

"Right."

"That's a mighty big accusation you're tossing around there. Public officials don't generally screw it to their own town like you're insinuating."

"You don't believe me?" Anger ripped through Dante. Figured. He tried to proclaim his innocence and his own father scoffed.

"I'm just saying your source is questionable. You're asking me to believe a man who immorally and possibly illegally bought property with the sole intention of damaging Santa Vera. And you expect me to take his word over one of our own."

The urge to put his fist through a wall was so strong, Dante had to shove his hands in his pockets to keep them still.

"You don't believe me," Dante repeated.

"I didn't say that."

"You didn't have to." Dante shook his head to clear the steam from his vision and gave a bitter laugh. "As usual, you'd take someone else's word—anyone else's word—over mine. And you wonder why I never stood up for myself before? It never mattered what I did or didn't do. Any accusation that came along, you sided with the other person. Right down to believing I was a thief."

"There was a witness." Maybe it was progress that Frank's voice held no conviction. But it didn't matter. He still wasn't supporting his son.

"Growing up, I'd have given anything, done anything, to have you support me," Dante said in quiet pain. "Just once. But it never happened. Obviously that hasn't changed."

He didn't know if it was because he'd opened his heart to let Isabel in, and in the process ripped the scab from a lifetime of wounds, or if this was a new ache brought on by his father's disbelief.

All he knew was he had to get the hell out of there before he did something he'd regret. Despite his mother's cry of protest, Dante turned and stormed out.

THE NEXT DAY, MARKING time until the emergency town-council meeting, Isabel stared at the list she'd been working on. The words blurred on the page. No matter how she outlined it, she didn't see a way to save her reputation.

As she'd done so many times already, she spread her hand over the ragged papers on the corner of her desk. Clearly spelled out was Dante's job description. Along with his signature on the inspection report and clerk's documents, they were pretty incriminating.

Lance had warned her. What a time for him to be right!

She'd spent twenty-six years following a plan, being careful. Worrying about what other people thought. And the one time, the one major time, she tossed aside her inhibitions? She'd lost her reputation, might lose her business. On top of that, her heart was in shreds and her self-esteem wilted.

Pretty freaking pitiful how badly her plan had crashed and burned. Oh, she'd had the fantasy sex. In spades. But the cost?

She traced a finger over Dante's signature and sighed. If she were honest with herself, she had to admit the truth. She'd do it all over again to be with Dante.

"Helloo," a voice called out from the storefront.

Isabel recognized Lorna's not-so-dulcet growl and groaned. She was closed. The sign said Closed for a reason. All morning she'd had a parade of "well-meaning" visitors, each spouting thinly disguised insults about her "mistake."

She'd had it with people. She didn't want to see, deal with or talk to anyone. At all.

She pushed back from her desk and trudged through the door to the store. Warm peach walls would be the perfect backdrop to a variety of plants and floral arrangements. A tastefully small walk-in refrigerator would hold delicate blooms. The candy counter gleamed, chrome and glass sparkling back the morning sunlight, while the checkout counter stood sturdy and welcoming. So close, and yet still not done. Would it ever be? Was there any point?

The perfection of her vision made reality hit her for a second, then she shrugged it off. It wasn't like it mattered now. Last she'd heard, Sweet Scentsations wasn't going to be allowed in the festival.

"We're closed," she said, hoping Lorna would get the message.

"Brought you more cake," the older woman said, slapping the sturdy white plate down on the beautifully inlaid counter.

Isabel licked her lips. She looked from the slice of

triple-layered chocolate decadence, again complete with sprinkles, to the older woman's stiff features.

She had no appetite for chocolate anymore. Damn Dante, it was all his fault.

"Why?"

"No chitchat? Just straight to the point?"

Isabel shrugged.

"No wonder the boy fell for you. He's the same way. Too many people like to play games, mess with the truth. You're just like Dante. Stubborn to the core."

After "fell for you" Lorna's words were an annoying buzz in Isabel's head.

"Dante didn't fall for me," she protested. Then she stopped and rolled her eyes. Pitiful. Juvenile and pitiful. If she didn't watch it, next thing she knew she'd be asking Lorna to go ask Dante if he liked her just a little.

"He's never fought for anything before. He's fighting this, for you. Dante Luciano wouldn't do that unless he'd fallen."

"I have no idea what you're talking about. Dante isn't fighting. Last I heard, he'd left town." And taken her heart with him. Faced with all the snide gossip that morning, she'd actually understood why Dante would have walked away. Nobody cared about the truth. Just about gleefully spreading their rumors.

"You should know better than to listen to gossip," Lorna chided. "You've seen for yourself how flimsy rumors can be."

"Oh yeah, I got that first hand when the lynch mob came through."

"Oh, pshaw. You gonna let that kind of thing run you off?"

"Who's running?" Not that she hadn't considered it.

"I don't see you at the meeting. You aren't there defending yourself. That's as good as running. Didn't you learn nothing from that boy's mistakes?"

"The meeting doesn't start for another hour," Isabel dismissed, not willing to discuss Dante.

"No. It starts in ten minutes. Emergency."

"I thought it was already an emergency meeting."

"Apparently the emergency was upgraded."

"How do you—" Isabel rolled her eyes and shrugged. "It doesn't matter."

But it did. Isabel wanted to scream. The urge to yell and kick and throw things terrified her. She didn't lose control. And yet, here she was, in the middle of no-control-central. Her life, her career, her emotions—all of them careened out of her reach.

"It matters if it's got you refusing my chocolate cake," Lorna claimed with a sniff. "I've only hand-delivered that cake twice in my life, and both times were here to you. That says something, girl."

With that, Lorna turned and stomped out. Leaving Isabel to deal with the fact that, somehow, despite the failure of her plan, she'd still ended up an accepted member of Santa Vera's community.

Or—Isabel reached out to press a finger to one of the chocolate sprinkles—at least Lorna's list of acceptable people.

Now what was she going to do about it?

Isabel glanced at the clock, then over at the stack of files and folders she'd been going through in search of an answer to give the council at the meeting. She hadn't found one, though.

For the first time in her life, Isabel was going to have to wing it. No plan, no backup. Just give it her best shot.

The idea scared her to death. But for Dante—hell, for herself—she had to try.

ISABEL SWALLOWED HER FEAR and, after a deep breath, pushed open the door to the town hall. The silence that greeted her was deafening, the stares lethal.

Unlike everyone else, from his place at the head of the table, Lance looked more surprised than angry.

"Isabel? What are you doing here? This is a closed session. And given the nature of the emergency, I'd have thought you'd wait to hear our verdict some-where…private."

"You mean cower in my store while you pass judgment on me? On Dante?" She shook her head and strode to the long table, planting her hands on the teak surface. "No, thanks."

"I'm sure you understand we can't justifiably discuss this problem with you here," Eileen said, her tone apologetic. "Especially given your relationship with Mr. Luciano."

Mr. Luciano, huh? And just a week or so ago, Eileen had been ready to lick Dante's toes.

"Sure you can. Zoning is, or was, my committee, after all. If you're going to try and nail this problem on my doorstep, I've got every right to be a part of the discus-sion."

She ignored the whispers and mutters and met Lance's angry gaze. She gave him a cold smile and raised one brow. "You didn't really think I'd hide away, did you?"

From his clenched jaw, Lance didn't appear to like being challenged.

Tough tooties. Isabel was sick of worrying about what

other people liked. She'd spent her whole life trying to fit other's perceptions, to toe the line. She'd finally dared to step outside her safe little box. And despite the results, she'd liked it. There was no way she was slinking back into it now.

"Nobody is accusing you of wrongdoing, here. We do realize your new position in town might factor into mistaken choices in companionship though," Eileen said, her tone snotty enough that Isabel considered taking one of the glazed doughnuts from the tray and smashing it in her face. Except that would be a criminal waste of good chocolate.

"I didn't make any mistakes," Isabel retorted. "And before you start your next round of accusations, neither did Dante."

"Look, Isabel, everyone makes mistakes. You simply trusted the wrong person." The only way Lance could have seemed any more condescending was if he'd walked over and patted her on the head. "While we obviously can't let it go, I'm going to recommend that the council not hold this against you."

Isabel opened her mouth to tell him to shove his recommendation up the same place his head seemed to be. But she was interrupted.

"That's damned generous of you, Anderson."

Isabel's gasp was drowned out by the murmurs and exclamations of the rest of the council. She spun around to see Dante standing in the door.

He hadn't left. Tears stung her eyes, but she blinked them away. She'd be damned if she'd lose control in front of all these people. Especially since she was pretty sure a couple of them were actually taking notes.

He was gorgeous, in his usual blue jeans and work boots. For the first time, he was wearing a button-up shirt, although in typical Dante fashion, he'd left it open at the throat and shoved up the sleeves.

Isabel's heart melted at the sight of him, his hair swept back from his forehead, a stack of folders in his hand. Dante's eyes met hers, emotions blazing in his green depths. She was afraid to read the message there. Nerves fought pleasure, her entire system going into overdrive.

It looked like she wasn't the only one who was willing to fight for her reputation.

16

DANTE CAST A CYNICAL EYE over the vultures crowded around the teak meeting table, picking over their heaping platter of doughnuts. Obviously they needed a good helping of sugar to deal with the emergency at hand.

"What's the meaning of this?" Lance's voice was knife-sharp, filled with righteous anger. But Dante could see the fear in the guy's pale-blue eyes. That was all he needed to assure him the dude was on edge.

Time to push him off.

"I'm here to clear up the bullshit you've been spreading," Dante challenged. He ignored the titters and whispers, only sparing a glance for Isabel. Her gaze held his, a smile of encouragement curved on those luscious lips. He gave her a quick grin before focusing on Anderson again.

"I thought you'd have run away," Lance said, leaning back in his chair in a show of control. "You know, like you always have in the past. Oh wait, you didn't run off last time, right? You were run off."

Nice one. Dante had to give the guy credit. He definitely knew where to twist the knife. From the quick glance Anderson slid toward Isabel, he figured on getting in as many damaging shots as he could.

"Last time I was wrong," Dante admitted. "I was too

young, too immature to deal with real life." He heard Isabel's intake of breath. "I guess you were banking on that not changing, huh? Too bad."

"This is a useless show of bravado," Lance said. "We've already examined the evidence, seen proof of your culpability in this situation. Why don't you leave, now, before the council decides to look into legal repercussions?"

The esteemed councilman made a sweeping gesture to indicate the rest of the town council. Dante's gaze scanned the faces, noting the bulging doughnut-filled cheeks and rapidly moving pencils.

But as fascinated as they all were, none of them looked ready to convict him to the big house. Most looked curious, a few encouraging. Huh, who knew. Maybe Lancey-boy didn't have the kind of power either of them thought he did.

"You try that," Dante suggested. "Better yet, why don't we call in the attorneys now? I've got one on retainer. Did you know that? He works for Tremaine Industries, of course, but he's mine if I need him."

Dante let the fury he'd kept on simmer surface then.

"You wanted to screw with me, that was fine. But this time you took it too far. You tried to set Isabel up. Not just screwing her over by making it look like she'd blown her job on the zoning committee, but in the gossip you spread about her. The way you tried to set people against her."

"This is all quite dramatic. I'm sure everyone is impressed with your dedication to your lady friend," Lance said with a sneer, indicating Dante's defense was going to hurt Isabel. That would have worked in the past, too. But not this time.

"Just like you're dedicated to... What exactly is it you do again? Bullshit people—and what else?"

Dante knew it was a calculated risk. Insulting Anderson could as easily backfire as goad the guy. But the dude's ego was like a house of cards, a fragilely built monument. If Dante poked a few holes in it, the guy might lose control.

"I'm a council leader," Lance pointed out. "Unlike you, I'm an integral part of this community."

"Right, and I'm trouble. Bet you'd like me to get the hell out of town, huh?" Dante took a cocky stance, a challenging sneer on his face. "Must drive you nuts that I've got everything you don't. Hot gal, great job." Dante waited a beat, then leaned forward, "Frank Luciano as a father."

"You don't give a damn about any of those things," Lance spat. "You're trouble through and through, and don't deserve any of them. If I wanted, I could destroy your chances with any of them, too."

"Just like you did back in high school," Dante goaded. "You were jealous then, wanting to be… What? Football star? Homecoming king? Too bad you sucked too much for both."

Lance shoved out of his chair, hands fisted at his sides. Dante almost wished he'd try swinging. It'd feel great to kick his ass.

"I didn't have a chance with you wasting all of Frank's time with your stupid games and rebellions. How was he supposed to coach the team if he had to keep leaving to deal with another one of your dramatic demands on his time?"

"So?" Dante shrugged. "He was my father. That's his job, to deal with my drama."

"He had other things to do. If you hadn't distracted him, we'd have won the homecoming game. I'd have won homecoming king."

Dante noted the spittle in the corner of Lance's mouth and the wild look in his eyes.

"So you figured you'd set me up? Pretty lame, don't you think?"

Lance sneered. "It worked, didn't it?"

Shocked gasps filled the room. But it was the roar of anger behind him that surprised Dante.

"You son of a bitch," Frank Luciano growled. His glare should have burned a hole in Anderson, it was so lethal. "Who do you think you are, messing with people's lives and manipulating the truth for your own devious means?"

Lance's eyes went huge, his mouth working as he shook his head. "I mean… No, I didn't set anything up. Not like he's accusing."

"Don't bother," Dante suggested. "You'll look like a bigger ass than you already are."

"Admit it," Frank demanded. "Did you steal from me and use the crime to set my son up?"

"I did no such thing," Lance snapped.

"I'll bet you did. Just like you set Dante and me up with this zoning issue," Isabel said. Her words were soft, quiet, but they rang with conviction. "You harp on about your reputation, all while you use gossip and backhanded games to try and ruin other peoples'."

"This is ridiculous," Lance claimed. He gave his patented good-boy smile and shook his head sadly. "Dante's poisoned your minds. He obviously has jealousy issues, Isabel. Surely you can see that? He knows we had a special relationship and is trying to ruin things between us."

"What's to ruin?" she asked with a confused frown. "We're over. We have been and it's not like we'd have ever got back together. This isn't about us, Lance. This is about you and Dante."

"Dante, Dante, Dante," Lance ranted, obviously snapping at her words. "You all think he's so damned perfect, but he's not. He's trouble. Always has been, always will be. Just look at the trouble he brought to Santa Vera."

"He didn't bring trouble," Frank defended. "I asked around. The trouble you're trying to pawn off on my son was created by you."

Speechless, Dante stared. Well, well. He swallowed, trying to get past the lump in his throat. Maybe it wasn't unconditional, given that Frank had checked his sources, but it was still support.

Lance sneered. "You might want to believe that, but you can't prove it."

While the angry accusations flew through the room, Dante's gaze met Isabel's, noting the pride in her soft gray eyes. He felt ten feet tall, like he could leap tall buildings in a single bound and make her come with just his tongue. He gave her a slow, wicked wink. He knew the last one was a guaranteed fact.

"You tried to blame the girl, to blame my son. It won't work," Frank stated, his voice raised over the noisy crowd. "I checked with the clerks' office, Lance. Not only did you set this up, you were the one behind the vandalism of Isabel's store. And yes, there is a witness. Only he, unlike past witnesses, is willing to make his statement public."

Dante watched Isabel pale, her hand flying to her mouth. She glared at Lance. Before she could say anything, though, the sullen teenager with an art fetish Dante had met doing trash duty stepped into the room.

As he listened to boy's words, to the town rallying around him, Dante's heart contracted. He realized he wanted a hell of a lot more than saving Isabel. He watched his father, and realized he wanted this. The connection. The family.

The feeling of coming home.

When Dante looked toward the doors again, Isabel was gone.

TWO HOURS LATER, ISABEL heard the roar of the Harley, but didn't move from her spot on the rock. She'd had to leave the meeting. If she'd stayed, she'd have humiliated herself by crying. Or worse, throwing herself at Dante. As she stared out over the lake, she tried to pull in some of its serenity. She was going to need it.

After all, Dante had fought for her. He'd broken tradition, stepped out of his comfort zone and saved her reputation. Quite a thanks, considering she'd done her best, right here in this very spot a few nights before, to hurt him.

And why? Because he'd made her lose control? Isabel sighed, tracing her finger over the rough granite. Was she really that weak?

"Somehow I knew I'd find you here."

His voice was a warm blanket, wrapping around her like a caress. Isabel glanced up as he joined her at the rock.

"People were in and out of the store, it was driving me crazy," she excused. Then she shrugged and met his gaze. "I figured you'd stop by here before you took off. I wanted a chance to talk to you in private. To thank you."

He winced.

"Seriously." She pushed on. "They were ready to run me out of town. Oh, sure, they were willing to think I was a dupable idiot, but that's hardly complimentary, now is it?"

"Dupable idiot is better than conniving cheat."

She shrugged.

"Despite that," Dante continued in a puzzled tone. "You defended me. Why didn't you let them believe I did it? *You* did."

She frowned, turning to fully face him, her knees drawn up and hands draped around them. "I never believed it. I guess maybe I acted like I did. And the sad truth is, part of me wanted to believe it."

"Why?"

"Because it made you the bad guy," she admitted. God, could she sound any more neurotic? "If you were in the wrong, then you'd pushed me to lose control. It was your fault things fell apart. Not failure on my part."

"Isabel, we were set up. This was all Anderson's fault."

"The zoning issues, definitely. Stirring up gossip and keeping people on edge, probably. But my fears? Those had nothing to do with Lance."

"*I* scare you?" The shock in his voice echoed off the lake.

"What you make me feel scares me. The way I lose control with you, the way you make me push boundaries. That's scary."

"That's why you used the sex-with-a-bad-boy card the other night? To try and push me away?"

She nodded. "Maybe my brain was fogged by the best sex of my life. Otherwise, I hope I'd have been able to move past the anger and realize sooner that the whole situation was fishy."

He grinned. "The best, huh?"

Isabel rolled her eyes. "Don't let it go to your head. You had pretty good directions."

Dante smirked. Then his face got serious. "There's no reason you should have suspected a setup. I knew I hadn't sold out the town. But given the evidence, I'd have called me guilty, too. Anderson was good at that. He twisted facts, presented the right information to create the picture he wanted."

"He's even better at planning than I am," Isabel admitted.

Dante snorted. "No, that's not possible."

She giggled and shrugged. "Maybe not, but his worked in this case. Even though you exposed him, forced him to admit his culpability, the sale is final. Without the contract, the damage to downtown is done."

"Actually, that's all taken care of. I talked to Tremaine. He won't back out of the sale, but he's willing to do things by the books. Go ahead and send him the paperwork and contracts, he's expecting them."

"He'll abide by the zoning contract? Leave the structure intact?"

"Yeah. He's not looking to mess with the downtown project."

Isabel's gaze traced the planes of his face as she considered his words. "He's doing it for you. I checked up on him, he eats small towns like Santa Vera for breakfast."

Dante frowned but didn't deny it. Instead he shrugged. "Don't forget, I'm usually the one serving them up with his cornflakes."

She'd thought plenty on that as she'd done her research. But she'd noted a common thread with the takeovers. While Tremaine left behind an ugly monstrosity after each turnover, he also left a sizable donation to the town. She wondered if Dante knew. Probably, he didn't let much get past him.

"I guess that's why you're such a bad boy, huh?"

"Well, *was*."

"Not when it matters."

He shrugged it off, but she could tell he was pleased.

"What happens now?" she asked.

"Don't you have a plan?" he asked. She couldn't tell if he was teasing or not.

"I think I might give up planning."

"Why? It works for you. Look at what you've accomplished because you carefully laid a path, knew what you wanted and made it happen. And not just with your business. Planning got you the best sex of your life, remember?"

Isabel snorted. It was probably a good thing he'd be riding out of her life any minute now. Otherwise she figured he'd be throwing that back at her forever.

"I've realized that planning can't take the place of actually living. You pushed me, dared me to step outside my comfort zone and really live. Even though I wrote that Man Plan, if it hadn't been for you showing up like you did, I'd never have gone through with it."

"You needed your fantasy guy, huh?"

She winced.

"No, don't be upset," he said, reaching out to wind one of her curls around his fingers. "I figured later you said that to piss me off."

"It's true, though," she admitted. "I had been fantasizing about you for years. Not because you were a notch I wanted for my scorecard, though. I never played those games. But—" She grimaced, then figured she might as well go for broke. "You were the hottest guy I'd ever seen. The first time I saw you at that party, I didn't even know what desire was. After kissing you, I finally understood what Audra was always raving about."

"I wish I'd gotten to know you then."

Isabel gave a rueful shake of her head, careful not to dislodge his hand. "No. You don't. I was way too young and way too busy meeting expectations back then."

"Already working on that reputation?"

She pulled a face. "Right, as Audra's sidekick? Those warnings to guard my reputation didn't matter. I don't care what everyone thinks. Just what the people important to me think."

"So what was that all about the other night? You can't deny you were pissed."

"It was about control. You'd taken that from me. Nobody ever has. It terrified me. To know someone could make me shed my inhibitions, completely lose my mind? That's a lot of power to let someone have, you know."

Dante frowned, his attention on the way her hair curled around his finger. Then he met her gaze.

"But you have that same power over me. It's good to know it goes both ways."

"I don't just mean sex," Isabel said with a laugh.

"Neither do I."

Her breath caught, then lodged in her throat to wrap around a ball of fear. The emotions, so clear in his vivid green eyes, were more than anything she'd ever imagined.

"Tell me," she whispered.

"You tell me first," he challenged.

A burst of laughter escaped her. Leave it to Dante to push her comfort zone.

Tears filling her eyes, she bit her lip, then she gave a smiling little sigh. What did she have to lose?

"I love you," she told him. "I love your sense of honor and your pride. I love your body and the way you bring fantasies to life. Your bad boy ways, the fit of your jeans, the way you make me laugh. I love—" she shrugged "—everything about you."

"Damn."

She pressed her lips together and waited.

"I've never had anyone—ever—accept me like you do. Appreciate me—all of me, like you do." He swallowed, then releasing her hair, he curved his hands around her waist and pulled her to him. "But that's not why I love you."

Giddy wonder swirled through her system at his words. Isabel blinked to clear the tears from her gaze. She wanted to see him clearly when he said this.

"I love the way you plan things," he said, obviously taking his cue from her words. "I love your sensuality, and the way you care about people. The cute way you wrinkle your nose when you laugh and how you make me feel like a better person."

He bent down to brush the softest of kisses over her mouth. His lips still on hers, he said, "I love you. It's that simple."

Then he took her mouth in a kiss so intense, so deep, Isabel swore she felt it all the way to her heart.

When he pulled away, she gave a deep sigh and smiled.

"So, you want me to go with you?" she asked, already planning things in her head.

"Why bother going anywhere? We've got the tree over there. Or," he cast a wicked glance at his bike, "the Harley."

"I meant when you leave town. Although I wouldn't mind trying that Harley thing again."

Dante pulled her tight to him, the warmth of his arms giving her a sense of homecoming she'd never had before. For this, she didn't need small-town life. She belonged with Dante. That was enough for her.

"Actually, I'm moving back here."

"What?" she gasped. She pulled back to stare. "Here?"

"Yeah. My dad's health isn't great. He needs to slow down. Honestly? I do, too. I'm tired of travel, tired of never knowing what's next."

"And given all the towns, all the cities you've seen, you want to settle here in Santa Vera?" Her words made it clear she'd follow him wherever he wanted.

"Yeah. This is home."

She sighed and settled her head against his chest, reveling in the feel of his arms around her. And more, in knowing they'd always be there for her. She'd never have been able to plan anything this wonderful. She'd never have dared.

"We never did do the tied-up thing," she murmured.

"I've got rope in my saddlebags," he said, pleasure warming his voice. "And a jar of fudge sauce with a little sterno heater so we could get it hot."

Laughter burst from her as she pulled back to meet Dante's eyes. "Planning ahead, were you?"

"I call it my Woman Plan." He brushed a soft kiss over her mouth and winked. "Looks like it worked. If it hadn't, I planned to use the rope to tie you to me."

"Tied up together, huh?"

"Together. Forever."

Isabel swallowed to clear the lump from her throat and gave him a sassy smile.

"Forever sounds good. I'll have to revise my fantasy list."

"I've already done that for you. Guaranteed to keep giving you the best sex of your life."

She laughed, her head falling back to glory in the warmth of the overhead sun, the heat of Dante's gaze.

Yup. He'd be throwing that at her forever.

She couldn't think of anything she'd ever wanted more.

HARLEQUIN Blaze™

is proud to present

Blush

Because sex doesn't have to be serious!

Don't miss the next red-hot title...

PRIMAL INSTINCTS
by
Jill Monroe

Ava Simms's sexual instincts take over as she puts her theories about mating to the test with gorgeous globe-traveling journalist Ian Cole. He's definitely up for the challenge—but is she?

On sale February 2008 wherever books are sold.

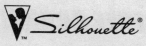

REQUEST YOUR FREE BOOKS!

2 FREE NOVELS PLUS 2 FREE GIFTS!

HARLEQUIN®

Blaze®

Red-hot reads!

You can lead a horse to water...

When Alyssa Barkley and Clint Westmoreland
found out that their "fake" marriage was never
rendered void, they are forced to live together
for thirty days. However, Clint loves the single
life and has no intention of being tamed, but
when Alyssa moves in, the sizzling attraction
between them is ignited and neither wants the
thirty days to end.

Look for

TAMING CLINT WESTMORELAND

by

BRENDA JACKSON

Available February wherever you buy books

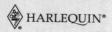

INTRIGUE

HARLEQUIN®

Blaze™

COMING NEXT MONTH

#375 TEX APPEAL Kimberly Raye, Alison Kent, Cara Summers
A sizzling Valentine collection—Texas-style!

Ride 'em, cowboys! Take a super-hot former rodeo star, a lust-worthy down-home boy and a randy Ranger, mix well with three Southern ladies who are each in need of a little action between the sheets, and what do you get? Tons of *Tex* appeal!

#376 MY WILDEST RIDE Isabel Sharpe
The Martini Dares, Bk. 4

Seduce the man you most desire? That's one tough dare for vulnerable Lindsay Beckham. But she can't resist hot bartender Denver Langston, a man known for serving up delicious cocktails…like Sex on the Beach.

#377 SHAMELESS Tori Carrington
Extreme

Torn between two lovers… Kevin Webster, Patrick Gauge and Nina Leonard are business partners and the best of friends. They share everything, including their sexual exploits. So when Nina complains about sleeping alone, Gauge and Kevin set her up with a stranger for a night of incredible anonymous sex. Only, the man in Nina's bed is no stranger….

#378 PRIMAL INSTINCTS Jill Monroe
Blush

Ava Simms's feminine instincts take over as she puts her theories about mating to the test with gorgeous journalist Ian Cole…who's definitely up for the challenge. But will he satisfy Ava's sexual curiosity?

#379 YOUR BED OR MINE? Kate Hoffmann
The Wrong Bed

Caley Lambert is making some changes. She's just dumped her boyfriend, and she's thinking about ditching her job. But she needs time to think, and attending a family wedding at the old lake house seems like the perfect solution. Only, waking up in bed with her first love isn't exactly what she was expecting….

#380 BURNING UP Sarah Mayberry
A month in a luxury location cooking for one man…it's the perfect job. But when Sophie Gallagher agrees to be actor Lucas Grant's chef, she's so not falling for his charm…until he pursues her with delicious intent, that is. And she discovers he is the hottest man alive!

www.eHarlequin.com

HBCNM0108

HENRY
AND THE
VALENTINE SURPRISE

NANCY CARLSON

PUFFIN BOOKS
An Imprint of Penguin Group (USA) Inc.

TO BARRY,

I AM GLAD WE BUMPED HEADS
34 YEARS AGO AT THE YMCA!

MUCH LOVE,
NANCY

PUFFIN BOOKS
Published by the Penguin Group
Penguin Young Readers Group, 345 Hudson Street, New York, New York 10014, U.S.A.
Penguin Group (Canada), 90 Eglinton Avenue East, Suite 700, Toronto, Ontario, Canada M4P 2Y3 (a division of Pearson Penguin Canada Inc.)
Penguin Books Ltd, 80 Strand, London WC2R 0RL, England
Penguin Ireland, 25 St Stephen's Green, Dublin 2, Ireland (a division of Penguin Books Ltd)
Penguin Group (Australia), 250 Camberwell Road, Camberwell, Victoria 3124, Australia (a division of Pearson Australia Group Pty Ltd)
Penguin Books India Pvt Ltd, 11 Community Centre, Panchsheel Park, New Delhi - 110 017, India
Penguin Group (NZ), 67 Apollo Drive, Rosedale, North Shore 0632, New Zealand (a division of Pearson New Zealand Ltd)
Penguin Books (South Africa) (Pty) Ltd, 24 Sturdee Avenue, Rosebank, Johannesburg 2196, South Africa

Registered Offices: Penguin Books Ltd, 80 Strand, London WC2R 0RL, England

First published in the United States of America by Viking, a division of Penguin Young Readers Group, 2008
Published by Puffin Books, a division of Penguin Young Readers Group, 2010

1 3 5 7 9 10 8 6 4 2

Copyright © Nancy Carlson, 2008
All rights reserved

THE LIBRARY OF CONGRESS HAS CATALOGED THE VIKING EDITION AS FOLLOWS:
Carlson, Nancy L.
Henry and the Valentine surprise / Nancy Carlson.
p. cm.
Summary: When Henry and his first-grade classmates notice a heart-shaped box
on their teacher's desk the day before Valentine's Day, they try to find out if he has a girlfriend.
ISBN: 978-0-670-06267-6 (hc)
[1. Valentine's Day—Fiction. 2. Teachers—Fiction. 3. Schools—Fiction.] I. Title.
PZ7.C21665Hcm 2008 [E]—dc22 2008001283

Puffin Books ISBN 978-0-14-241682-2

Manufactured in China
Set in Avenir

Tomorrow was Valentine's Day, and Henry and his classmates found a heart-shaped box on Mr. McCarthy's desk.

"I wonder if Mr. McCarthy has a girlfriend," said Sydney.

"Teachers don't have girlfriends. They never leave school," said Henry.

"That's not true!" said Tony. "I once saw Mr. McCarthy at the grocery store!"

"Let's find out if Mr. McCarthy has a girlfriend," said Henry.

So during recess, they spied on Mr. McCarthy

talking to Ms. Olson, the playground monitor.

At lunch, they saw the lunch lady

give Mr. McCarthy an extra tuna melt.

Later, Tony spied on Mr. McCarthy

eating lunch with the French teacher!

"Wow! Mr. McCarthy has a lot of girlfriends," said Henry.

At the end of the day, Henry asked,
"Who is that valentine for?"

"I will tell you tomorrow at the party," said Mr. McCarthy. "Now it's time to go home and work on valentines for all of your classmates."

"Even girls?" asked Henry.
"Yes," said Mr. McCarthy. "Please make
a valentine for everyone in the class."

After school, Henry made valentines for
everyone in his class, including the girls.

Henry even put an extra candy heart in
Sydney's valentine.

The next day, everyone was excited about the party,

and Mr. McCarthy was looking sharp.

When it was time for the party, Henry asked
again, "Who is that valentine for?"

"Well, this very special valentine is for . . .

". . . all of you!"

"Is that fish food?" asked Sydney.
"And that's a net!" said Tony.
"But we're not fish!" said Henry.

"No, but your new class pets are!"
"Yay!" cheered the class.

"There are twenty fish. One for everyone in
the class to name. You can even make a special
valentine for the fish you name!"

"Yippie!"

"See, I told you teachers don't have girlfriends," said Henry.

"Yeah," said Tony. "Teachers are too busy . . .

". . . teaching!"